TROUBLE COMES IN THREES

Fairytale Anthology #5

www.YeOldeDragonBooks.com

Ye Olde Dragon Books
6909 Ackley Rd.
Parma, OH 44129

www.YeOldeDragonBooks.com

2OldeDragons@gmail.com

ISBN 13: 978-1-961129-86-3

Published in the United States of America May 1, 2025

Table of Contents

FOREWORD

Hey there, loyal readers! Yes, Ye Olde Dragon Books has done it again. With the help of our fabulous authors, we've slaughtered… er, manipulated… uh, TRANSFORMED yet another fairy tale into ten very twisted stories. Some will make you laugh, some will shock and terrify, but all of them will be well worth the time it takes to read them.

We have one new author in the mix, and he's been delightful to work with. I love those precious "newbies"! (And it's amazing how many of them we steal… er… commandeer… well, wrangle (?) from *Havok Publishing*!) We get one now and again, and I always get super-excited to see another author added to our ranks. So, Arlan Gerig, **welcome**! Now I cannot say enough about the rest of the authors in this book, because they are all returning warriors, armed with the **BEST** fiction in the universe! Stoney Setzer has not missed one anthology since we started five years ago! Yes, this is year **FIVE**! Can you believe that!?! I think he's the only author (besides Michelle and me) who has been in every volume! And while his stories have connective thread, they can be stand-alone tales too. So get ready for another Sardis County story! Michelle Houston, Jim Doran, and Kathleen Bird have been steadfast in their submissions, and they score big with every story they submit. Kathleen gives us a touch of "real world" but weaves in aspects of the fairy tale with such grace, she leaves us breathless. Oh, how happy I was to see Jim Doran join our team. I was the resident "horror" writer until Jim showed up. He excels at the thriller, and we've loved his stories. And Michelle Houston — she's the jack of all trades around here! We've seen science fiction, fantasy, mainstream, and even a touch of horror. She does it all! We are so proud of all our writers! Not so many issues ago, we gained new authors Jordan Campbell and Etta-Tamara Wilson. Wow! We've been especially proud of the work they've done with us. Jordan usually scares us silly with his tales, but in a real turn-around, he submitted a hilarious treat for this edition. Etta-Tamara has given us laughs and scares in equal measure in true fairy tale style. This time, she added a touch of reality with a hurricane and a very "wolfy" insurance man! And lastly… oh, what can I say about the Dynamic Duo, Pam Halter and Rosemarie DiCristo?! They wrote individual stories for our early anthologies and we were delighted. THEN, they teamed up to write together and BAM! It's like the old 1960s *Batman* television show where they put up bubbles with WHAM!" and "POW!"

to show they'd walloped the bad guys. These two ladies have knocked it out of the ballpark *every* time. Can you tell how very proud I am of all these wonderful people? We would not have lasted for five minutes, much less five years, without each and every one of them. They've stuck with us through the learning curves of the publishing "stuff," and helped us to look like we knew what we were doing. (even when we didn't!)

I can't finish this off without mentioning my "partner in crime" … hm… "partner in publishing," Michelle Levigne! There wouldn't BE a Ye Olde Dragon Books without Michelle at the helm. She does all the bookkeeping, the formatting and negotiating with the printers… in other words, all the "tough stuff"! I'm so grateful to her for guiding us in this wonderful, often-frustrating, nerve-wracking world of book publishing.

And you, beloved reader! If this is your very first YODB anthology, welcome to our wild and wacky world! We hope you'll enjoy the ride. If you've been around for a while, welcome back for another crazy edition. I think this might be the wackiest volume yet. I mean, the Three Little Pigs? Who wouldn't have fun with that?

This is going to be a great year for our company! In a few months, we'll start working on the fall "Monster" edition which will be Dracula! I've been saving this mesmerizing guy for a landmark year and this is IT! So, hang onto your hats and get ready to tag along. Three Little Pigs — ready, set, GO!

Deborah Cullins Smith
March, 2025

PART II

What she said!

I should mention Deb's contribution. She deals with the contracts and the biographies so you get to know our authors behind the stories, and edits and makes the anthologies visible in social media and comes up with promotion ideas and …. Yeah, we'd just be sitting here, looking at our computer screens and wishing someone would notice we have a bunch of stories out there, without Deb!

And for your reading pleasure, her story this time around brings back some beloved characters from previous stories. Not going to give away their identities, because they're both living under their own nom de guerre, but you'll have a "howling" good time figuring out who they are while reading about some very justified if painful justice visited on some very brutish piggies of the worst kind.

Thanks for reading. We think you're going to have a great time with these stories. And remember to come back for more. We're gonna be around for years to come!

Michelle Levigne
March 2025

NOBODY GNOMES THE TROUBLE I'VE SEEN
Arlan Gerig

I cared about scientific advancement as much as the next gnome—which wasn't much—so when Hamcake burst into my kitchen crowing about breaking the laws of time and space, I didn't get excited. I ignored him. I also wondered if this would mirror the time my brother created a mechanical dragon that nearly burned down the village.

Hamcake frowned. "Are you listening, Loopy? It finally works!" He spread his chubby arms as though encompassing the entire room, his eyes sparkling, and spittle dribbling into his beard. "This could be my big break."

I yawned and tried to change the subject. "I hear you, brother, but I spent an awful morning getting rid of fairies from the garden. They're so annoying when they get all sugared up from dandelion nectar and swarm anyone who crosses their path. I only want a swig of ale and a nap."

"Don't you care about the mysteries of the universe? There could be hidden dimensions all around us, and you only want to sleep your life away!"

I grunted and slurped my ale. "*You* try keeping those fairies out of the garden. Not easy, I tell you."

Hamcake threw his hat onto my table. "Maybe Greasy will understand. This could be our chance to explore other dimensions. There's no telling what we'll find!"

"You say *we*, brother, but I say you go for it alone, 'cause you're giving me a headache."

He looked ready to slug me, but my creaky front door distracted him when our sister Greasy shuffled in.

She looked down her nose at us. "You two aren't fighting again, I hope."

I grinned. She was short and pudgy like most gnomes, complete with a bulbous nose and round, red cheeks. I admired Greasy's sense of style, the way that daisies and petunias draped over her oversized straw hat and covered her large ears. Her hat overshadowed Greasy's otherwise serious personality.

I pointed at our brother. "Hamcake says he's got another awesome invention that will take us to other planets—or maybe someone's closet across town. I wasn't really paying attention. Maybe you can figure him out."

Greasy pushed her hat back and squinted at Hamcake. "Are you squandering our inheritance trying to prove your goofy theories?"

Hamcake's cheeks turned red. "Not what I said at all, but they're not goofy theories. Definitely *not* a waste of time and gold." He clenched his fists. "I can prove it to you."

Without another word, he stomped out the door, leaving Greasy and me to shrug at each other and follow him along our meandering forest path. I liked my cozy log cabin, furnished sparsely with a bedroom and a small, homey kitchen. A door at the far end led to an underground tunnel that descended into the rest of my home, used mainly for entertaining my siblings and storing my ale.

Hamcake's house resembled a big, unwieldy box. It annoyed me with its total deviation from gnome culture. He had used so much gold to finance his experiments that his house was meager, consisting of compressed wood and a thatch roof. His constant desire to test and observe had killed all the weeds and most of the grass in his yard. Even the birds resting in the withered trees seemed off, like they were too tired of Hamcake's experiments on their habitats to do more than give an occasional tweet.

The door swooshed open into Hamcake's lab, complete with tables of pipes and mechanical arms, gears, metal tubes, and complex circuits. I shrank back from all this metal and science, more comfortable with my gardens and flourishing fruit trees. Different dimensions and quasi-scientific theory strained my brain. It wasn't natural.

Hamcake wove around the collection of tables to a large device in the center of his lab. "This is where the future happens."

He yanked on a lever, and the machine shrieked as wheels and gears slowly turned. As the machine gathered momentum, a large, middle wheel spun and gyrated. It spun so fast that I wondered if it might break off and fly in our direction. The monstrous scream and growl the machine emitted made my nose hairs quiver. At the same time, I was impressed. My brother had actually invented something that didn't fall apart when turned on.

My awe turned to horror as the wheels and gears spun in a blur with sparks that sizzled and popped. A flash of lightning blinded me, leaving a burn mark on the ceiling.

"Turn it off!" I yelled, my voice lost in the screech and whir of the wheels. Hamcake jumped at the levers, cranking them, pushing buttons, and striking a red button over and over.

Greasy had her hands over her ears, her screams indiscernible from the noise of the machine. Whether from the lightning or Hamcake continuously hitting the red button, the screech lessened and the spinning wheels slowly wound down. No more lightning appeared.

A seat had appeared in the middle of the wheels. A hunched figure in a black hooded cloak sat there, covering its head with furry paws.

The wheels slowed, and the figure turned to us with gleaming, red eyes peeking from the hood. A grimace exposed large incisors. My blood ran cold. Had my brother just pulled a wolf from a different dimension into ours? Or maybe an angry wolf from a distant village? The wheels stopped with a creak, and the cloaked wolf leaped from the machine.

Standing to his full height, he towered over us. His voice rolled like thunder. "This is a most fortuitous event that has released me from that awful, life-sucking prison that shriveled my soul. May those rotten guards never learn that I, Devlin, am finally free!"

Devlin? A name like that certainly didn't sound familiar to our dimension. He let loose something between a chortle and a howl that froze us in place. It reverberated throughout the large lab, gaining in volume rather than lessening. My knees almost buckled under his scrutiny.

"Back away," I said. My voice squeaked, and I winced. Why couldn't I sound more intimidating when I wanted to?

Saliva dripped from Devlin's sharp, yellow teeth. I grabbed a pipe and brandished it as a sword. Hamcake held my arm back, pure rapture in his eyes. I stomped on Hamcake's foot, and he released my arm.

Devlin wiped his mouth. "In exchange for freeing me, I will give you three an extra twelve hours to enjoy your meaningless lives." He licked his lips. "I am so very hungry after my long imprisonment."

He leaped over us and sprang out the open door.

We tottered after him, which was fast for us, but Devlin had already disappeared into the forest. A little too chubby for his own good, Hamcake puffed from the exertion and grinned weakly.

"Looks like we made a friend from another dimension."

Greasy whirled around, hands on her round hips. "A friend? Rethink who your friends are."

"Will you help me find him?" Hamcake bit his lip. "He may feel lost in a strange world."

"He didn't look lost by the way he flew out of here. More like a predator. I'm going home before he changes his mind and returns." She snorted, gave me a brief wave, and shuffled along the path to her home.

I hated uneasy silences, but I hated dancing around the truth even more. "I have to agree with Greasy. He's not in the forest looking for a burger or a friend." I locked my hands together, giving my brother my best disapproving glare.

Hamcake stared through the fading sunlight with a stupid grin. "My machine works! Think of the possibilities."

"If you mean death, destruction, and utter chaos in the streets, I'd say you're right."

Hamcake sighed and placed a pudgy hand on my shoulder. "Our first attempt may not have gone exactly as planned, but there's so much we can learn from him. He can enlighten us on life in another dimension. Think of it, Loopy. Another dimension!"

He hopped forward, rubbing his hands together. I'd seen this same reaction when he'd taught fairies to pick gooseberries. Some fairies had gotten berries into the bucket, but most gooseberries became a pulpy mess when the experiment turned into a food fight. Despite that, Hamcake insisted the fairies were close to cooperating.

I waddled into the deepening forest shadows, then turned with a scowl. "Will he enlighten us before or after he tries to eat us?" Without another glance, I scurried into the fading twilight.

In the daytime, the forest exuded piney smells amongst mossy dankness, full of growth and overflowing life. At night, it was a maze of traps and terrors. Due to our slight size, we were careful of bears, wolves, and witches. Equipped with only my oil lamp from my handy fanny pouch to guide me along the winding forest trail, I shuddered whenever I remembered Devlin's sharp teeth and piercing eyes.

At each creak or rustle, I stopped to hide the oil lamp, listening for more. Besides an owl announcing its presence and a deer galloping through the woods, I heard little more. Relief filled me when I finally spied my cabin, a light still merrily shining in the window. Everything looked in perfect order when I got inside. With my doors firmly locked, I climbed into bed.

My disturbing dreams of running from red-eyed wolves, running but always feeling their hot breath on my heels, were interrupted by a banging on my front door. I staggered to open it, still shaking, as Hamcake rushed inside.

"I need help, Loopy! This could be the worst thing ever to happen to Flagen Woods. The worst." Hamcake paced in my small kitchen, muttering other things I couldn't make out.

"Speak up, brother," I said. "I'm not awake yet."

Hamcake wrung his hands. "They're blaming me because Devlin's eating gnomes! He's just misunderstood, I'm sure, and not familiar with our culture. Plushpot's gone, Fuzzlegob's gone, and so is Hooey, but the Gnome Council can't blame me for that." He stopped to wipe away a tear and blow his nose in a loud honk. "I don't know what we're going to do."

I clenched my fists, upset that we'd already lost some close friends, the sun not even over the horizon yet. "We? You created that horrible machine that brought him here. In the main interest of saving our village, and only because of that, I'll help you stop him."

Hamcake brightened. "He's also some kind of wizard, which is incredible, right? We just have to teach him not to eat gnomes."

I shuddered when I remembered my past dealings with wizards. The ones I'd met were grizzled, humorless fellows with little consideration for other people's viewpoints. They weren't power-hungry, though. If Devlin managed to catch gnomes, who mostly resided underground, he must be powerful indeed. If he was as evil as I suspected, we were dealing with a serious problem.

"You must promise to destroy your confounded contraption once we get rid of this menace." I folded my arms and thrust out my lower lip.

"That's not fair." Hamcake intertwined his fingers and stared at the floor. "Just because the first person we find in another dimension is possibly homicidal..."

"You must promise."

Hamcake glanced up, then down at the floor again, still mumbling in barely discernible words. "Don't glare at me like that, and don't make me promise. I love inventing."

I lowered my arms and pointed at him. "Look at the trouble your inventing has caused! You brought something back you can't control, and we've already lost precious gnomes from our village. The Gnome Council could banish you to live in mountain caves, so consider this a decent alternative."

Hamcake said nothing but kicked at an imaginary pebble.

A sharp knock pulled our gazes to the door. I shivered, took a deep breath, and shuffled to open it. Devlin stood there, still dressed in his black, hooded cloak that hung past his knees. His smile revealed sharp teeth and a large red tongue. Hamcake bounced on his heels, twiddling his fingers nervously.

"Ah, I believe we've met," Devlin said and chuckled. "I'm making my rounds, getting collections. So nice to again see the brothers who released me from my miserable prison. As thanks, I'll merely collect two hundred gold pieces and let you continue to live in your humble abodes."

I gulped, gave a quick glance at my bug-eyed brother, and leaned forward. "I appreciate your kind offer, but we're fresh out of gold pieces."

With a swipe of his paw, he pulled a wand from his cloak. A black cloud whirled up behind Devlin, spinning like the tornadoes that I'd heard stories about, including one that dropped a house on a witch. A chill trickled down my back. We could use a flying house right now.

"Mr. Devlin, sir, I-I don't have access to any gold. Perhaps Greasy does."

Devlin's red, wolfish eyes narrowed. "You have no gold? In the absence of the White Wards, I do what I want." He gave a sharp bark that ended in a howl. "And they don't seem to have followed me. In my dimension, gnomes are known for their gold, and this one seems no different. Certainly one of you three, probably that female, has plenty of gold to trade in exchange for your lives."

The whirlwinds behind him grew stronger and larger. I ground my teeth in anger. How dare he make us barter for our lives! Fear of losing everything gnawed at my brain, but I couldn't back down.

"Do what you will, you miserable wolf. I'm not giving you any of my gold, and neither is anyone else. Hamcake, go downstairs where it's safe."

Hamcake nodded and rushed for the door leading down to the tunnel to my living room. I slammed the reinforced door and waddled down after him.

The ground shook. The sound of a hundred winds barreled overhead. Dirt particles trickled down the walls and through the door leading to the surface. The shaking continued. My bookshelves emptied their precious contents. Dishes smashed on the floor, and paintings of our ancestors fell and cracked their frames.

I led Hamcake to the dining room and backed against the wall with my eyes shut, waiting. The quakes and winds ceased as quickly as they started.

Devlin's maniacal laughter rang longer in my ears, penetrating even this far underground. "Next time, give me the gold."

Hamcake and I glanced at each other, and I nodded. "Let's investigate."

We struggled up the stairs and worked to shove open the door, which we discovered was blocked by the fallen beams of my ceiling. I frowned in dismay at the damage. The top part of my house was gone! Everything had turned to rubble, everything destroyed. I screamed in frustration and kicked pieces of what used to be my favorite chair, now broken and covered in debris.

Hamcake stood beside me with quivering lips and his hands tightly folded together. "I'm so sorry, Loopy. This is all my fault."

Angry as I was, blaming Hamcake wouldn't help. "He didn't kill us, and he couldn't destroy my underground dwelling. That's something to be glad about, isn't it?"

Hamcake turned pale. He gripped his beard with both hands. "My house! Do you think he destroyed it?"

My shoulders drooped at the thought. "I hate to think he did, but let's find out."

As we waddled along the road to Hamcake's boxy house, something kept rattling in my little gnome brain. "What do you think he meant about the White Wards? Never heard of them."

Hamcake gulped and tried to smile. "Does it matter? He said none of them followed him into our dimension."

If Hamcake's house was destroyed, he deserved it. If it still stood, though, maybe we could use the machine one more time to pull a White Ward through, if they were powerful enough to stop Devlin.

I waddled faster to catch up to Hamcake, my mind racing. If the machine was destroyed, how could we get Devlin back to his own dimension? Was that even possible? If not, I had no idea how to stop him.

I scratched my beard, brow furrowed. My worst fears were confirmed. Hamcake's home lay in ruins. Other homes lay untouched. Hamcake wailed.

I grunted as we examined the damage. The machine no longer existed, torn apart and metal shards scattered. "That's what's decorating the countryside," I muttered.

Hamcake continued to wail and cry, waving at the damage. "I know I should have listened to you about building below ground, but I never expected this."

"Yeah, we can debate your stupidity later," I said with a glare. "Right now, we need to get rid of this wolf."

"We can't return him, and he's too powerful to stop," Hamcake cried. "I hate this as much as you do, but it would take months to rebuild my machine. That's assuming we can even find all the parts."

Taking a deep breath and stepping away from my stupid brother, I decided the bigger problem was saving our community from this methodical maniac. There was only one person I trusted, only one who could create a decent plan for stopping Devlin.

"Come on." I grabbed Hamcake's arm and tugged. "We need to find Greasy. She can help us develop a plan."

Hamcake nodded and wiped his eyes. He blew his nose again into his sizable handkerchief and followed me at a distance, head down. He occasionally wiped away more tears and blew his nose.

Greasy's home sat further away, cleverly nestled into the hillside. Her door was hidden between gorse bushes.

As we drew near, Devlin sat on a shattered tree stump. He gave a wolfish grin. Those yellow teeth and red eyes gave me the shivers, but I bravely thrust my chest forward.

"You'll not threaten us again, you mangy wizard."

Devlin sneered. "And why not? I've already feasted on several of your kind. Rather tough meat, if I don't say, but juicy. Two more wouldn't hurt."

"That's the thing," I said, rubbing my hands together to prevent them trembling. "If you want any measure of gold, Greasy has plenty, much more than Hamcake or myself. However, you'll get nothing if we can't talk to her. She'll never listen to you."

Devlin thought a moment, licking his lips around his sizable snout. "You make sense, my little gnome. Pity your machine was destroyed. Since going back to my own dimension is not an option, I'll need some gold to establish an empire here." He snickered, and I kept myself from rushing him, choosing instead to spit in his direction. "Take some time. However, I'll kill you all if you take too long. I am a creature of much patience until I get hungry again."

Hamcake and I scurried through the gorse bushes to Greasy's door. Barely two knocks in, her door opened. She glowered and pulled us inside. Monitors next to her door showed Devlin sitting on a little mound, relaxing in the sunshine.

"You've got nerve bringing that gnome-killer here," she said, jabbing a finger toward the monitor. "I keep up with Gnome News. You might be interested to know that Hamcake's home was the first one hit."

"The first?" Hamcake looked like he would burst into tears again.

I patted his back. "Houses can be rebuilt."

"But my machine! Years of research and gold, just gone like that." Hamcake snapped his fingers, tears spilling down his face.

"Get it together, you sap," Greasy said, shaking him. "We obviously can't use your machine, and he's too powerful for us to stop."

"He wants gold, two hundred pieces," I said. "Maybe then he'll leave us alone."

"You really think he'll stop at that? No, we need a way to destroy him. Either of you know any wizards?"

Hamcake shook his head, and more tears dampened his cheeks.

"He mentioned White Wards," I said, shivering at the thought of meeting wizards from any dimension. "In the absence of any wizards, maybe a White Ward will show up."

Greasy's eyebrows twitched. "If they had him in a prison in his dimension, they must be very powerful. But are they good? You assume a White Ward imprisoning an evil beast would be good themselves, but that might not be the case."

Hamcake paced. "We need to fix my machine. It's the only way."

Greasy slapped him on the arm. "Wake up, brother! It's up to us. No White Ward or anybody else is coming to help us. We need to find a way to stop him before he destroys our whole land and enslaves anyone he hasn't eaten."

I nodded. Coming to Greasy was the best way to stop this wolf wizard. Besides, her whole house was underground, an added benefit. I pointed to the monitor.

"He's starting to look restless. Will your house sustain a whirlwind?"

She snorted. "There's no tornado or storm yet that's been able to infiltrate my abode. Now don't interrupt me."

Greasy waddled to her bookcase and pulled out a couple thick tomes. "If there's anything written about White Wards, it'll be here."

She handed me a book, giving a sardonic glance at Hamcake. He still paced, wringing his hands. We both knew he would be useless.

Greasy had given me Wizards, Magical Creatures, and Other Useful Beings for Gnomes. I flipped through the contents page, sneezing at the dust. There weren't any useful headings, and nothing about White Wards.

I sighed and started down the listings again. One listing caught my eye: "Contacting Wizards in Times of Emergency." Turning to page 395, I ignored the hand-drawn pictures of gnomes and ravens, but the wizard drawing caught my attention. It accurately captured everything, from the condescending eyes to the wispy beard around sneering lips. The drawing included a gnarled hand gripping a staff that no doubt had whacked its share of gnomes and other creatures too distracted for his liking.

Wizards were difficult, snobby people who looked down on gnomes—which nearly everyone did, anyway—but ravens were just as bad. They were loud, obnoxious birds; I didn't relish messing with either one.

I sighed again. This was an emergency. "Greasy, do you have any ravens?"

She glanced over her glasses with a frown. "Nasty birds like that would never last underground. Are you considering ways to contact a wizard?"

I nodded. "There's nothing here about White Wards, but plenty about contacting wizards."

"Yes, White Wards seem relegated only to Devlin's dimension."

"Um, Greasy?" Hamcake fidgeted, pointing at the monitor.

The wolf shook the camera, yelling at it. "I've been patient enough. Your time is up."

Devlin twirled his wand, and a black whirlwind rose behind him. With a flick of his wrist, the tornado gained size and speed and rushed at us.

I gulped when the familiar rushing sound surrounded us. The ground shook, several books fell from Greasy's bookcase, and the chandelier rocked slightly. We had each found a wall to lean against, and we all smiled as the whirlwind's whoosh died away. Cries of frustration from the monitor added to our glee.

Devlin glared into the camera. "My first whirlwind failed, but the next one will surely destroy your house. As my reward, I'll eat the female first."

I glanced at Greasy, but she only scowled. "It'll hold," she said, crossing her arms.

As the wind picked up again, I shuffled to her and spoke in a whisper. "Do you have anything we can send to contact a wizard?" I pointed to the page I'd been reading. "Besides ravens, it looks like we could use magic mushrooms, dogs, weasels, or pigs."

Greasy's face brightened. "My P.I.G. Why didn't I think of it sooner?"

She rushed to her closet and pulled out a little pink device that resembled a vacuum cleaner with legs. She carried it to a chute built into a wall and opened it. Although carved into dirt, the tunnel looked solid.

"This is my Pink Instant Gasbag. It will take any magical message to the wizard's dormitory. I just have to open it here and inject a message."

The whirlwind had started again. The chandelier rocked precariously side to side, and several more books fell. Greasy opened the back end of the gasbag and spoke into it. As the shaking grew worse and the whirlwind louder, faint cracks formed along her ceiling. She shut the gasbag and shoved it into the tunnel. Greasy closed the chute, pushed a button, and hung onto the wall as another tremor shook her home.

I hid under the table and shut my eyes. Hamcake muttered desperate prayers from his corner. When the shaking stopped, I looked around. Everything was still in place!

Cursing came from the monitor, as well as bangs to the camera. More cracks had spiderwebbed across Greasy's ceiling.

I grimaced as Devlin's wolfish face filled the monitor. "This is where I destroy you once and for all. I will eat all three of you in the public square, enjoying you morsel by morsel so that your whole community knows not to mess with me." His guffaws sent chills down my spine. "I will rule this land with a mighty fist. All will serve me, giving me whatever I ask."

He stepped away and waved his wand. A tornado larger and blacker than the others sprang from the earth, headed right for us. I frantically scanned the room, hoping for anything that might protect us.

"We're not going to make it," Hamcake wailed. "I am so sorry I caused this. This is all my fault."

"It's about time you admitted it," Greasy snapped. She scowled, facing the monitor with her arms folded. "I just wish you'd said it way *before* we're killed by a wolf you brought here. As though we don't have enough predators of our own!"

Hamcake crumpled into a heap, sobbing into Greasy's carpet. I swallowed my anger and glanced at Greasy. "Where's the wizard you called? Did your message make it?"

"I wondered the same thing." She glared at the monitor. "If I make it out alive, the Gnome Council will hear how they should have protected us better."

I giggled. Maybe it was the overwhelming tension, maybe knowing we were going to die. I couldn't stop giggling. "What would the Gnome

Council do? Not the International Council of Wizards? Not High Gnome Fluzzpot?"

My giggle became a laugh. Her glower turned to a smile, then a laugh. "Why not the Ultra Spectacular Grand International Chief Council of Wizards and Gnomes?" She plopped into a chair, laughing harder than before.

Hamcake stopped wailing to frown at us. "Have both of you lost your minds? There is no Ultra Spectacular Council Chief… whatever…"

The screaming wind of the tornado grew in intensity. Its image filled the monitor. I laughed all the harder, wiping away tears. Impending death had made me giddy.

A voice boomed through the monitor and the vibrations shook the room and Greasy's whole house.

"Cease!"

The whirlwind went from black to gray to white and fizzled away. The face of a wizard with a long, white beard filled the screen, speaking in a friendly voice one might use to coax a kitten from a box.

"Greasy? You and your brothers can come out now. The danger's over."

"Bermelthus!" Greasy exclaimed and raced for the door. I followed her, Hamcake close behind.

A tall, thin wizard dressed in typical green robes grinned and bowed as we exited. Devlin stood next to Bermelthus, frozen stiff. Only his head moved as he cursed at us.

On the other side of Bermelthus stood a stern figure in white robes, holding a sword that glinted in the sunlight. The figure spoke in a deep, penetrating voice.

"Devlin, you have broken your sentence of imprisonment and terrorized yet another race in yet another dimension. Therefore, you are banished to the lower levels of our prison, where the fires burn hotter and darker, and there you will remain."

Devlin's howl cut short in a bright flash. When we looked again, Devlin and the white stranger were gone.

Greasy ran to the wizard and hugged his knees. "Thank you, Bermelthus. You couldn't have come at a better moment."

The old wizard chuckled. "I left my dormitory as soon as I got your message. I met that White Ward on the road, who said he followed Devlin's time signature to this location. He brought me here instantly. His magic is even more powerful than mine."

I removed my cap and bowed. "Thank you again, dear wizard, but I have a question. Why didn't the White Ward appear earlier to stop Devlin? I don't understand."

"Nor do I," Bermelthus said, rubbing his hands together. "Perhaps it took him time to follow Devlin's path. Some things we will never know. But I am assured that this wolf will never bother you again." He turned to Hamcake with a stern glower. "And you, my bright, ambitious gnome, must do your research before opening up more unknown dimensions."

Hamcake blushed. "Of course. Yet…" He scratched his ear. "… there must surely be dimensions that don't contain ferocious wolves."

After all that, my brother still wanted to explore! Bermelthus chuckled. I snickered and smacked Hamcake's hat off. "You dolt."

If such a dimension existed, my brother would surely find it.

The End

PASS THE BACON
Michelle Houston

The alarm rang out, sending notes of ACDC's *Thunderstruck* blasting through my brain. I hated that song, the only one from the band that I didn't like, so I slammed the snooze button and closed my eyes again in the blissful silence.

But somewhere in my skull my hindbrain, running on instincts smarter than my civilized self, started yelling at me that I was missing something important. My logical cognitive center groaned in displeasure but was eventually prodded into action. Synapses sluggishly fired, trying to determine why on earth I set an alarm last night

Not a job. That wouldn't be important enough. Not an interview, for similar reasons. All bills nearing due dates were paid, so I wasn't trying to hide from a collection agent. Maybe family? Mother and Father weren't supposed to come by today but sometimes they surprised me. No cousins or friends were needing help…

Uncle Rupert!

My eyes flew open, blearily taking in the time.

Horror rushed through me, jolting me awake faster than McKensie's famous double espresso mocha energy drink.

I had thirty minutes before Uncle Rupert's plane took off without me, thereby depriving me of a free two-week vacation.

I scrambled out of bed, shoving my feet in the first two shoes I found, thankful that I slept in shorts and a t-shirt.

No time to pack. I grabbed my wallet, passport and phone from the dresser, my toothbrush and toothpaste from the bathroom, and scrambled out the door.

The elevator in my old Victorian apartment building was slower than the development of dirt, so I jumped down the stairs, three at a time, praying I wouldn't sprain an ankle.

The last set was long and straight, down to the middle of the courtyard. If Teddy were with me, he would have insisted on sliding down the railing, saying that was faster than running. But my cousin never did have a mind for puzzles and wouldn't have realized that sliding was slower than falling. So I simply leapt the railing and let gravity pull me down before I set out running again.

Out the door, round the corner to the metro, apologies thrown out to those I shoved aside in my hurry. I swiped my card and then jumped the barrier, not wanting to waste the precious two seconds for the plastic doors to open. I squeaked between the doors to the tram just before they closed, then collapsed into an empty seat.

My phone informed me that I still had twenty minutes before Uncle Rupert left. I might just barely make it. I sincerely hoped so, and not just because I wanted a free vacation. My father said Rupert was kooky, but I thought his different approach to life was refreshing. He was enthusiastic, generous, and not inhibited by others' opinions. He was also one of the few in my family who overlooked my failures and enjoyed my company.

My phone buzzed, still on silent mode. Uh-oh. My father was calling.

"Hey Pop! What's up?" I tried to sound breezy, not out-of-breath. Mentally I flipped a coin. Was he calling about a responsible job for me or inducing a guilt trip to get me to visit?

"Martin, get your lazy butt out of bed and open the door! I've been knocking for several minutes!"

"At my door?"

"No, at the Sistine Chapel! Of course your door! Open up! I got a friend to agree to interview you for an engineering position at his company this afternoon, and I'm not going to let you screw this one up. We're going together."

I crossed one leg over the other, ignoring the annoyed look my seat neighbor shot at me.

"Sorry, no-can-do, Pops-a-roni. I'm not at my apartment."

"What do you mean? Of course you are. You never get up before noon."

It's times like this that I wish we still lived in a cash system. It would be so satisfying to dig a coin out of my pocket and flip it in the air while avoiding my father—just like in the movies.

Unfortunately, credit cards did not flip well.

"Though I do admit to a propensity to nocturnal life and avoiding mornings, at this present time I'm on my way to do my familial duty to Uncle Rupert and Aunt Jane."

An annoyed sigh came through the speaker. "Martin, you know he's not your real uncle, it's a distant relationship via stepsisters. And I'm sure he'd agree it is more important for you to get a good job."

If my father thought it was a good job, I probably wouldn't last a couple of months at it. Not that I usually stayed at any job longer than six months, but I'd probably hate those months from day one. Father and I didn't tend to have the same viewpoint on life. A fact that he pointed out to me every time he lamented the engineering degree from Oxford that I was not using.

The sign for the airport flashed by. I was grateful for the excuse to get off the phone. My father meant well, but we were like water and an oil-based flame. The more we tried to mix, the more we spread disaster around.

"Sorry, I'm at my stop. I'll call when I can. Tell your friend thanks but maybe later. Bye!"

I hung up and stood ready to exit, clutching my phone in one hand and my passport in the other.

Ten minutes now to make it to the plane.

As soon as the doors opened, I started running. Thanking the powers-that-be that my uncle had his own plane, so I didn't have to go through customs, I sprinted down the corridor past the commercial airlines, past the stores and food stalls, and past the checkpoint, flashing my passport at a confused attendant.

That last one was a problem. They yelled at me and probably called security.

I didn't dare slow down. If I could make it to Uncle Rupert in time, he would take care of it. If I didn't, I'd probably be in detention for the day and possibly jail for the night.

I burst through the doors to the tarmac, Uncle's plane in sight with the stairs still attached. I was going to make it!

I put on an extra burst of speed. Honestly, I think the track I ran at Oxford was more useful for my life than anything else.

I ducked into the plane, pulling air into my lungs like it was the ambrosia of life. *Which it is,* the logical part of my brain insisted. The same part that got me into and through Oxford before I woke up to the fact that my future was days of sitting in front of a computer, helping oil companies get richer and more powerful while they threw more pollutants into the environment.

Shaking that depressing thought from my mind, I gave a cheery grin to my uncle and aunt sitting in their plush chairs near the door, too out of breath to speak. Uncle Rupert was in his usual pressed khakis and polo shirt, his dark grey hair slicked back into a short ponytail, smiling with delight at me. He was the only person in my family who didn't look down at the choices I was making or try to change my path. I had heard him say to my father more than once, "Martin will find his way. He's a good lad. Just give him time." It was always amusing to see the conflict on my father's face when he said this. My father disagreed, but he didn't want to be rude to anyone with money and power.

Holding hands and snuggled into his side was Aunt Jane. She was a sprite of a woman, with sharp pointed features set in a diminutive frame and surrounded by a halo of white fluffy hair. I wouldn't be surprised to find out she had a fairy somewhere in her family tree. They had only been married for five years, but she loved adventure and my uncle equally.

They were a great match.

"Hey…Uncle…Rupert…could…you…call…off…the…guards?" I panted, waving toward the tarmac where security personnel were boiling out of the building.

Uncle Rupert peered around me out the door and snorted. "Looks like your usual, Martin." He called out to the pilot to contact someone for him.

While he took care of the ball and chain threatening to take me in, Aunt Jane looked me over in concern. "No luggage? You know we'll be gone for two weeks and there are no stores on the island."

Rupert came back and indicated I take the seat behind them, swiveling his and Jane's chair around to face me.

"I'm sure Martin will figure out something. He'll probably spend most of his time on the beach anyway. We're about to take off, so buckle in. Snacks are in the fridge if you want any." He settled into his chair, gently taking Jane's hand in his before closing his eyes.

Uncle said he didn't mind flying, it was the taking off and landing that unnerved him. Therefore, he always closed his eyes during those times.

I buckled up, then leaned over to open the small refrigerator attached to the wall between our seats. Yogurt, apples, some type of nut bar hung out beside bottles of water and kefir. There was also a bag of crispy bacon. I snorted in amusement. Uncle tried to eat healthy, but bacon was an alluring siren's song for him. He had to have some every day.

I snagged two apples for breakfast, determined to use the facilities as soon as possible to brush my teeth. They always felt fuzzy in the morning, a sensation that drove me crazy.

The flight to Uncle's island took five hours. He snoozed while I passed the time reading magazines on board. There was *Science*, *Lancet*, *Architecture Today*, and *Vanity Fair*. Aunt Jane spent the time playing *Clash Royal* on her phone. Apparently, she was "Hogtime," one of the top twenty players in the world.

In *Architecture Today* I found an article talking about the challenges of building in remote locations, which included Uncle's house. It went into the impossibility of shipping supplies and laborers in, due to the lack of sea-worthy docks and Uncle's solution of sending interested youth to the mainland to learn the necessary trades. It also talked about how Uncle had invested in the local infrastructure to facilitate the movement of rock quarried in the southern part of the island up to his property. What it didn't say was that there was similar rock at the north end; Uncle had simply wanted an excuse to pump money into the island to help the population.

Once he woke up, Uncle pulled me into an in-depth discussion about some supply issues he was facing with his nanoscale development company. One of the things I loved about my Uncle was that he was brilliant and had more esoteric facts hidden in his brain than I learned in five years of college. He was always surprising me with his knowledge about one subject or another. The other thing I loved was that he didn't care about conventional behaviors; he said and did what he thought was best no matter what anyone else said.

We compared alternative materials and different vendors for two hours before he sat back, satisfied.

"That's my conclusion too, Martin. I'm glad you agree. You always did have a great head for complex details within a Gordian knot puzzle."

I basked in his praise. My father might say similar things, but it was always in preface to a lecture of why I was wasting my time working odd jobs in various sectors. He saw no value in learning about hospitals by being an orderly, or supply and demand by managing a restaurant, or ecosystems by pruning forests.

Uncle Rupert pulled out his phone. "Have I shown you our skydiving pictures yet? Jane and I went again last month." He passed me his phone.

I chortled as I flipped through the pictures. There were several of him and Jane kitted up in the plane, one of Jane as she started to jump, and then a whole bunch, obviously taken by a third party, of both of them in free fall. The best one was of him and Jane from below. His hair had come out of his ponytail and streamed behind him like a dark silver tail. Their goggles made their eyes look big, and they both displayed a lot of teeth with their delighted grins. I could tell they were having a grand time.

I passed the phone back, shaking my head with a grin. "I don't understand how you can enjoy falling out of a plane but landing on a runway makes you nervous."

He chuckled, putting his phone away in his bag. "When I'm landing with a parachute, all the laws of physics are working for me. Even if I screw up, the worst is some broken bones. But with a plane, there is so much that has to go just right. One mistake can cause a crash, which is hard to walk away from." A somber, far-away look came into his eyes. I suspected he was remembering some of his experiences in Iraq. "I'll leave the planes to the experts."

Hoping to draw him away from the past, I quipped, "I'll leave jumping out of perfectly good planes to crazy folk like you two. I like my adventures on the ground."

He grinned at me and I felt relieved. Mission accomplished.

The pilot announced we were approaching the island. Uncle closed his eyes as I stared out the window into the choppy Atlantic waters. It had been four years since I was last able to come here.

The island flew under us, cliffs rising above the water, trees covering the land like petticoats concealing a lady's form. Waves broke upon the rocks, sending huge plumes of spray into the air. A single road snaked through the forest off to the right, empty of cars. Gasoline was an expensive luxury here.

The plane lurched as the pilot touched down, then rolled to a sharp stop. My uncle looked decidedly pale.

He quickly unbuckled and opened the door, waiting for the staircase to be wheeled into position. A man my age greeted him with a hug and helped him to the ground. Another similarly helped Aunt Jane.

We strolled away from the plane, Aunt Jane with three large suitcases trailing her, Uncle Rupert with one being carried by a porter, and me with my wet toothbrush stuck in my pocket. We piled into an extra-large SUV with a chauffeur at the wheel.

Uncle immediately started asking him questions about his mother, his kids, and how the island had weathered the summer storms.

He was like that. Always into the details of the lives of those around him.

As they chatted, the chauffeur drove us across the island to Uncle's house.

His property was sprawling, going from the hilly forests inland to the cliffs at the ocean's edge. I had seen pictures of the old mansion that used to exist on the property. A large, blocky structure that perched right on the cliffs. I'm sure it had a great view from inside, but from the outside it seemed to defy its surroundings, denying the beauty of the area. It was destroyed in a storm shortly before Uncle bought the land. I am sure the residents of the island were thankful for that storm.

In contrast, Uncle's house snuck up on us. It was hidden in the forests and we had to slow down to look for it. It had a sprawling structure, half-buried in the loam and bushes, made of local stone and wood. Each section was short in stature and had a steep roof. The first time I saw it I was reminded of a clan of wood gnomes, all grouped together in friendship.

My father would have called me daft if I told him that. My uncle had roared with laughter and pounded my back in approval.

We pulled up the dirt drive and the housekeeper, Mrs. Rosie Swift, opened the door. She was backlit from the soft electric light inside. She had been with Uncle for years. She was a medium woman, with medium brown hair, medium figure, and medium height. But her smile was a million watts. She greeted Uncle with open arms, joy lighting up her face.

"Mr. Laurent, Mrs. Laurent, welcome! Let Charles take your bags to your room. Everything is ready. The horses would love to run, the footpath to the cliff has been cleared, snacks are waiting by the fireplace. And what's this?" She noticed me hanging back. "Is this Martin?" She clucked her tongue at me, turning me around in a spin. "Look at you, not an ounce of fat on you. I'd better warn the families to keep their daughters away or you will break some hearts. Do you want your old room?"

I felt simultaneously like an adult and a little kid when she fussed over me like that. "Yes please." I wondered if I could borrow some of her son's old clothes while there. We had the same build and I couldn't care less that they would be worn and out of style. I could almost hear my father lecturing me about proper appearances at all times.

~~~~~

The next morning, I woke up feeling like a million euros. I had two weeks of an all-expense paid vacation where people would pamper me, I could do what I wanted, and there were no parents to complain about my sloth. The only thing I had to do was keep Uncle entertained on occasion with conversations about whatever caught his interest. I really enjoyed those discussions. Uncle had an eclectic mind, stuffed with gems of esoteric knowledge and overflowing with curiosity. Between the two of us we delved into the swirling currents of internet facts and fiction, turning over ideas and philosophies for hours on end.

~~~~~

The two weeks passed quickly, like a dream. Every day was filled with activities, and yet it seemed like I just drifted easily through each one, enjoying them without feeling any pressure. It was the best vacation. There were early mornings watching the sunrise on the cliffs, large breakfasts of eggs and bacon and biscuits, long horse rides and swims, helping the natives clear out brush or fix fences, and chatting by the fire at night with dinner on our laps. It couldn't get better.

But unfortunately, it could end.

We were two days from leaving when a fierce storm, typical of the area, blew through. We stayed in our snug house, secure that nothing could touch us. The next morning at dawn, we came out to a changed world. Several of the trees were down and debris was everywhere. We found three lawn chairs, a sign for two-for-one beers from a pub, and four dead fish in our front yard.

As usual, Uncle and I joined with the island people to clear the debris from the roads and houses. Later that night, Uncle got a call informing him that the airport had been damaged enough that we needed to delay our departure by a week.

Someone in heaven must have liked me. One more week that I didn't have to hear about getting a "real" job.

The next morning, we went for breakfast as usual. When Uncle opened the plate for bacon, though, there were only two crisp slices staring up at him.

Uncle was pretty easy going, but he was addicted to bacon.

"Rosie!" His voice carried to the kitchen. She hurried into the dining room, wiping her hands on her plaid apron. "Where's the bacon?"

She grimaced. "I'm sorry, but we have to ration the bacon."

Uncle fell back into his chair with a gasp. "Ration? Bacon? But why?"

"The storm brought down some trees on Finley's pig pens. They all escaped and so far, nobody's been able to catch them. Which means no pig slaughter this month and no piglets next spring. We have to conserve our pork until they are caught."

Uncle looked so distraught I had to offer a solution. "Why don't you just airdrop a barrel of bacon?"

He sliced his hand in the air. "Temporary solution at best, Martin, and an expensive one at that. It wouldn't solve the pork problem for all these good folks here. Besides, the winds make airdrops difficult." He thought for a moment. "No, we need to fix this." He paused dramatically, then thrust his finger in the air. "We need to recapture those pigs!"

"Yes, but Rosie said that people have tried that without luck."

He put his finger along his nose, his eyes twinkling. "Ah, but they didn't have the knowledge of a Laurent! What do you know about pig wrangling, Martin?"

I looked at him blankly. "Absolutely nothing. Oxford didn't cover it in their engineering courses."

He tsked and shook his head, his grey ponytail swishing around his neck. "What a shame. Give me a couple of hours and meet me back here. I want to plan our best strategy, then consult with you before we get started." He abruptly stood and grinned at me. "Mark my words, by tomorrow night we will have caught our first pig!" He turned around and strode out the door.

Aunt Jane watched him go and sighed in admiration. "I love it when he gets fired up."

I spent the time talking to Rosie and googling pig habits. I was alarmed by several things. First, Rosie said the pigs were Duroc, which are large and mean. Second, she said two of the pigs that got out were an old sow and a boar, known for being especially large and mean. Third, they were brown rather than the typical white, so they could hide better in the woods and ambush us (in other words, sneaky and mean).

When I googled escaped pigs, I learned four very useful things: One, they can run **really** fast. We didn't have a chance catching them. Two, if they become feral, they could wreck an ecosystem. Three, they were wary of traps. And four, they liked Doritos.

Oh, and they had been known to kill unwary people and even eat their corpses.

So I rounded up all the Doritos bags I could find. I figured maybe Uncle could use them, and at the very least I could scatter Doritos in my path to distract the pigs while I escaped.

A little while later, Uncle bounced back into the dining room, several papers with hand-written diagrams and a map of the island in his hands. He had an enthusiasm and energy that I hadn't seen in him for years.

"This is it, Martin! We will capture the pigs, restore the island to its normal function, and remove the bacon rationing during our last few days of vacation. We will return to England as heroes."

I really was worried about Uncle. I didn't want him hurt, and there were no large firearms on the island to use if things got out of hand with the pigs.

He spread the map on the table. "Here is Finley's farm." He pointed at a central location. "Fortunately, there are several choke points that should keep the pigs in the forest near him." He rubbed his hands together with glee. "It will be child's play."

I cleared my throat. "From what I've read, our best chance is to open the gate to the repaired areas and call them in with treats like Doritos."

Uncle stilled and stared at me in disbelief. "Doritos."

I nodded. "Doritos." I picked up a bag and shook it. "Like these."

He stared another moment, then chuckled. He patted my arm in a condescending manner. "We don't need those. There is lots of food in the forests for pigs right now. Definitely more tasty than those, those, things." He poked a bag with distaste.

I sighed. I was sure I was going to regret my next question. "What do you suggest?"

He beamed. "Straw!"

It was my turn to stare. "Straw?"

"Yes, straw. Granddaddy Beamus said his grandfather always used straw to get the pigs to come back after foraging. They love it."

I wanted to massage my temples. Uncle knew a lot, but this seemed like too much, too far. "You mean Great-granddaddy Beamus whose logic was as crooked as an inchworm in his last days? Who never farmed in his life?"

Uncle scoffed and waved away my objections. "He learned at his grandfather's knee." He leaned forward to impart some secret information. "His grandfather was so well known for his pig knowledge that he was called The Pig Whisperer."

"Are you sure Beamus wasn't just remembering *The Three Little Pigs?*"

Uncle Rupert gave a one-shouldered shrug. "Maybe, but you know that fairy tales always have a kernel of truth in them."

"So we just lay out the straw and the pigs come?"

He waggled his hand back and forth. "Kind of. But the straw is the most important part. Come on, let's get out there. We need to get everything ready before dusk."

~~~~~

Several hours later as night approached, we stood a few feet away from the gate to the repaired pig pen. Two bales of straw had been dumped inside and then thoroughly soaked with water and red wine vinegar. Uncle claimed the smell of rotting fruit from the vinegar would draw the pigs in.

I figured this would be a waste of time, since the pigs had not been seen here since their escape. They were probably halfway across the island by now.

But it was a pleasant evening, with a gentle wind that played with my clothes and occasionally brought the scent of vinegar and hay wafting to me. I was actually looking forward to watching the stars come out during our uneventful vigil. I didn't even mind Uncle's admonition to stay perfectly still. He claimed pigs had horrible vision but would detect any motion we made.

I never saw anything emerge from the woods. One moment we were alone, Venus twinkling near the horizon, the next, several large, dark pigs appeared four meters from us, snuffling and acting nervous.

I froze, more concerned about attracting attention and getting attacked than catching them.

One turned its head toward us, beady eyes roaming over the farm. Its mouth was open, large canines visible. I gulped and was tempted to reach for the Doritos bag. Rupert snagged my hand and held me still.

The breeze shifted, driving the smell of Uncle's concoction straight toward the pig.

I swear it smiled.

It ran right up to the hay and started tearing into it, snuffling around and snapping. The rest of the pigs enthusiastically followed suit.

Uncle quietly slipped around me and closed the gate. In the gathering dark, he grinned. "Ten down and two to go."

~~~~~

The next day at breakfast I asked Uncle if we would use the same pen tonight.

He shook his head. "Pigs are smart. The other two were watching from the forest. I'm sure they learned to avoid that area now."

I stared at him, sure he was joking. "The other pigs were watching."

He nodded solemnly. "Yes."

"And they saw their friends captured, so they will avoid the same trap."

Another nod. "Yes."

I closed my eyes briefly. "Okay, so we have a couple of genius pigs. Do we need to spread the straw somewhere else?"

He frowned slightly in annoyance. "Pigs aren't geniuses. Where did you get that idea? No pig has ever won a Nobel Prize or Pulitzer." He shook his head at the folly of my youth. "No, no straw. Like I said, I'm sure they have learned. They'll know it is a trap. This time, we use wood!"

I sighed, wondering how this adventure would go. I was sure last night had been a fluke. "Is this from Great-grandfather Beamus? 'Cause it still sounds like he was channeling *The Three Little Pigs* story."

Uncle Rupert gave me a saddened gaze. "Oh, you of little faith."

~~~~~

We spent the day constructing a hut of wooden sticks. I say hut, but really it was more like an A-frame lean-to. As we carefully laid the sticks together, overlapping them with lots of brambles and a few ropes, Uncle Rupert explained.

"Granddaddy Beamus said the reason this works is that it plays into the pigs' natural desire to root among fallen wood for insects. They can't resist a pile of wood, sure that somewhere in there is a tasty worm or grasshopper or lost acorn."

My hand got tangled in a bramble. As I carefully extracted myself, another piece seemed to whip out and catch my shirt. If I had been a different man, I would have been swearing a blue streak. Out of the corner of my eye I watched Uncle weaving the brambles around the branches without getting a single scratch.

"So the pig comes to look at the wood. How does that help us catch it here in the field?"

Uncle stood back to gaze at his creation, then reached for another branch. "If we have constructed this correctly, it should collapse and catch the porker when it explores the interior."

I managed to free myself from the pile. "Why on earth would the pig go inside?"

He frowned at me. "Come on, Martin. You usually are quicker than this. I just told you it will be looking for food. Which hides in the darkest, dampest corners."

I pricked my thumb on another thorn and stuck it into my mouth, keeping my doubts to myself.

The hut was finished well before dusk, allowing us to take a breather and eat the snack Rosie sent with us. As I munched on a turkey and tomato sandwich, and Uncle eyed his baconless BLT with dismay, I tried to critically look at the hut from the viewpoint of a pig.

It certainly didn't look like a trap. It was so haphazard and fragile that it seemed like it would collapse from gravitational forces at any moment. And the dark hole at one end didn't seem to deliver any promises of juicy worms. But maybe my brain ran differently from piggish ones.
~~~~~

Once again, the weather favored us, almost as if it was trying to make up for the pork disaster it had caused. The temperature was unusually mild with a brisk breeze that ran from the forest edge past us. The sun delivered a cascade of colors painted on the clouds as it lowered behind the hills.

And once again, a large boar appeared out of nowhere.

This one never looked at us, a favor granted by the universe at large. Because I was still sitting on the ground and the Doritos were several meters away from me. If the pig decided to charge, there would be no chips in my attempted escape.

The boar snuffed around the hut, sometimes going right up to it, sometimes circling it at a short distance. At last it stopped at the entrance and stood gazing at it, as if it held the answer to the ultimate piggish question of existence.

The answer must have satisfied it, because it moved forward, slow but steady, into the interior.

By this point I was nervously glancing from the hut to Uncle. Because if we didn't succeed in capturing it, I was pretty sure we would have a hungry and annoyed boar looking for revenge for the empty promises the hut provided.

It was probably only seconds, though it seemed like hours, before the hut suddenly collapsed, squeals coming from the inside. The larger branches surged around, but the weight and uncertain footing kept the pig down. Uncle jumped up, running to the hut and shouting for me to grab the ropes. We pulled from opposite sides, effectively making a wooden version of pig-in-a-blanket.

I panted from fear and adrenaline while Uncle called the farmer to come bring his truck. We had successfully caught another one of the pigs.

~~~~

The next morning, breakfast only contained one piece of bacon. Uncle stared at it sadly until I motioned for him to take it.

"What next, Uncle? Will we use the wood or straw again? Or will it be a brick house this time?" I was partly sarcastic and partly wondering if the trend would hold true.

"Oh, definitely a sturdy house. The last pig is the sow, and she will be looking for somewhere safe for her litter. Grandpappy always said there was nothing more dangerous than a pregnant sow. I don't want to chance straw or branches failing to hold her."

My fork fell out of my fingers and clattered onto the plate as I stared at him in horror. "You mean there was a chance one of those others could have gotten loose?"

He waved my fears away. "Miniscule, I assure you."

"And what about this time? Is there a chance of failure?"
~~~~

He ignored the question. "Normally I'd build the house out of wood, but all of the planed boards on the island have been used in repairs. We'll have to use some spare brick and the quick-drying mortar I keep at the house." He looked at me and motioned at my neglected plate. "Hurry up and eat. We need to get started to give the cement time to set before dusk."

I hoped this wasn't going to be my last meal that I was gulping down. I also hoped, just this once, that Beamus was wrong and pregnant sows had a quiet and demure disposition.

Uncle chose to build this house right up next to the woods. From previous jobs I knew how to lay bricks, but Uncle showed me how to slant them into a Roman arch, the weight of the bricks increasing the stability of the walls. At the door we included several slots that would hold rebar to keep the sow from escaping. I suggested we create a pulley system whereby we could move the rebar from a remote location. Uncle agreed with worrisome alacrity.

I also noticed he programmed his phone with both Farmer Finley's number and the hospital number on speed dial.

We finished early and scouted out some trees we could wait in. Neither of us wanted to be on the ground if the sow rejected the house. I suggested we throw in some Doritos, which Uncle firmly vetoed.

I discovered that waiting in a tree was much less comfortable than waiting on the ground. My leg fell asleep until I shifted positions, at which point my other leg fell asleep. I got very tired of hanging onto the rope connected to the rebar.

Again, the sun was just setting when the old sow appeared. She was huge. She was mean. I imagined she hungered for human flesh. I wish Uncle had let me leave the Doritos on the ground.

She peered into the house while we held our breaths. Then she backed away. I'm sure my face was just as dejected as Uncle's. But then she came back to the door. Then circled the house. Then the door. Then around a tree. She kept glancing up at us. I'm sure she was deliberately playing with us.

Uncle was right—pigs were smart.

But she finally walked into the house and I loosed the rope. The rebar fell into place just like we planned (my engineering classes were finally useful).

Uncle and I cheered and hollered as the pig squealed and Farmer Finley joined us to take over the situation.

We went home that night victorious. We recounted the story to Rosie and to Aunt Jane and to the horses. We shared stories of other victories in our lives, both big and small. It was a wonderful time, and I could feel something strong and wholesome growing within my chest. It was long after midnight before we finally collapsed for the night.

~~~~

"Pass the bacon," Uncle Rupert said with a wolfish grin on his face the next morning.

I was playing with my phone at the table, and when I gave him a full platter of crispy goodness his face transformed to a look of triumph.

I couldn't resist. I snapped his picture.

Between his salt-and-pepper hair escaping his ponytail and framing his face and his teeth-revealing-smug grin, he looked like the wolf that had gotten all three of the little pigs.

I later shared it on Instagram, along with the story.

~~~~

I paused for a moment on the stage and clicked the remote, causing the photo to appear on the giant screen overhead. As the audience laughed, my eyes were drawn to the front row, where my now-ninety-year-old Uncle Rupert sat laughing with everyone else, his hair a short white halo around his jovial face, making him look even more like a wild animal than usual. Apparently, he had lost a bet recently with a friend over the effects of marijuana gummies on the gut microbiome and had to cut off his ponytail.

"As you know, the story and picture went viral and brought me to the attention of *The New Yorker*, which launched my career in journalism." I continued my speech.

I saw my father beaming with pride, his eyes on the prize in my hand. Uncle Rupert, in contrast, was staring at my face, his gaze full of confidence in me.

"So as I accept this Pulitzer Prize, I want to give a huge shoutout to my family, but especially to Rupert Laurent, the wolf who always believed in me and who, in defeating the pigs three times, started the chain that led me to this place."

The End

RISE OF THE PIGS
Rosemarie DiCristo and Pam Halter

Kara pushed her hair off her sweaty brow. She blew out a long breath.

"Be careful," her best friend, Elsbeth, said. "Otis is on watch today. If he or any of the other pigs catches you not working, you'll get tossed into the Hole."

"I know," Kara said. She struck the ground between the rows of corn plants with her hoe. The plants were about knee high right now. Even though it was early spring, it had been warm enough that the humans were told to plant corn two weeks before normal. "But sometimes, I wonder if that would be better than this."

The girls fell silent as the Mindoro overseer, Otis, strode down the row of corn adjacent to where they were working. His snout twitched as he snorted and sniffed over the growing corn. Kara kept a sly eye on where he was as she hoed her row with more energy than she had done a minute ago.

She wondered, not for the first time, why humans were under the rule of the Mindoro. When she mentioned it to her mother, she was shushed. None of the adults would listen to her questions or talk about it at all.

The massive Mindoro Compound was surrounded by a high, smooth brick wall. The only plants allowed were crops, the tallest being corn. There was one gate, which the Pig Patrol guarded day and night. The pigs opened it once a day to bring in logs, which the human men chopped and split for fires.

Kara, Elsbeth, and the other human females continued to hoe the rows until the afternoon bell rang. They all trudged home, home being houses made from straw and sticks, which didn't offer much protection from the weather. Or bugs. Bugs fell almost constantly from the straw roof starting in spring and continuing through autumn. Kara's mother had worked for two years to piece together linen fabric scraps with thread (when she could find that) to stretch under the ceiling over their table and beds. She could only get one or two pieces at a time off the trash heap, and only when no one was watching.

The Mindoro were, as was typical of pigs, wasteful and sloppy. But they didn't allow their human serfs to take anything they threw out. It was a risk, to be sure, for them to have anything they were not given by the

Mindoro, but Kara felt the thin pieces of linen blended into the straw nicely. A pig would have to actually come into their house and take a careful look up to see it.

The male pigs guarded the wall and oversaw the humans. The females sat home and ate and got fat and did whatever female pigs did for fun. Kara caught a glimpse of them once in the salon as she walked home from the gardens. She had shivered in disgust as there wasn't one who wasn't grotesquely fat and obnoxious. But they were pigs, after all. Now when she walked home, she averted her eyes when she went past the salon.

Liv, Kara's mother, smiled as she came through the door. "Kara, love, how was your day? Did you see Zeb on your way home?"

Kara shook her head. "It was hot, and no, I haven't seen Zeb at all today."

Liv frowned. "He's usually back before you. I hope he hasn't gotten himself into trouble."

"Wouldn't we get notified if he did?"

"We should, but you know the pigs don't always go by their own rules," Liv said. "Set the table, would you? I managed to get some mushroom stems, turnip tops, and a small rabbit carcass off the trash heap today. I have stew simmering in one pot and swamp grass in another."

Kara grinned. "If I wasn't so hungry, I'd be mad at you for taking the chance. What if a pig *smelled* the stew? You know how they can sniff things out!"

Liv gave her a playful swat on the backside. "That's why I'm simmering the swamp grass. And I have the stew as covered as I could get it."

"Sneaky *and* smart. You better not let anyone see that side of you," Kara said. "Are we waiting for Zeb?" She hoped they wouldn't, but then she felt guilty. Of course, she wanted her brother home and safe. But she was so incredibly hungry.

Liv spooned stew into bowls. "No, let's eat while it's warm. We'll save him some."

Kara got a small crock from the shelf and set it on the table. "Looks like our coltsfoot ash is getting low. I'll see if I can pick more on the way home tomorrow."

They sprinkled some coltsfoot ash into their bowls and ate the stew in silence. Kara didn't mind the hot meal on a hot afternoon, it tasted so good. Her mom could make most things delicious. She knew all about the different plants and herbs that grew wild; how they tasted and what to do with them. Coltsfoot was Kara's favorite. The salty flavor made almost everything taste better.

They guarded this secret, though. Picking wild herbs from the side of the road and using them in cooking was forbidden. If anyone knew, they could inform the Mindoro. The pigs didn't allow humans any kind of luxury. Their rule was harsh. No kindness of any sort.

All except the curly-haired Mindoro couple, Liem and Litza. While they weren't exactly friendly, they treated any human who worked for them in the hair salon, particularly Liv, decently. And as long as no other pig was watching, their children, Olow and Chickie, were also pretty decent to most humans. They were careful, only treating well the select few humans they trusted; Liv, Kara, Elsbeth, Zeb, and his best friend, Grady.

Kara had just finished her meal when Zeb came through the door. He had a black eye and a ripped shirt.

"Oh, what now, Zeb?" Kara sighed at the same time her mother ran to Zeb, touching his face and chest. When she pushed back a lock of his white-blond hair, Liv found drying blood from an inch-long scrape.

"Son, are you okay?"

Zeb's smile was more of a sneer. "What, that? It's nothing. A price well worth it, considering what I found."

"Who did it to you? Dexter? Roscoe?" Liv's voice was quiet, as if she was afraid one of the guards would overhear.

"Hamlet and his goons. Who else? And they were so glad to be able to knock a few human heads together, they didn't even report it to Potam or any other of the Pig Patrol."

Hamlet and his friends, Percy, Hugo, and a couple others, loved tormenting the human boys. They'd definitely grow up to be on the Pig Patrol.

"Report what?" Kara asked.

"Nothing really," Zeb answered. Then he grinned. "I might have grunted a little when they walked by."

Kara started to laugh but then cleared her throat and coughed.

"Why, Zeb?" Liv asked. "Why are you always getting in trouble? And don't you know grunting at pigs could be considered subversive?"

"Someone's gotta fight for our dignity. *Besides,*" he said before either Liv or Kara could interrupt, "I also made it seem like I'd been rooting around for truffles, and Grady and I got smacked around for that."

He actually sounds proud of himself, Kara thought, and felt a mixture of frustration … and pride. Or maybe it was longing, a wish that she—or someone—really could do something subversive and end the domination of the pigs.

"And what were you *really* doing?" Liv sounded resigned.

Now Zeb's smile was smug. "I found a way outside."

Kara saw her mother squinting at Zeb as if she, like Kara, were wondering if she'd heard right. Then Liv said exactly what Kara was thinking. "There is no outside."

Zeb's lips twisted scornfully. "Of course, there's an outside. The pigs bring in logs every day!"

"Maybe, but no one—no humans—can go there," Kara said.

"Of course we can! Outside! The real world! Freedom!" Zeb was almost shouting.

"Shhhh!" Liv warned. "Do you *want* us all thrown in the Hole?"

"Ever hear that old joke about a fate worse than death?" Kara swallowed hard. "Leaving the Mindoro Compound for any reason means death and dismemberment, for you and your entire family, down to the sixty-fifth cousin thrice removed."

"Yeah. Try not exaggerating, Kara. The punishment's bad, but not that—"

"Bad? Only 'bad'? Zeb! The pigs use DNA to find and dismember every member of a rebel's family. *No human* goes outside."

"They would if there was a way," Zeb countered.

"There *is* no…" But even as Kara said that she knew there was one or Zeb wouldn't have said what he did.

"We'll have no more of this talk!" Liv's voice was shrill.

"But, Mom," said Zeb.

"No! Silence!"

Kara knew what she meant: the pigs hadn't bugged humans' huts—yet—but a passing patrol…

"There's a tunnel." Zeb's words were so urgent, Kara and Liv couldn't stop him. At least he whispered. "It's old. Someone dug it out decades, maybe a hundred years ago."

"That's not possible." But Kara's heart swelled with the hope that it was, and what that might mean for humans.

Then Zeb said, "Frisk dug it."

It was like he'd punched her in the gut. "Frisk is dead—killed for challenging the Mindoro."

"Yeah." Zeb's voice was mocking. "Killed and dismembered through his sixty-fifth generation. But Frisk did all that before our great-grandparents were born." Before Kara could respond, he added, "He left writings."

It was getting worse and worse.

"Do I have to remind you, simpleton," Kara hissed, "that humans are forbidden to read or write? We shouldn't even know how."

"Then I'll take those half-dozen story papers you've got hidden under your bed."

"Story papers aren't like Frisk's subversive, political—"

"They're still forbidden—"

"Children!" Liv's voice was still shrill. "Stop this now. This talk *and* this bickering."

Zeb shook his head. "Grady's dad has one of Frisk's writings. And they're practically sacred, not subversive."

Liv interrupted, "I've heard the rumors, too, of what Frisk wrote, but *anything* humans write is—"

Zeb waved her off. "Mom, you don't know. You don't know how they tell of great things humans have done. That's how Grady and I found out there's a tunnel that goes to the outside world."

Liv's hand rose to her throat. "You didn't actually go... out?"

Zeb rolled his eyes. "I didn't *see* the tunnel. I just read about it."

"I can't believe Harro let you read those writings," Liv said.

"He didn't! Grady found them in his dad's bedroo—I mean behind the—er, under the couch, I think." Zeb shrugged. "Anyway, we read them behind Grady's house. In the shadows."

Kara rubbed her temples. "You had them outside? Don't you know that's the easiest way to get caught?"

"Naw. We heard Hamlet and Percy and all the *piglets* coming, and I swiped the truffles Harro had dug up as a cover while Grady stuffed the journal through the window." He shrugged again. "Hamlet doesn't need an excuse to rough us up."

"Sit down," Liv said. "I'll get a wet cloth while Kara spoons you out some stew."

Kara smacked the back of his head. "We saved you a little."

Zeb grinned. "Thanks."

Kara set the bowl before him. "You and Grady should burn that journal."

Zeb laughed. "But we intend to read the rest of Frisk's journal soon. And what's more..."

Liv wiped the gash on his head with the wet cloth. "What's more is I'll be talking to Harro," she said. "What is he thinking, keeping something like that in his hut?"

"But—"

"No more talking about it," Liv snapped. "This life isn't the best, but it could get worse real fast. Eat your stew so I can wash up the evidence. We haven't had a surprise inspection for a while. We're about due."

They spent the rest of the evening cleaning up the kitchen and throwing the leftover scraps into the cooking fire. Liv dumped the swamp grass out back. Then they all got ready for bed. Dawn came early, and even though most of the pigs slept in, the humans were expected to be up and working by sunrise. Unless they were sick in bed, and even then, a human better be pretty darn sick to not be working. Anyone caught faking went immediately into the Hole.

Kara shivered thinking about it. A literal hole in the ground, deep, dark, and damp. She had overheard Elsbeth's cousin, Mik, talking to one of the men about being in the Hole.

"I could hardly breathe. The dirt kept crumbling around me, and when I tried to push it away, worms came out."

Mik had only lived a month before he came down with what the humans called Hole Sickness and died. It was a rare occurrence for someone to get put into the Hole these days. But still …

If Zeb and Grady got caught, they were definitely going in.

~~~~~

A week went by with no incidents or trouble with the Mindoro. Liv questioned Zeb every night at dinner about Frisk's journal, but he just shook his head. Kara knew Zeb wanted them to believe he hadn't read any more. But she wasn't fooled. She knew her brother too well.

Their mom hadn't talked to Harro yet. No opportunity. Since it was late spring, and a warmer than usual one, she worked more hours in the hair salon as the longer-haired pigs were getting their summer shearing early. Kara and Zeb did their best with the little food they had in their allotment. Soon, the early crops like peas and asparagus would be harvested and they would be able to have some variety. Although, they had to be sneaky about it.

One afternoon, as Kara noticed asparagus tips poking up from the ground, the bell rang early, followed by a siren. That meant everyone, humans and pigs alike, were to gather in the center square. These gatherings were never good.

She and Elsbeth got to the square, where Elsbeth joined her Gran, Lottie. Lottie was standing erect, as she always did in public, but Kara saw how tightly she gripped Elsbeth's hand for support. Partly so as not to call attention to that, Kara looked for her mom and Zeb. Liv joined her a minute later, but there was no sign of Zeb. Kara got a sick feeling in her stomach.

Big Bill, the giant forest hog leader of the Mindoro, stepped up onto the platform. He was flanked by Otis and Mortimer. Dexter and Roscoe, the other leaders of the Pig Patrol, stood in front looking angry and, according to Zeb, stupid. Kara wondered where Tremen and Gargan, Big Bill's personal bodyguards, were. She hoped they didn't have Zeb.

Before Big Bill spoke, Kara saw movement to her left and snuck a look. Zeb and Grady slipped in from behind the leather crafter's building. That made her feel less anxious.

Big Bill narrowed his piggy eyes and scanned the crowd. He gave a grunt. "I've heard some disturbing news." *Snort!* "Seems there's been digging going on at the west wall."

The people murmured and shifted nervously.

"Whoever's doing it needs to stop." He grunted deep in his throat
~~~~~

and spit on the platform floor. "If there is any more digging, we *will* find you and put you in the Hole. Ya hear?" *Snort!*

No one responded, so Roscoe whipped off his glove and smacked the nearest human so hard, he fell face-first to the ground. Blood spurted from the gash on his cheek.

"Ya hear?" Big Bill repeated.

The humans nodded while the pigs shuffled their feet and grunted.

"The guards will be doubled on the wall, as well. In fact, if the digging continues, we'll pick three humans at random and throw *them* in the Hole."

More nods from the humans. Louder grunts from the pigs.

Big Bill stared them down again. "And to show you I'm serious, I'm puttin' one of ya in *now*."

There were gasps and a few outcries as two Mindoro guards trotted into the crowd and dragged a woman out.

"Deena," Liv whispered. "Oh God, it's Deena."

Kara didn't know Deena, but the horror playing out before her eyes made her knees weak. She stood helplessly as Deena was hauled away screaming.

Big Bill gave one sharp snort and shambled off the platform. Kara heard the creaking of the boards. One of these times, Big Bill was going to crash through. She'd take grim satisfaction to see that happen.

Liv took her hand, and they walked home. As they passed Zeb and Grady, Liv flicked her wrist and pointed. Zeb fell in step with them.

At home, Liv shut the front door. She raised her eyebrows at Zeb. "Well?"

"What?"

She just waited.

"It was a joke!" Zeb burst out. "A joke!"

Liv stood and stared at him a moment. Then she shook her head and went to her room.

He turned to Kara who gave him a disgusted look. "Really, Zeb? Are you *trying* to kill Mom?"

"I ..."

"Didn't you see what Big Bill just did to one of us?"

"I did! That's why—"

"Go to bed."

~~~~~

Liv went to her room, but not to sleep.

After about an hour, she quietly left the hut, wearing her dark cloak and hood, trying to hide herself as much as possible from any pig patrols.

Since Kara also wasn't sleeping, she saw Zeb follow their mother. So of course, Kara followed Zeb.
~~~~~

Liv went straight to Harro's hut and tossed three small pebbles against his window.

Humans weren't allowed to gather in groups, but that didn't stop them from sneaking out to meet with each other when something was urgent. Fortunately, Harro's hut was only four huts away, which lessened the possibility of discovery. It helped that it was a dark night with very little moonlight. It also helped that years of prowling in darkness had enhanced humans' night vision.

Harro silently came outdoors. His cloak and hood were pulled far forward, to hide as best he could his bright red hair and pale face. "Liv." He sounded both relieved and puzzled. "What...?"

Liv didn't hesitate. "I cannot believe you not only have Frisk's writings but read them and allowed your son and mine—"

"I didn't allow, exactly, but now that they've found them, I'm not displeased."

It was clear from her manner that Liv wasn't expecting that, but before she could speak, Harro added, "I've also gone into the tunnel."

Liv jerked as if she'd been slapped, then moaned, "Oh, dear heaven."

"The boys told me how concerned you are. But don't you see? We had to do it."

Zeb, from behind her, added, "Grady found it. Much of Frisk's writing was in code, at least parts like the location of—"

Liv turned on Zeb, and Kara couldn't tell if her fury was because he had followed her or because of what he said. "I do not care about codes, or... Harro! Bad enough you, but do you want your own son to be put in the Hole? Like Deena?"

Grady had come outdoors, too, and now he placed a hand on his father's shoulder.

Harro patted it, then said, "I don't want anyone killed, let alone my son. Or yours. But if we're to escape subjugation..."

"You'll get us *all* killed." Liv had turned and spotted Kara. Her tone grew scornful. "Not that I seem to be able to stop anyone from doing anything rash." Now her voice was nearly a sob. "Kara, why?"

Kara just shook her head. She had no idea why she'd followed her mother and brother into the night.

Actually, she did. She needed to learn more.

"Liv. Listen to me." Harro's frustration was evident from the way he moved closer to her. "*I want freedom.* For myself, yes, but mostly for Grady, and his future children, and every child that's born to our people. But sometimes death *is* freedom. So be it, if it must be."

Liv's laugh was humorless. "I'm not so careless with my children's lives."

"Mom." Zeb touched her hand, but she pulled away. "I'm sorry you're upset, but… he had to go in the tunnel. Can't you understand?"

"Then why did you come back inside?" Liv's voice indicated her shock that, given the opportunity, he hadn't fled for good.

Harro answered. "The cursed thing only goes some hundred yards, then stops. A cave in. Several probably, before we reach Outside. I'll need digging tools." And he eyed Liv.

"No!"

"Your job gives you access to scissors, clippers…"

"*No!*"

"Sharp instruments. We only have our hands." He held out his: rough, calloused, with broken, jagged fingernails.

"That, and desperation," Grady added.

His father continued, "We need things we can dig with. You can sneak them out, Liv."

"Just how do you think scissors and hair clippers could help you dig through a cave in?" Liv asked. "Not that I'm going to get them for you. Just like your tools, mine are all counted. They assign them to me, and I have to turn them back in when I'm done."

"They can slash at roots, pry out stones! Woman, even a teaspoon would be of use." Harro threw up his hands in frustration. "You know there's no way I can sneak an ax out. Scissors can be pocketed!"

Kara spoke up. "Elsbeth can maybe help."

She could see a sort of bewildered hope in Harro's eyes. "I just remembered. She mentioned once that her gran had taken a metal spoon from the trash outside Rap's Deli. That would work better than scissors, wouldn't it?"

Zeb's face glowed. "I'll talk to her tomorrow."

"No," cried Liv, too loudly. In a fierce whisper, she continued, "You're involving Elsbeth and Lottie? No."

She didn't have to say, the Hole. The Punishment.

After today, everyone knew the pigs were serious. And maybe a little scared? Of what, Kara had no idea, but the thought was there.

She also didn't have to say that Elsbeth's gran had enough trouble: debilitating arthritis that was slowly crippling her. So far, Lottie had hidden it from the pigs—a crippled human was a useless human, which meant a dead human—but if the pigs ever had reason to observe her more than casually, it would be disastrous.

Zeb's voice turned wheedling. "I'll just talk to Elsbeth, Mom. Talk isn't action. Talk is talk."

Liv spat out the words. "Even if you could get digging tools, the wall is being guarded! Did you not hear Big Bill?"

Zeb smirked. "We have ways of neutralizing the guards."

"What, kill them?" Liv sounded as sick as Kara felt. "Do you know the punishment for *that*?"

"Incapacitate, then." Zeb grinned at their baffled faces, then turned to Grady. "Care to elaborate, oh trusted assistant to Big Bill's personal chef?"

Grady's grin matched Zeb's. "A little dried lavender and purple passionflower mixed into the fruits, berries, and bark of the Pig Patrol's energy bars causes sleep within a half hour or so. A lot of it gives them diarrhea. Either way, three little piggies, *not* patrolling for a little while, at least."

"No," Liv said. "No, no, no, no."

"Imagine what would happen if we could slip it into their barley ale," Grady said. "They drink more of that than they eat energy bars."

Zeb snickered.

"How do you know this?" Kara asked Grady.

Grady started to answer when his dad broke in.

"Liv!" Harro's voice shook. "Why do I have only one child?"

He didn't have to ask; everyone knew. But he answered anyway. "Because Grady's six months younger than your Zeb. Born after the Limitation was enacted."

The Limitation that allowed only one child per human family. If it died—and to pigs, all humans were "it"—they didn't get a do-over. The pigs wanted to make sure humans didn't outnumber them.

"We have to end the subjugation," Harro said again.

"By escaping to an outside world we know nothing about?" Liv said.

Grady jumped in then. "I found the information in Frisk's writings. Apparently, he was a botanist, among other things."

"But *where* can you get them?" Kara asked. "Not that I think we should."

Zeb winked. "They grow in Big Bill's wildflower fields."

Kara gave a short laugh. "What, the ones in front of his house?"

"Yep," Zeb and Grady said together.

"No!" Liv snarled. "No, this is not going to happen."

"It's easy for me to get them!" Grady said. "I work in the kitchen in Big Bill's house! Chef Ramsey sends me outside all the time to pick herbs."

Zeb spit on the ground. "Pig lover. Imagine how easy it would be if Chef Ramsey was on our side—the human side—*his* side!"

"Zeb!" Liv cried.

Zeb lifted his hands. "Well, it would!"

"Liv, we have Frisk's writings about the tunnel. They contain all we need to know," Harro pleaded.

There was silence for a moment. Then Harro looked at Grady and Zeb and they nodded.

"And we're going to gather the rest of Frisk's writings," Harro said.

"They're scattered among our people. We just have to find who has each piece, get them to trust us enough to put them all together. It tells a story, an answer to all our questions. It will save us."

Liv moaned softly; her hands pressed to her lips.

"We're going to dig out the tunnel."

"No," Liv said again. "No."

They made plans anyway.

~~~~~

A week later, Kara, Elsbeth, Zeb, and Grady met behind Elsbeth's and her gran's hut at midnight. It had been Elsbeth's idea.

"I'm not saying I'm in," Kara said. "But I want more info."

"Me, too," Elsbeth said.

The boys nodded.

"Did your dad get any more of Frisk's writings?" Kara asked Grady.

"He did. Not many. Maybe three or four?"

"Can we see them?"

Grady hesitated.

"What?" Kara said.

"I think so," he answered. "But he's still reading them. Studying them. I'll ask him when he's done."

"Well, have you at least dug farther into the tunnel?" Elsbeth asked. "Using my gran's spoons?"

The boys were thrilled when Lottie produced two large, bent spoons. That meant quicker digging.

Again, the hesitation. This time it was Zeb who reluctantly answered. "A little bit. It's still blocked."

"I can help unblock it," Elsbeth said.

Zeb hooted—so loudly, Grady elbowed him in the gut. So, Zeb whispered his derision. "A *girl* dig out the tunnel?"

Elsbeth's eyes narrowed. Kara knew that look well. Elsbeth had wanted to tell the boys something important, but now she wasn't going to. "Fine." Her voice was tight.

Yes, Kara mused. The boys just lost their chance at… something.

They stood quiet a minute. Then, without saying anything else, the boys crept silently back to their homes.

Kara's frustration and fear grew as she grudgingly turned to follow. What was the point of meeting secretly and taking the chance of being caught if the boys wouldn't give them information to make it worth it?

Kara turned back to Elsbeth. Elsbeth just shook her head and went indoors.

But the next day, she whispered to Kara as they passed each other in the tomato garden. "I have something for you."

Kara scratched her right ear; a signal she saw and understood. The
~~~~~

girls had worked out several communication signs that required little to no talking. Whatever Elsbeth had, Kara would get tonight at 1am at the shed behind the scrap heap.

~~~~~

Elsbeth handed Kara a book wrapped in skunk grass leaves. Kara took it without a word and slipped back home, although she did wonder what it was, and how on earth Elsbeth had gotten something so dangerous as a book.

In her bedroom, she quickly unwrapped it and ran her hand over it. There were no raised marks or writing that she could feel. How she wished she could chance lighting a candle, but as dark as the night sky was with no moon, she might as well broadcast to the entire compound that she was looking at something when she should be sleeping. She would have to wait until morning, and even then, she'd have to be quick; humans had to be at their workstations no later than a half hour past sunrise.

Kara slept fitfully until dawn, then she threw the sheet off, grabbed the book, and read the title: *Human History and the Rise of the Pigs.*

She drew in a sharp, quick breath, then read the title again to be sure she'd seen it correctly. Human history? Humans had no history. And "rise" of the pigs? The pigs were always in charge.

Weren't they?

The book was fairly small and looked ancient. She flipped it open randomly and saw brittle pages and tiny type. She could read, but not perfectly, so she was tempted to bring the book to Zeb. But no, he and Grady were clearly hiding something; maybe it was *her* turn to have a secret.

She turned back to the first page.

In the beginning, before the rise of the pigs, humans were the higher life form, second only to the wolves.

Kara nearly dropped the book. *Human beings* were…? No. Not possible. Humans were subservient. And wolves? Was the writer talking about the Big Bads? Once, Kara had seen a little pig tell his kid sister, "The big bad wolves will get you if you don't behave." Instantly his mother smacked him so hard, he nearly flew across the room. "Never say those words again!" she'd thundered. Kara didn't get it. Wolves were extinct, like too many of the animals that had once roamed the earth. At least, that was what they'd been told. And of those animals that weren't extinct, none came into the compound unless they were brought in to be eaten by the pigs. Even the stray bird that flew in was shot down by the Pig Patrol.

She shook her head as if that would clear her confusion and skipped ahead a few pages.

In those days, we built a network of roads, fine cities, glorious civilizations…
~~~~~

A few more pages.

We ruled supreme…

She skipped ahead several chapters.

Back then, pigs were associated with negative human attributes like greed, gluttony, and general uncleanliness. These connotations occurred across all the then-known human languages…

Human languages? As in "more than one"?

It was not uncommon for humans to use terms like fat as a pig, you live in a pig stye, you sweat like a pig, and more. Not to describe pigs, but rather human failings associated with alleged pig behaviors. "Swine" was a particularly pejorative term…

She could hardly take a breath as she turned the page.

Pigs could be useful to humans. Many lives were saved when pig valves, harvested from freshly killed pigs, were successfully implanted into human hearts…

Gag! Pig parts inside humans?

Again, she skipped a few pages ahead.

Although some cultures did not indulge for religious reasons, there was a time when humans dined on pig, feasting on spare rib, pork belly, loin chop, and a favorite of almost everyone, bacon…

Kara shut the book but opened it again a moment later, turning to nearly the end, to the beginning again, back and forth, trying to find something that made sense. Nothing made sense.

Finally, she turned to a random page in the middle. What she read caused her to shut her eyes tight, press the book to her chest, and murmur, "Oh, dear God!"

Calling out to the ancient god felt strange on her lips, but that was exactly what it was: a desperate pleading. Only the oldest humans mentioned this god. Prayer, she learned, had been forbidden for generations, and while random humans kept trying to start underground churches, no one except nearly senile elders believed any more. But praying, even clumsily, was all Kara could think to do. Then she got up and ran to Zeb's room.

"What?" he said. "It's time to report to work. You'd better hustle to the gardens."

She said nothing, just thrust the book at him. This was a secret she now didn't want to keep.

Head cocked, eyebrows raised, he took it.

Kara trembled as Zeb had the same reaction she had: a sharp intake of breath as he read the title. Only he exclaimed, "This is the lost work Frisk spoke of! But where did you —?"

"Elsbeth."

"But how did she —?"

"I don't know!"

Zeb snapped the book open to the first page, glanced at Kara in surprise, then, as she had done, began turning to various pages… But she had no patience for delays and commanded, "Read page 112."

Zeb said with a sneer, "Yes, boss."

"Just *do* it."

Zeb did and read exactly what she had. All the color drained from his face.

"This … this …" He could hardly get the words out as he dropped back down on his bed. "We *have* to show this to Harro. And Grady. And Mom."

"I know."

He flipped back a few pages. "Can this be true? I mean, it *has* to be, right?"

Kara shrugged.

"Do you know what this *means*?" His voice rose to a tinny pitch on the last word. Then he took a deep breath. "Kara, we *have* to get out and soon."

It was still too disturbing to think about, so Kara said, "We have to get to work before we're late and our hut gets raided or worse."

Work that day was a special kind of awful. Kara and Elsbeth tried not to exchange looks whenever they saw each other, but they couldn't help it. Any excessive communication, even in the daytime, was forbidden for humans. Most of them had learned how to speak without moving their lips, but now Elsbeth murmured one thing, "Girls can do as much as men. More, probably."

Kara pulled her earlobe—meaning she *didn't* understand.

"Harro's. Tonight," was Elsbeth's swift response.

Then they separated.

By lunchtime, they were both sweating and almost sick to their stomachs. Kara prayed Mortimer, who was on duty today, wouldn't notice.

If there *was* a god somewhere, he just said no to her prayers.

As she and Elsbeth sat nibbling on their lettuce sandwiches, a shadow came over them. Kara squinted up at the pig overseer.

"You! Wenches!"

Mortimer.

The girls scrambled to their feet before he kicked them.

"Chief?" Elsbeth said.

Kara couldn't have said a word if her life depended on it, and it just might. She nodded and tried to pull herself together.

"What are you up to?" Mortimer growled.

"Having lunch, chief," Elsbeth said with a small curtsey.

"Nah, the looks. What are the looks for?" He glared at each of them in turn.

Kara's knees went weak. She tried in vain to think of a good answer, and Elsbeth stood silently, as well. Which was a mistake.

Smack! Smack!

Both girls spun and fell as Mortimer's gloved front foot caught their cheeks. Kara cried out and grabbed her face. No blood. That was because of the glove. Something to be thankful for, she supposed, but she was definitely going to have a bruise.

"No more looks, ya hear?" he snapped. "Or I'll take my gloves off next time."

"Yes, chief," they answered together.

"Now get up and get back to work!"

Neither of them dared to say their lunch break wasn't done yet. They got up and moved to opposite sides of the garden. Kara hoed around the growing lettuce. Her cheek throbbed with each hit of the hoe on the dirt.

If she had any doubt about finding a way out, it was now gone.

~~~~~

Harro read silently as Kara, Zeb, Grady, and Elsbeth sat on the couch. The only sound was when he turned a page. His face in the candlelight was grim. Kara looked at the window. They needed to get that candle out soon.

Finally, Harro spoke. "I should have known Lottie would have something important."

"Gran would've been here to explain, but..." Elsbeth sighed. "Tonight, the pains are too great."

"Where did she get it?" Zeb beat Kara to the question she'd been desperate to ask.

"Mik."

Kara couldn't stop the sharp intake of breath. Mik, the cousin who'd died of Hole Sickness. That made her think of Deena, who they had no news about since she was thrown in the Hole.

Elsbeth nodded. "I don't know where *he* got it. I don't know how long he had it. But Gran says that it will save us."

"Save us or kill us," Grady muttered. But from the look in his eyes, Kara could tell he relished being able to take up Mik's cause.

Harro's laugh was sharp and humorless. "Ironic that Mik died for providing meat to the humans when his actual crime was much more treasonous."

"It was a cover," Elsbeth said. "He sacrificed himself, Gran says, so no one would know about the Resistance. He got the book to her just before they destroyed his hut."

And tossed him into the Hole. No one said that out loud, but Kara
~~~~~

knew they were thinking it.

They sat silent a moment.

When Harro spoke, his voice was solemn. "Lottie kept the book from everyone all these years? Even from me?"

"Even from *me*," Elsbeth said. "But Gran says it's time."

"Then we need to get this to Mavis or Solomon. They'll know who will be willing to help us. People trust them more than anyone. Most of us go to them, when we can, for advice. And the pigs believe older humans are dotty, so our elders are not under any kind of suspicion. They'll pass the information along." He paused a second. "They also know who to keep it from. There *are* humans who would inform the pigs."

Grady gave a sharp laugh. "Pig lovers!"

Zeb hit him on the arm. "*Swine* lovers!

Both boys cracked up.

Kara shushed them. "Do you want us to get caught? We need to go. Now."

They slipped out of Harro's hut and crept from shadow to shadow toward theirs. Elsbeth got safely into her hut, but Kara and Zeb were one hut away when a bright light shone in their faces. Two voices spoke.

"Well, well." *Snort!* "What's this? Out after dark?"

"Looks like it."

Kara suppressed a groan. Dexter and Roscoe. She tried to think up a story, but her mind went blank with fear.

Zeb didn't seem scared at all. "Hey, chiefs. Sorry. We know we're not supposed to be out, but I heard something. Sounded like something was hurt. It howled."

Dexter shoved a lantern closer to Zeb's face. "What? What howled?"

Did he actually look nervous? Why?

"Don't know." Zeb shrugged. "But it scared Kara, so we came out to see what it was."

Roscoe swung his lantern around. It wavered a little. "I don't see anything."

"Yeah," Zeb said. "We didn't, either. So, I told my sister we should just go back to bed."

Dexter shone the light into Kara's face. "That right, girlie?"

Kara shivered and nodded.

The Mindoro guards stared at them for a few seconds. Then they shone their lanterns around again. And again, Kara thought they looked nervous.

"Humph," Dexter grunted. "Get on back, then. And if you hear it again, come and report it. We'll handle it."

Zeb nodded. "Yes, chief. C'mon, Kara."

They walked quickly to their hut, went in, and shut the door. Their mom was still sleeping. Which was good. She would probably have hurt them more than the pigs.

Kara followed Zeb into his room. "What just happened?" she whispered. "I thought we were both going into the Hole."

"Harro got a few more of Frisk's papers from Mavis and Solomon," Zeb whispered back. "Frisk wrote in them that the pigs are terrified of the Big Bads."

The Big Bads again. "Maybe. Some. But wolves are extinct."

"No. They're not."

"But the pigs say—"

"Get it in your head, Kara; the pigs lie to us about everything." Zeb added, "I decided to use howling as a reason I was out after dark in case I got caught."

Kara let her breath out in a huff. "What if it didn't work?"

"It *did* work." He snickered. "You know what that means? It means we have an advantage now."

<div align="center">~~~~~</div>

Kara wasn't as convinced as Zeb that howling would work as a reason every time they were caught out after dark or needed an excuse for something.

Then again, either because the pigs were lazy or because they thought they'd cowed the humans, their patrols were regular—and predictable. And, thinking back, Kara thought she had smelled fermented barley— barley ale—on Dexter and Roscoe's breath. Maybe they'd been doing something forbidden, too. That might explain why they were so willing to ignore Zeb and Kara's indiscretion.

But even if Kara and Zeb knew when to time their prowling, if they continued to go out after dark—particularly two nights after being caught by Dexter and Roscoe—they *would* get caught. Didn't Zeb think he and Kara wouldn't be watched?

Maybe he did, but he went to Harro's hut anyway, just like Kara did.

Once again, they didn't dare tell their mother about the meeting.

This time, Mavis was there along with Grady and Elsbeth.

"This will be short," Harro said, and Kara gave him a sharp look. He nodded. "Yes. I know. We're taking too many chances."

"But chances must be taken," Mavis said. "Risk is necessary if one is to live free." She was just about the oldest person Kara knew, and every human thought of her as wise, but Kara guessed none of them realized she was... what? A rebel?

Now Mavis leaned forward to pierce each of them with a searing gaze, and it seemed to Kara that in that short time, she made an instant assessment of each of them. Kara, frightened. Elsbeth, indomitable, just like her Gran. Zeb, hot head. Grady, ditto. But all Mavis said was, "We

47

need to ascertain who will be involved, what skills they can offer, what liabilities they might have, if we are to flee to the Outside."

Outside, outside. It sounded so easy, and so impossible.

"There are five others so far in my group," Mavis said. "Of course there are other groups."

"If…" Kara began, then stopped.

"Yes, young one. Go on."

Kara chewed her lip. "I don't mean this to sound cruel. Of course, as many of us who can escape, should. But if there are many… well, a lot of us?"

If there are *too* many. Kara didn't have to say the words, or what would happen if "too many" caused them all to be caught.

Elsbeth made a small sound, and Kara realized she must be thinking of her gran: was Lottie strong enough to make it Outside?

Mavis seemed to know what each of them was thinking. "That is one of the things we are determining," she said. "How many of us will want to go—are able to go. How many we can trust. Who we cannot trust." She shook her head. "But now is not the time for that detail. Tonight, I merely need a head count. Is this…" She gestured to the five humans in the room. "Is this all of you?"

"No," Liv said as she slipped into the hut. "I'm fleeing, too. I cannot let my children go Outside without me."

Kara almost burst into tears. Liv had refused to read the book. She hadn't taken part in any midnight meeting. Kara didn't want to leave her mom behind, but how could she have forced her to go? She reached out and squeezed Liv's hand and Liv squeezed back. Zeb grinned like an idiot.

"I knew you'd come to your senses, Liv. Right now," Mavis continued, "that makes six?"

"Seven," Elsbeth said. "I can't leave my gran behind."

Mavis nodded. "Good, good. Now, to be safe, let's leave the hut in five-minute intervals."

Kara barely took a breath until they were safe in their hut. They stood staring at each other by the light of the low burning fire for several moments, then without a word, they went to bed.

The next morning during a short break to get a drink of water, Kara put her cup back in its place and reached for the towel that hung by the cup case. She started to wipe her sweaty face when she heard voices coming from inside the tool shed.

"Big Bill is stepping up the guard patrol."

Kara sucked in a breath. That was Mortimer's voice. She should move. Get back to work. But her legs wouldn't budge.

"Yeah, there's talk about howling. Bill thinks the Big Bads are on the move again."

That was Otis. And what did he mean by the Big Bads on the move *again*? Kara's stomach clenched and her legs trembled. *Get going!* she told them. With an effort, she forced herself back out to the lettuce garden. Elsbeth was still working on the other side by the peas. Kara took the long handle scratcher and roughed up the dirt around the plants. She needed to keep her head down and work until it was time to go home. She couldn't have spoken if her life depended on it.

~~~~~

"They said *what?*" Zeb's voice was incredulous.

"You heard me," Kara snapped.

Zeb practically howled with laughter as he fell back onto his bed.

"Stop it," Kara gritted through her teeth. "If any of the guards are nearby, they'll hear you!"

"This is the best! I mean, Kara. Come *on*! They believed us! This is sweet!"

Kara rolled her eyes. "Just because you got lucky doesn't mean we're free and clear. Don't get cocky. That *will* get you caught."

Zeb calmed down with only a chuckle now and then escaping his lips. Kara gave him a scathing look but then grinned herself. "Okay, so you started it, but really, Zeb, do not let this make you sloppy."

"I won't." He paused and thought. "I gotta think of something to add to it for the next time we're caught."

"Oh, now you are *wanting* to get caught?" Kara threw up her hands. "You really are crazy."

Zeb sat up. "I know! I won't wait to get caught. I'll go and report something, just like I told Dexter and Roscoe I would."

"No! No, no, no, no! I swear, Zeb, I'll tell Mom and Harro and Mavis. You will not do anything so incredibly risky and, well, stupid. You won't!" Kara's breath caught into a sob, and she clapped a hand over her mouth.

"Hey, okay. Okay. I won't report anything. I promise."

Kara just shook her head and left the room.

~~~~~

The next three days were quiet except for the news Deena had died inside the Hole. Kara had no idea what the pigs did with her body. There were more guards on the walls, just like Kara had heard there would be, but overall, things were calm. On the outside, that is. Inside, Kara felt as though a hundred eyes watched her, and a thousand beetles scuttled around in her stomach as she worked. It took all her strength not to burst into tears.

Liv was working well into the night at the salon lately, so it fell to Kara to fix dinner. Even though she felt sick with fright, she managed to pocket some pea pods as she harvested them. And she found some wild spring onions by the trash heap. She'd make pea and onion gravy with the beef bone Zeb snagged from Big Bill's trash. Liv just about fainted when he came home with that yesterday, but he assured her he was totally alone when he found it.

As she stirred the gravy, Kara wondered when they'd hear something from Mavis. She wondered if anyone had found a way to dig out more of the tunnel. And she worried the silence meant trouble.

She and Zeb ate their potatoes and gravy quickly. Kara put Liv's portion on the stove to keep warm.

As she started to get ready for bed she heard an owl hooting. She pulled her shirt back on and collided with Zeb in the hall.

"Finally!" Zeb whispered.

"I know!" she whispered back.

They slipped out of the hut and tiptoed to Harro's, keeping in the shadows.

"What's the news?" Zeb asked as soon as they got inside.

Harro nodded. "Mavis and Solomon have set the date. One week from tomorrow. They're working on a diversion that will give us the chance to get out."

Kara leaned in. "Is the tunnel clear?"

"Almost."

"Do Elsbeth and Gran know?" Kara asked.

"They do," Grady said. "Mavis gave them the news earlier."

Kara crossed her arms. "And are you going to tell us where the tunnel is now?"

The boys looked at each other, their faces grim. "We can't," Zeb said.

And Harro said, "The fewer people who know, the safer we'll all be."

Kara glared at them. Drat, that made sense. But she didn't like it one bit.

~~~~~

One week. One week to prepare everything.

Kara shook her head. It seemed impossible. And to flee from a place they'd lived their entire lives to survive somewhere no one knew anything about? It *was* impossible.

For years, humans had sewn inside pockets in their garments to make taking things from the garbage heaps easier. Now they were expected to use them to hide things they'd need, like slivers of soap, small bits of food that wouldn't spoil, clean underthings… and they were told to wear beneath their clothing an extra set.

Not that they had much extra of anything.

"We can't possibly bring enough to survive," she said to Zeb that evening when they were alone in their hut. Their mom was working late again.

"You don't realize what's out there." He sounded exuberant. "Fruits
~~~~~

and vegetables you've never dreamed of, a countryside full of small game, waterways teeming with fish. And all of it ours."

Kara felt like stamping her foot. "You think it'll be easy? How will we catch and cook the small game? Will we have kettles, pots and pans? Will we have drinking water? Places to live?" She swallowed before saying the one thing she couldn't stop thinking. "And what if we're caught?"

Zeb took from beneath his shirt a handful of sharpened sticks.

Kara stared at them a moment before squeaking, "What? You expect us to attack the pigs?"

"Use your brain, Kara. Thin sticks against pig hide? These are to hunt small game, or to roast them on spits."

"And where in the world did you get...?"

"No questions."

Only the fear of being overheard kept her from screaming the words. "I'm tired of 'no questions.' I'm risking my life, too. I want answers."

"Okay, okay. Olow gave them to us."

"Olow?" The pig son of their mom's employers. He'd always been nice to them, but...

Zeb continued, "He thinks the pigs have gone too far."

"Olow." It was as if repeating his name would make everything clear. "He... knows...?"

"Knows and wants to help. He's even given us some supplies, like those pots and pans you were yammering about. Harro and Solomon and some of the others have been slowly bringing them into the tunnel."

"A tunnel that's not fully cleared out yet."

Zeb's voice rang with confidence. "It will be. And then we'll start bringing those supplies Outside." Before she could ask, he added, "There are caves, for temporary places to live, and stories of brick homes that were abandoned, for us to move in to."

"Abandoned? For what reason? By who?"

Zeb just shook his head.

"Does that mean you don't know? Or won't tell me?"

"A little bit of both. You have to trust."

He hadn't answered her question about being caught because they both knew the answer, just like they also knew the answer to the other question she'd dreaded asking. *What will the pigs do to those of us who stay behind?*

Trust? Yes. That was all any of them could do.

~~~~~

Two more days passed. Word came that the tunnel was clear.

Kara wasn't sure if that terrified or thrilled her. All she knew was that working in the gardens these final days, as if nothing were happening,
~~~~~

was torture.

She'd just risked a glance at Elsbeth to see how she was coping when Chickie, Olow's sister, approached.

"The crops are looking fine, human," Chickie told Kara.

Kara curtsied. "Thank you, miss." Chickie didn't often come to the gardens unless… she slanted a questioning gaze at the box in the pig's hands.

Chickie's nod was subtle. "I have some old towels for my mother's treasured employee."

Kara's breath caught in her throat. Pigs were allowed to give humans fairly useless things, like the towels from Litza's hair salon. They were torn, worn, and — as Zeb liked to say — stinking of pig. They could be used for minor, unimportant things: scrubbing, usually, or possibly for patching up holes in the straw huts. But Chickie, Olow and their parents tried to help the humans in small ways, if they could. When Chickie used the word "treasured," it meant that something was hidden in the box.

Story papers, usually. That was how Kara had gotten hers. Chickie had taught her to read.

Kara again curtsied and said, "Thank you, miss."

The moment she was safe in her hut, she pawed through the box, Zeb looking over her shoulder.

Candles. Boxes of matches. And a note.

It read, "The Big Bads are real. They hate us so much, they'll help you. Find them when you're Outside."

~~~~~

The next morning as they headed to work, the bell rang, and the siren followed. A general meeting was being called. Kara, Zeb, and Liv stood side by side as Liv said they had to stay together as much as possible. "I don't want to be separated from you," she had said.

All the humans stood in a tense silence, shuffling from one foot to another. A meeting again so soon after Deena … well, Kara didn't want to speculate what was coming next.

Big Bill strode out to the podium, which was flanked by Potam, as usual, but today he was joined by Gargan and Tremen. Kara's mouth went dry. She didn't dare glance at Zeb for fear of being noticed.

Big Bill cleared his throat. He tapped a foot on the podium as if to get everyone's attention, as if they weren't all standing and waiting for him to speak.

"Listen up," Bill snarled. "If y'all think you're being funny or sneaky, you're not. And because you didn't take me seriously about the digging, *two* of you are going in the Hole today. One in each Hole." He turned to Gargan and Tremen. "Go get them."

All the people shifted as though they might start to run, but the entire
~~~~~

Pig Patrol surrounded them. Gargan and Tremen grabbed a man and a woman and carried them off to the Holes while a child screamed out, "Mama! Daddy!"

An older woman ran to the child and held her close. Kara couldn't breathe for several seconds.

"And if ya don't stop the digging, there will be worse repercussions."

Big Bill and Potam walked off the stage. "Get to work!" Bill flung over this shoulder.

Liv gave Zeb a glare. He shook his head, his eyes wide with fright. It wasn't him, Kara knew. If it had been, he'd have admitted it. She trudged to the gardens, wondering who was purposely making the pigs angry and what they might do next. And would that help or hinder their escape?

~~~~~

For the next five days, the oppression, which Kara thought pretty bad before, became unbearable. Pigs were *everywhere.* In the streets, behind their huts, and on the walls. Every time Kara turned around, there was a pig. The humans couldn't even go to the outhouses without a pig escort.

The heat and humidity exasperated everything. Fights broke out between humans. Fights broke out between pigs. Zeb mumbled under his breath one night that something had to give, or the entire Compound was going to explode.

On the sixth day, which should have been the day of escape, the meeting siren sounded mid-morning. *What now?* Kara thought. Could things really get any worse?

Turns out they could.

Big Bill stood and stared at the humans who were pressed close to each other because the Pig Patrol surrounded them, forcing them to smash up against each other. The stench of sweating bodies caused several people around Kara to gag. She was one of them.

Finally, Bill spoke. "Where are they?"

No one answered.

"Where are they?"

Silence.

Bill slammed his front foot on the podium. "**Where. Are. They**?"

Kara felt Liv grab her hand, but she couldn't turn to look at her mom. Where was who? Was someone missing? They were supposed to go through the tunnel in small groups all during the night, but Harro had managed to send a message telling them to wait. Had one of the groups not gotten the message?

Bill turned to his guards. "Otis?"

Otis stepped up to the podium. "The humans from three huts in the B sector are missing. None of them showed up for work this morning. After a thorough search, the Pig Patrol found nothing."
~~~~~

Bill shoved Otis away from the podium. "I'm going to ask y'all one more time; where are they?"

Again, no one responded. Kara certainly didn't know anything. Did Mavis or Solomon know? Did they send the group out on purpose? And what about Harro? It was all so frustrating. They hadn't been able to meet, so she had no idea what was going on.

"That's fine then," Bill growled. He nodded to Tremen and Gargan. "Since the Hole obviously hasn't stopped your subversion, maybe this will." He pointed to the front of the group of humans. "That one. Take it to the hot mud pit and throw it in headfirst."

Tremen and Gargan jumped off the stage. Tremen pulled a length of rope from his pocket. Gargan grabbed a woman, who screamed and begged to be let go.

"You sniveling, grunting, slobbering cowards. Picking on a woman half your size. Are you scared to come for me?"

Liv gasped. "That's Taylor!"

"Who?" Kara asked.

"Mavis's brother."

Zeb leaned in. "Why is he doing that? Is it on purpose?"

"It must be," Liv whispered back.

The pigs roared, flinging people away as they tramped toward Taylor. Gargan knocked him to the ground, then Tremen tied his hands behind his back.

"How gallant," Bill sneered. "I hope it's worth it. You won't be spouting off any brave words in the mud. And even if you tried, we'd never hear." *Snort! Snort!* "Take him away!"

"Get back to work," Roscoe shouted.

The people moved off in a daze to their jobs. Liv grabbed Kara and Zeb and hugged them hard, then jogged off toward the salon. Kara and Zeb looked at each other for a second, then moved away themselves.

~~~~~

The next day repeated. More people missing. More people enraging the pigs to take them to the mud pit. Kara wanted to ask Mavis or Solomon how people were getting out. Where was the tunnel? How did they get past all the pig patrols?

The escape plan was moving forward even though no one could meet after dark. Olow and Chickie continued to smuggle supplies. Now that she was committed to the escape plan, Liv worked long into the nights making a syrup she created to drug the pigs, even though that required having a candle lit. She set up a lid from her cooking pot on one side of the candle so it wouldn't reflect on the window. But the fragrance? What if the pigs smelled it? There was no shielding that.

So far, though, Liv managed to get it done without detection.
~~~~~

What has happened to Mom? Kara wondered for the tenth time. *It's like a brave confident woman has taken over her body.* Not that that was a bad thing. It was just surprising, and even a little dangerous.

Or a lot dangerous.

It seemed everyone had something to do but Kara. Liv made the syrup with the herbs Grady brought. Zeb reported suspicious sounds and movements to the Pig Patrol, which allowed Harro to take the smuggled supplies to wherever the tunnel was while the paranoid pigs checked out Zeb's report. Even Elsbeth got involved by passing notes from Mavis to Harro and Liv.

"Mom," Kara said. "I need something to do. I feel useless. Why have I been left out?"

Liv looked up from the steaming pot of syrup. "You haven't been left out. We have a job for you." She took the pot off the fire. "This is the last batch. It needs to cool before I pour it into the bottles. Tomorrow night, you must take them to Grady."

"By myself?"

"Yes, Kara. We can't risk more than one. You know that."

Kara swallowed. She had asked to be involved. She had to be brave.

~~~~~

She'd barely gotten past her hut when a pig shoved a lantern into her face.

Dexter and Roscoe again.

"Human." Dexter moved so he stood inches from Kara. "Why are you out?"

He didn't say "again." Did he not recognize her from the last time? Or was it because of his interest in the box she carried?

"I—" The clay bottles of syrup, hidden by a mass of white truffles, were securely wrapped in Chickie's towels. But Kara's hands shook so badly she thought they might still clink together.

Roscoe saved her from answering. "With so many humans disappearing, some have taken the tasks of others. Right, girlie?"

She nodded.

Dexter snorted. "So, what are *you* doing?"

"Gr-Gr-Grady." Kara swallowed hard, then said clearly, "Grady forgot to bring Chef Ramsey the white truffles."

Was God finally with Kara? The pigs took just one glance at the truffles overflowing the box, then gestured for her to proceed. At the last second, Roscoe reached toward the box. Kara caught her breath. But he only snatched a truffle, which he popped into his mouth.

"Get going, wench."

She started off.

"Hey!" Dexter cried, but Kara didn't stop walking, and although her
~~~~~

legs shook all the way across the compound, she walked straight and tall like Lottie would. Maybe that was why no other pigs stopped her.

Finally, she reached the kitchen.

"About time," Grady whispered. "Ramsey is freaking out."

Just then the head chef yelled from across the kitchen. "Is that the truffles? Bring them over here *now!*"

Grady scooped them up and hurried over to Ramsey. Then he came back and huffed out a breath. "That was close."

Before Kara could leave, Ramsey said, "And you, girl. You can stay and help. Those dratted assistants, Virdon and Burke, have vanished. There's a lot of work to be done for Big Bill's wife's birthday feast tomorrow night!" Then he mumbled to himself, "Don't understand these humans who aren't grateful or loyal to the pigs. They've housed us and fed us. There needs to be more respect."

Grady pushed some ears of corn to Kara. "Here, start with these. The corn has to be cut off the cobs."

Kara worked with Grady for the rest of the night. Between the prep work, taking ingredients to Ramsey, and putting bowls and sheet pans on shelves, they managed to slip the syrup in the open bottles of barley ale and push them to the back so they wouldn't get mixed up with the bottles for the party. Harro made it clear none of the tainted bottles should be served there. If the pigs attending started falling over, it would definitely create suspicion.

Kara hoped her mom had made it strong enough to keep the Pig Patrol asleep long enough for them to get through the tunnel and far away from the Mindoro Compound.

When she got home, she only had time for a nap before her mom was waking her up to go back to the kitchen. Because of Big Bertha's birthday feast, more humans were pulled from their normal jobs to help with the birthday party prep.

Kara splashed cold water on her face and set off. Halfway there, she met Elsbeth and some other girls. They nodded to each other as they passed, but Elsbeth, who was last to walk by her, grabbed her hand and squeezed it.

The kitchen was hot, crowded, and busy. Ramsey barked out orders above the din as people struggled to follow them. The chaos proved to be an excellent cover for Kara and Grady. Under the guise of food prep, Grady explained to Kara how they would get the barley ale with the syrup to the Pig Patrol.

"Big Bill sends one bottle to each of the guards on his wife's birthday. But one bottle each is enough. We'll get Zeb and Elsbeth to help us carry the boxes. That way, we'll be together. When the pigs are asleep, we'll meet my dad at the garden supply sheds and go to the tunnel from there."

Harro had finally told them the location of the tunnel, which Kara still could hardly believe. Directly under the stage that held the podium where Big Bill made his announcements. It was crazy. Risky. But who was going to be at the stage during the party?

The kitchen slowly emptied out as people carried finished dishes up to the dining hall. Ramsey looked around to check if all the food was gone. He nodded to Grady and Kara.

"You two, get some help to get those bottles to the Pig Patrol. Big Bill wants everyone to toast his wife whether they're at the party or not."

"Yes, chef," Grady said.

Ramsey went up the stairs.

"Let's go," Grady said.

They loaded the boxes of barley ale into a cart. Elsbeth and Zeb joined them, and they started for the gate where Otis, Mortimer, Dexter, Roscoe and the others would be waiting. About halfway there, Grady said, "Wait."

"What?" Zeb asked.

Grady pointed and counted the boxes. "We're missing a box. Kara, were all the boxes out of the kitchen?"

"Yes, I carried the last one out."

"Oh boy, this is bad," Grady said. "That means one of the boxes of barley ale with the syrup somehow went up to the party."

Elsbeth started pushing the cart. "Well then, we need to get these bottles to the Pig Patrol and fast!"

They hurried the rest of the way. Mortimer met them in the road.

"About time," he grumbled. "You two!" He gestured to the guards. "Help me carry these boxes!"

Grady turned the empty cart around, and they walked back up the road. Kara wished they could run, but that would draw too much attention. As they walked, they heard the party in full swing. That was a good sign. Maybe no one had drunk the tainted barley ale yet.

They approached the garden supply sheds and looked around. Grady whispered, "Dad?"

"Here." Harro stepped out from behind the shed.

"What about the others?" Zeb asked.

Liv and Lottie came around, too. "We're here," Liv said.

"Okay," Harro said. "Mavis and Solomon went about half an hour ago. It's just us now. Let's go one at a time. Liv, you're first. Then Kara and Zeb. Elsbeth, you help your gran. Grady will follow, and I'll bring up the rear."

Liv slipped smoothly across the grass and behind the stage. Kara was about halfway behind when she heard shouting from the gate. She stopped and looked. Mortimer and some of the Pig Patrol barreled down toward them. Before anyone could move, the siren went off.

At the same time, pigs and humans raced from Big Bill's mansion toward the meeting place.

"Zeb!" Kara called. But their group got separated as pigs and people swarmed into the area. The pigs screamed in anger, calling the humans despicable names, even trampling over them as they charged forward. The humans who were shoved and punched, tried to fight back, but to no avail. The pigs were drunk and angry. Not a good combination.

Big Bill shouted from the podium to silence the mob. It took several minutes to get some order, and in the end, Mortimer and the Pig Patrol finally had to use their cudgels to beat back the furious pigs.

The pigs quieted, but still surrounded the humans, pushing them close together. Kara saw a flash of red hair, which she hoped was Harro's, but saw no one else from their group. Had her mom gotten into the tunnel? Gotten away? Kara hoped so.

"Boss," Mortimer shouted. "Half the Pig Patrol is down. Something in the barley ale smelled off. I tried to stop them from drinking, but—"

"The Pig Patrol, too?" thundered Big Bill. "So, that's what happened to my wife and children!" He turned to the humans. "If slow death in the mud pits wasn't enough, how about we kill as many of you as we can, right here, right now?"

That nearly set off another riot. The pigs started clamoring. Mortimer and the remnants of the Pig Patrol surged forward as if they couldn't wait to use their cudgels on human heads.

Despite being jostled, Kara caught a glimpse of a white-faced Zeb and a frantic-looking Elsbeth, then Grady, then, yes, that was Harro several feet back. But no sign of Liv or Lottie.

"Ya hear?" Big Bill raised his front right foot. "Don't you know by now to answer when spoken to?" Before anyone *could* answer, he whipped his foot downward. "Mortimer! Now!"

That's when Kara heard Lottie's voice. "Get away from us, you stinking, dirty pigs."

There was total silence, then Lottie, from far back in the crowd, spoke again. "That's right, *pigs*. You're just pigs. But we once ruled over you. It says so right here." In her hands, she held the book.

The book! Frisk's writings! How could Lottie allow the pigs to see it? Know about it? Kara tried to cry out for Lottie to stop, but only a choking sound came from her throat.

"What's this?" Big Bill roared.

"Pigs were one of the lowest life forms," Lottie went on. "Humans used you *for food*."

The pigs squealed out in shock.

"Ribs, roasts, chops!" Lottie shouted. "*Bacon!*"

"That's enough!" Big Bill shrieked. "Enough!" Then he gagged and snorted and coughed.

"Pig farmers used to feed their swine slop. *Garbage!*" Lottie gave a harsh laugh. "And you gobbled it up!" She paused, then put a hand to her mouth, threw her head back and called out, "*Suuuuuuu-Eeeeee!*"

Squealing, oinking, and grunting broke out from the pigs. Some of them dropped to all fours and began madly racing in circles. Big Bill tore from the platform, closely followed by Mortimer and the Patrol. Humans scattered, screamed, fought back, but the pigs had one target: Lottie.

"*No!*" screamed Kara, although no one could hear her above the squealing of the pigs. "Run! Get away! *Run!*"

Someone tugged Kara's arm. She yanked away, trying to see Lottie, but Lottie was surrounded by incensed pigs.

"Kara! We have to go! Now."

It was Liv.

"No, Mom. Lottie—"

"*Now*, Kara."

Harro was able to push past the milling humans, who stood stunned, staring at the mob attacking Lottie. "Go, go, go, all of us, now, go." He shoved Zeb, Grady, and Elsbeth along as if shooing pigs.

Elspeth broke free. "*Gran!*"

Harro grabbed her around the waist and stopped her. He sent the boys a searing look. "All of us. Now."

Liv pulled at Kara, but she broke free at the same time Zeb cried, "Mom, we can't leave Lottie."

Liv shook her head. "In the tunnel. Outside. Before it's too late."

And Harro said, "Don't you understand? Lottie planned this. If we refuse to go, her death…" His voice faltered.

"Will be in vain," Liv said.

Mortimer charged back toward Kara and the other humans, calling for the Patrol to fall in behind.

"Now!" Harro started off with Grady helping him drag a struggling Elsbeth.

"Kara, follow them!" Liv reached out to grab Zeb's arm, but Hamlet and Percy got between them.

"Didn't learn anything from those times I cracked your head open, human?" Hamlet sneered to Zeb.

Percy knocked Liv to the dirt. "Filthy humans! *We* rule *you*."

"Don't," Kara cried, but a laughing Hamlet's slap sent her staggering. And then Mortimer was so close, Kara could almost feel his breath.

He leered at the fallen Liv. "A useless human is a dead human," he chanted, and lifted a foot.

With a guttural cry, Kara rammed the now-empty barley ale cart into him and the closest pig. They toppled to the ground.

Zeb walloped Hamlet, knocking him backwards into Percy, who fell flat when Grady raced over and leapt on him.

Harro, looking resigned but proud, hauled up Grady and once again ordered, "All of us. *Now.*"

And then the other humans, most of them at least, roared forward, tearing at Mortimer and the Patrol, at Hamlet and Percy.

"Liv! Get up!" Harro cried. Then to Kara and Zeb, who still stood motionless, "Go!" He waved frantically. "For Lottie's sacrifice," he said to Elsbeth, who wiped her eyes and said, "For Gran!" before racing toward the stage.

Liv pulled herself up. She grabbed Kara and Zeb's hands. They glanced back at the pig mob for a moment. Then they ran.

~~~~~

The group pushed out of the tunnel, gasping and coughing. Kara could still hear the screaming and fighting on the other side of the wall.

"Come on," Harro said hoarsely. "We have to keep going. We're too close."

So, they kept going. For at least two hours, they ran, then walked, putting more and more distance between them and the Mindoro Compound. At last, Harro told them to stop.

"Here's a stream," he said. "Let's get a drink."

They all drank deeply. Then without saying a word, they fell asleep on the bank.

~~~~~

Kara heard something. What was that sound? She opened her eyes and stretched. Then she sucked in a breath. "Mom!"

Liv sat up, yawning. She opened her eyes and gasped. "Harro!"

One by one, the rest of the group woke up. No one moved or said a word. There, standing before them were three giant creatures. They were covered in dark gray and black fur and had striking yellow eyes. What were they? Kara wondered if they escaped from the pigs just to get eaten by monsters.

Harro stood and raised his hands before him. "Are you wolves?"

The biggest creature stepped forward. "We are. I am Kapil, leader of the Apennines. Some of your people have reached us already. Mavis and Solomon and others. We've been looking for you."

Elsbeth burst into tears. Kara put an arm around her shoulders.

Liv's laugh ended in a sob. "Thank God you found us."

Kapil nodded. "Come with us."

They followed the wolves for what Kara figured was an hour. About the time she felt like she couldn't take one more step, the wolves stopped.

"Just over this ridge," Kapil said.

They scrambled up the small hill and gazed in amazement. In the valley sat a massive village with high, smooth brick walls exactly like the Mindoro Compound. Kara noticed the corn fields where women hoed between the rows. There was a center square in the exact same place as in the Mindoro Compound. In the far distance, she saw a large building. A mansion? She couldn't tell for sure from here.

There were many huts, not made from sticks and straw, but bricks. They looked a lot nicer than the huts at the Mindoro Compound. Even so a sick feeling started in her stomach.

Then she noticed wolves and humans working together. Children and young wolves romped and played together. The gate in the brick wall stood wide open. There were what looked like guards standing by them, but none on top of the walls. Kara started to breathe a sigh of relief when she had a thought.

Where were Mavis and Solomon? Why weren't they waiting at the gate to greet them?

Kapil turned his yellow eyes on them. "Welcome to the Apennine Compound. We're happy to have you here." He grinned a toothy grin and added, "You can call me Chief."

The End

VENGEANCE IS SWINE
Stoney M. Setzer

Three Years Ago

Marshall Ritch wondered if his three targets felt safe.

The two-story brick home was the closest thing to a mansion that Matheson, Mississippi had to offer. Countless cars passed by on the two-lane state route every day, glimpsing the house but never getting a good look. It sat atop a hill just beyond the western city limits, looking down on its surroundings. A brick fence with an iron gate and a keypad ran parallel to the road, keeping it cut off from the outside world--or so it seemed from the road. All it really meant was that Ritch had to park his RV elsewhere and make his final approach on foot, which he would have done anyway.

His client had given him items with the Swilling brothers' respective scents, always a part of the arrangements. Ritch then used his artificially enhanced sense of smell to track them. No fence in the world could have hidden their combined stench from him. Once he was locked in on a target, he always found a way.

In this case, he did so with surprising ease. A little exploring on foot revealed that the brick fence only ran along the side of the property adjacent to the road. The other three sides were surrounded by woods-- no challenge to Ritch in his wolfen mode.

His original plan had been to do surveillance first to determine the best time to strike Hamilton, the brother living in the brick house. He had been behind the house in the pool and patio area, grilling steaks. The other two brothers, Ned and Ben were there as well. Three young women were there also, all of them appearing to be over the age of twenty but still considerably younger than any of the brothers, no doubt more attracted to their money and their power than to the men themselves. The three women put together might not have weighed as much as any one of the brothers. Another familiar smell drifted to his nose, that of alcohol. The three Swilling brothers were having a party.

Pigs, he thought in disgust. The appalling living conditions that they put their other residents through were bad enough. Only God Himself could calculate how much misery their practices had caused their tenants, and these men were living it up. Nevertheless, it presented a golden opportunity, and Ritch changed his strategy. He would take care of all three of them in one fell swoop.

The familiar hunger rose within him, mingling with his desire to see justice served. As much as Ritch hated what Dr. Lockhart's experiments had done to him, this was the only way he could reconcile it with his conscience. If his exposure to caprinium had made him a monster who had to kill periodically, the least he could do was make sure his victims were people who had victimized others.

Ritch hunkered down, his muscles tensed like a spring as he waited for the moment. Waited for when at least two of the brothers would be standing near each other and in line with his vantage point, without any of their guests in his path.

When the moment came, Ritch didn't hesitate. The wolfman charged forth like a shot out of a cannon, covering the distance and jumping on one of the brothers before anyone realized what was happening. Ritch made short work of the first Swilling, and jumped on the second before his impaired state allowed him to react.

In under sixty seconds, he had fulfilled two-thirds of his contract. Now he just had to find the third brother, who was nowhere to be seen. However, an open patio door gave him all the information he needed. The unmistakable aroma of adrenaline and terror accented the scent of his quarry, making it more pungent. Ritch hustled through the door, following his nose into the house.

The scent led him into a windowless study with bookshelves lining each wall. He entered just in time to see a section of the shelves was ajar, like a sliding door. Ritch could just glimpse a dark space beyond as the section began to slide into place. His nose told him that the other Swilling brother had gone that way, into the darkness.

Ritch sprang forward, but he was too late. The wall closed a second before he could get there, sealing off Swilling's escape route. Canine instinct urged him to try to reopen it with brute force, but his human mind reasoned that a secret passage would also have a secret control. It might be triggered by a book on the shelf or somewhere inside the furniture or decor. He just had to find it…

Distant sirens wailed, rapidly growing louder. Closer. Either his quarry or one of the guests must have been clear-headed enough to call 911. Ritch couldn't let himself get caught here, even if it meant letting his third target escape.

Seeing no other way out, Ritch retraced his steps back out to the pool area. No time for anything but retreat now. The sirens were too close. He sprinted back into the woods, plunging himself as far into their cover as he could.

As he slowly crept back toward where he had left his RV a quarter of a mile away, he lamented the outcome of his mission. Partial success wasn't much different from failure in his book. The third Swilling brother had gotten away, and now the police would know about the deaths of the other two. Hanging around to finish the job later was not an option, even if the survivor would stay in the area. Ritch saw no reason to assume that Swilling would do so.

Besides that, a stranger in an RV was too conspicuous. Ritch needed to get out of Matheson as quickly as possible and hopefully never come back.

Present Day

Marshall Ritch braced himself. Since Dr. Lockhart's experiments had turned his life upside down, he had faced off against a variety of formidable opponents. One of them had even become his ally--Dallas Boyle, the skin-grafted behemoth who stood with him now, another of Lockhart's test subjects.

Somehow, none of his previous confrontations seemed as daunting as this one.

"There ain't no way I'm doing that," Mrs. Hazel Dell said flatly. The short old lady looked almost as wide as she was tall, but Ritch had learned she could be a formidable presence. When she crossed her arms in defiance, any hopes of this being an easy interaction wilted. "No. That's final."

The two men exchanged morose glances. Boyle's brute strength and Ritch's abilities as an artificially engineered werewolf made for a powerful team when they were facing a true enemy, but they weren't much use in debating matters of survival with their comrade.

"Mrs. Dell, look at the facts," Ritch said, gesturing with his maimed right arm. "Val's already tried to kill you once, with that Mindbender. After everything you've told us about the Other Side and everything else, do you really think that's the end of it, that she or they or whoever is just going to give up?"

She clenched her jaw instead of responding right away, a sign that Ritch's words had hit home. Boyle saw it too and ran with it.

"It wasn't long ago you told us to think of this as a war and of ourselves as soldiers. That makes you like a general, doesn't it? Yes, you're our leader, but that also means we have to protect you at all costs, right?"

"Sheriff Carter seemed to know what he was doing when he took out those mutant frogs in the bait shop," Ritch said. "It's not like you'd be leaving Sardis County completely unprotected. You'd probably have to tell him that you're not going to be here, but…"

"I don't like it when you two are right," Mrs. Dell sighed. "Fine, we'll go, but only temporarily. We come back once we think things have cooled down some."

Who knows when that might be? Ritch wanted to ask, but he knew better than to push their luck. "All right, fine. Let's go."

They left Mrs. Dell to gather some necessities while they readied Ritch's RV.

"Any idea where we're going?" Boyle whispered.

"I don't know yet. I guess I didn't expect to get this far."

~~~~~

"Are you absolutely sure this is the right address?" Searcy O'Dell asked, her brow knotting in consternation as she looked at the shabby cinder block building across the street.

"Yes, I'm certain," Dr. Kelvin Lockhart said over the Bluetooth connection. "If you're asking that, then I presume you must be looking at it."

"Afraid so. It's not…well, there are lights on and vehicles in the parking lot, old pickup trucks mostly, but…"

"But not what you pictured." Lockhart chuckled. "Not exactly what you young people would call a happening place."

"Not in the least."

"I know it's dark, but look for an older model white Ford pickup with Mississippi plates, HMM 120. Let me know if you see it."

Like looking for a needle in a haystack, Searcy thought. *I'm in Mississippi, so that's on all the plates, and just about every truck here is older than I am--wait.* "Okay, I see it."

"You have the physical description of your target?" Lockhart asked.

"Got it," she replied, dreading the task. Nevertheless, she knew her mission. Mustering her courage, she strode from her vehicle and crossed the street to Pierce's Tavern, her boots crunching as she crossed the gravel parking lot.

The inside was everything she feared it might be. Cigarette smoke hung in the room like a fog, looking weird in the low lighting. There was a pool table, a pinball machine, and a dart board, all ancient. A few booths lined the walls, but most of the patrons were gathered around the bar. This wasn't the kind of bar where people came to party; it was where despondent people came to drown their sorrows.

Searcy was the youngest person in the building by at least twenty years. Worse still, she was the only female. The men gazed at her, first in shock but then their expressions became something more familiar. Searcy tried not to squirm. Her turtleneck and jeans covered everything, but the way these rednecks were ogling her, she might as well have been wearing a bathing suit.

Men can be such pigs. An ironic thought, given what she was about to
~~~~~

do. She suppressed a chuckle.

She spotted her target quickly. The fat man sat alone in the far corner, at a booth that could barely accommodate his girth. He was separate from everyone else--ostracized, according to intel. All because nobody believed his wild stories. Ignoring everyone else's stares, Searcy sauntered over to his table.

"Is this seat taken?" she asked, batting her eyelashes at him coquettishly.

His beady eyes widened a little. Between his inebriation and his shock, it took him a moment to find his voice. "Go right ahead."

"Hey babe, why do you want to fool with old Ham there?" protested a man at the bar. "Come back over here and pick out a real man!"

"Yeah, he ain't gonna do nothing but tell you a bunch of crazy stories about the Boogeyman!" another man added. Raucous laughter erupted from around the bar. Searcy's target balled up a fist but made no move.

Searcy patted his fist as she sat down beside him. "Never mind them. They're just jealous, that's all."

His face brightened a bit. "Yeah."

"So, your name is Ham?" She already knew the answer, but she had to play her part.

"Yeah. Hamilton Swilling, but you can call me Ham, little lady." Now that he was getting used to her presence, he was trying to turn on the charm. Trying and failing. He sported a long goatee, and she tried to ignore the pieces of food stuck in the hair on his chin.

Play the part. Stay in character. "So, I hear that you know something about a big, bad wolf?" she asked, doing her best to act like she was warming up to him.

Ham scowled. "You here to make fun of me? Which one of them put you up to this?"

"Nobody!" Searcy patted his hand and leaned in closer than she would have liked. Whispering, she added, "I've seen one too. A wolf-man with a messed-up arm."

Ham's eyes widened again as his mouth fell open, and she forced herself not to look at his teeth. "Was...was it his right arm?"

Searcy gasped. "You've seen the same one, haven't you?"

"Three years ago. He killed my two brothers and tried to get me. Dan and Joe and I ran a construction business together, Swilling Brothers, but now...well, it can't be Swilling Brothers with them dead." Sloppy tears rolled down his drunken face. "Killed the two of them right in front of me, at my own house!"

"Don't let him fool you, Missy!" a man at the bar shouted. "They were the shoddiest builders you ever did see. Cut every corner they could. Their properties were slums and ghettos, with everything that goes along with that. Yeah, his brothers got killed, but it was probably somebody who got tired of living in a slum while them Swillings lived high on the hog!"

"Shut your mouth, Jake Dalton!" Ham shouted. "You weren't there!"

Not exactly denying any of the accusations, Searcy noted. *No wonder Marshall Ritch went after them.* She sidled up to Ham and gave his hand a squeeze with one hand as she reached into her purse with the other. "I'm so sorry that monster did that to your brothers, Ham."

He looked at her with disbelief, his argument with Jake temporarily forgotten. "You mean you actually believe me?"

"I do. That monster has done all kinds of things like that, and I'm out to put a stop to him. Thing is, I need somebody who can help me. Somebody who wants to take him out as bad as I do. Somebody big and brave and strong." Searcy batted her eyes again, keeping his eyes locked on hers while stealthily drawing a tiny syringe from her purse. "Will you help me?"

Ham nodded solemnly, his lower lip quivering. "Count me in, little lady. There's nothing I'd love more than to avenge my brothers."

"She's as crazy as he is," Jake announced.

Ham looked up toward him, giving Searcy her chance. Quickly she jabbed the needle into his arm.

"Ouch!" he squealed, gaping at her. "What did you do?"

"It's called caprinium," she whispered. "You'll thank me later…maybe."

Ham doubled over, his head hitting the tabletop as violent tremors shook his body. Moving quickly, Searcy slid out of the booth.

"You guys might want to get out of here," she said to the men at the bar.

"What's wrong with him?" the bartender demanded. "What did you do to him?"

Searcy hustled away from the booth, getting out of the way just before the table flipped over. Ham stood. The caprinium she had injected into him had already done its work. His facial features had transformed, making him look like a man with the head of a pig. In particular, his nose had unmistakably morphed into a pig's snout. The only thing about his face left unchanged was his long goatee. On either side of his mouth, long tusks began to push through his skin.

Exclamations of shock and horror erupted from the bar. In spite of her admonition, Searcy knew these were not the kind of men who would tuck tail and run. At least that would give her a chance to put her new recruit to the test.

"Ham, can you hear me?"

"I hear. What you want?" he grunted.

Always a side effect with caprinium, Searcy thought. *In this case, it's his mind.* She looked at the bar and shrugged. "Don't say I didn't warn you." She pointed to the bar and tried to keep her words as simple as possible. "They laughed at you. Get back at them."

"I get them!" Like the boar he now resembled, he charged toward the men at the bar, snarling in fury.

The rednecks didn't stand a chance. In a matter of minutes, it was over, and Searcy led Ham outside. Nobody was left to follow them.

"That's good, Ham, very good," Searcy said, using the same tone that she would use to praise an obedient dog. "Good job."

"Want to hunt wolfman now," Swilling huffed. "Get revenge."

"Soon, soon. Do you see that white van on top of the hill?"

"I see it."

"Good. Now, go to it and get in the back."

As she had hoped, Ham obeyed perfectly. His girth prevented him from moving too quickly, but Searcy had expected as much. Once they reached the van, she opened the rear door and let him in. There were no side windows, and all of the rear seats had been removed, a little blanket spread out across the floorboards. Ham entered without hesitation.

Searcy slid into the driver's seat and handed him a flask. "Very good. Now, drink this and rest for a bit."

Ham opened it and chugged it down obediently. Moments later, he slumped over as the sedative took effect. Keeping him asleep until he was needed was probably going to be the only way to keep him under control. Once she was confident that Swilling was out, Searcy tapped her earpiece.

"Searcy to Lockhart."

"This is Lockhart. Report."

"Target acquired, and I have administered the caprinium," Searcy replied. "Effects were immediate."

"Nature of the mutation?"

"Subject transformed into a porcine-like mutant with extraordinary strength. Side effect is diminished cognitive function and heightened aggression." None of that had caught Searcy by surprise at all. Unlike Lockhart, she knew exactly what effects the caprinium would produce. Even the side effects had been by her design. Naturally, she saw no need to let Lockhart know that. Let him continue to believe that he knew more than she did.

Let him continue to believe that he was the one in charge.

"Good, good. Are you ready to proceed with the next phase?"

"Absolutely," Searcy replied, unlocking her cell phone. "Setting the trap now."

~~~~~

"I still don't like this idea," Mrs. Dell said, scowling and crossing her arms. "Not one tiny bit."
~~~~~

"We know," Ritch said, gripping the steering wheel with his one good hand. "You've mentioned that a time or two."

"Or twenty," Boyle quipped from the rear of the RV.

The old lady paid them no attention. "It's not right for us to be leaving Sardis County at a time like this! The Other Side is active, we don't know where Val Owens ran off to or what she might be planning…"

Ritch chuckled. "All you're doing is making my point for me. Val's already tried to kill you once when she brought in that Mindbender from the Other Side. There's no reason to believe that she won't try it again. Take it from me, the best way to keep from getting yourself killed is to be a moving target. I learned that from my lone wolf days, no pun intended. This RV came in handy when I was still drifting through the Southeast looking for people who had escaped justice."

Mrs. Dell broke the silence. "We can't go very far. We need to be able to get back to Sardis County in case we're needed."

"Fair enough."

"So where to?" Boyle asked.

Ritch shrugged. "I don't know. Memphis isn't too far, and there's plenty of places to hide…"

A sound like a bullhorn interrupted him. Immediately Ritch braked and pulled off to the side of the road. "I haven't heard that notification in a while," he said as he grabbed the phone and gazed at the screen.

"What is it?" Mrs. Dell inquired.

Ritch took a deep breath. "Apparently somebody wants to hire my services. I haven't taken any contracts since I came back to Sardis County. Maybe now's the time, since we need to be on the move anyway."

Mrs. Dell and Boyle looked at each other. "So, where is this job going to take us?" Boyle asked.

"A place called Matheson, Mississippi." Ritch paused, frowning. "I did a job there before, maybe about three years ago. I usually — well, used to avoid going back to places that I've already done a job. I'd probably better decline this one…" His phone went off again, and his eyes bulged in the light of its screen as he read the next message.

Mrs. Dell leaned in as close as the seat belt would allow. "Something's wrong." It was a statement rather than a question.

"Swilling," Ritch muttered, his jaw tightening.

"Is willing to do what?" Boyle asked.

"No, it's a name. Swilling. That job that I had to do in Matheson. My targets were the three Swilling brothers. I got two of them, but one got away." Ritch took a deep breath. "I didn't pursue him because I didn't want to stick around too long and risk getting caught. Only took half the payment even though technically I guess I was entitled to two-thirds. I haven't heard a peep from anybody in that area since, until now."

"And now this Swilling is making a peep," Boyle guessed.

"Message says that he just killed eight people. That's more than a peep." Ritch looked at his two companions. "All because I didn't finish business the first time around. And if he can kill eight people just like that, how many more could he destroy if he goes unchecked?"

"I take it your mind is already made up," Mrs. Dell remarked.

"Isn't our whole purpose in fighting the Other Side and Dr. Lockhart and everything else supposed to be to protect innocent lives? How is this any different? Wouldn't we still be trying to protect the innocent?"

"Never said it was," Mrs. Dell replied. "I just hope you aren't about to get into more than you bargained for."

They drove on without any more debate, but her last statement resonated in Ritch's ears for many miles.

~~~~~

Matheson was the type of town best defined by the phrase *used to be*. A plethora of abandoned buildings suggested that there used to be plenty of jobs here, that it used to be possible to make a living and support a family. In all likelihood, it probably used to be a decent place to live. Now, it looked to be the sort of place where people driving through made sure their car doors were locked.

The GPS guided Ritch's RV past a weathered sign that proclaimed the area beyond to be the industrial park. In truth, it was more of a ghost town than the rest of Matheson, a desolate labyrinth of dormant industrial structures.

My client might as well have picked a cemetery for our rendezvous point, Ritch thought.

"Do you know where we're going?" Mrs. Dell asked, a hint of uneasiness in her voice. "I mean, did you ever go to this address the other time you were here?"

"Can't say that I did. The Swillings may have had some properties near here, but don't quote me on that."

"So what did these Swillings do in the first place?" Boyle asked. "They had to have done something bad for somebody to have hired you to take them out, right?"

Ritch tightened his grip on the steering wheel. "They called themselves a construction and property management company, but that was sugarcoating. Slum lords would be more accurate. Cutting corners on construction, shoddy maintenance, you name it."

"That doesn't sound like much of a reason for someone to take out a contract on them."

"Directly, maybe not. Indirectly, their negligence opened the door for a boatload of suffering. Residents getting pneumonia in houses that weren't insulated properly. Vermin go unchecked, carrying disease with
~~~~~

them. Gas leaks, lead-based paint, faulty wiring, that sort of thing. But apparently the Swillings and the local building inspector had themselves an arrangement in place, so they never got held legally accountable for what they did--or didn't do, depending on how you look at it. Then when you factor in the other things that tend to crop up in such a setting, gangs and drugs and so forth...well, you get the idea. In this particular case, somebody just happened to hear about me and decided to do something..."

"Turn left in two hundred feet, and your destination will be on the right," the GPS announced.

The brick and mortar carcass of Thompson Mills still looked sturdy enough, despite the fact that it had clearly been forsaken for quite some time. It looked as if it might still be serviceable, should some business need a structure to call home. A water tower stood like a monolith pointing to the sky. Railroad tracks ran directly to a loading dock, suggesting that they had once been a major artery for the mill.

"Okay, so now what?" Boyle asked.

"Let's find out." Ritch grabbed the phone and started to type. "I'm...here..." he muttered as his fingers hopped around. After a few seconds, he got a response notification. "I'm supposed to go inside."

"Is that how you usually did things, back when you were ...well, you know?" Mrs. Dell inquired.

"No, ma'am. Usually, it was in wide open spaces, like RV parks or campgrounds. But I've never had to go back for one that got away, either."

~~~~~

Getting into the building was easier than Ritch would have expected. Most of the doors were boarded up, but whoever had done so had not bothered with the loading docks. Corrugated metal doors were rolled down over them, but one had been vandalized, leaving enough of a gap for an adult to pass through easily. The damage didn't appear to be terribly recent. Maybe the culprits had been homeless people desperate for shelter, or maybe they had been gang members claiming this place for a new hideout. Either way, whoever owned this property didn't seem to care enough to do anything about it.

Ritch used his flashlight to dispel the inky darkness that enveloped the inside of the shipping area. If homeless people or gangbangers had indeed come inside the building, they were nowhere to be seen now. Cobwebs adorned every nook and cranny of the cavernous room like bizarre party streamers, suggesting that nobody had disturbed them for quite some time. If anyone had been in here recently, they either were not here for long or had been peculiarly fastidious about leaving as little evidence of their presence as possible.

Still, his artificially augmented sense of smell picked up something.
~~~~~

Sweat, lots of it--human, yet somehow slightly different. He gripped his flashlight tighter as his body tensed. Nothing about this sat right with him. If there was ever a prime setting for a trap...

A bellow of animalistic fury broke the silence, reverberating off the walls so that it was impossible to discern its source. Ritch spun around just in time to see something charging toward him--something human-sized but not human-shaped. He dodged it seconds before it ran into him. Somehow it skidded to a stop before slamming into the opposite wall.

Ritch shone the flashlight at the creature. It was built like a burly man, but the head looked like that of a boar. Curved tusks flanked a distinctly piglike nose. The creature held one meaty arm up to shield his beady eyes from the glare of Ritch's flashlight, and his hand looked almost exactly like a cloven hoof.

With another yell, the pig creature charged again, his tusks coming at Ritch like a pair of scimitars. Ritch dove again and narrowly missed getting impaled. Quickly he doused his flashlight and moved from the spot where he had landed. Pitch blackness wasn't ideal, but neither was the creature tracing his flashlight beam to locate him.

However, he did have one option that was ideal. Concentrating, he focused on shifting into his wolfen mode. Ritch's hair transmogrified into fur as his teeth reshaped themselves into canine fangs.

"You wolfman must pay!" a husky voice growled. "Pay for my brothers! Me Swilling kill you wolfman!"

At least now I know who I'm up against, Ritch thought, quietly backing away from where he had been. Darkness could work in his favor as long as he kept moving and didn't give his position away. But what happened to Swilling? What had he become?

Rushing footsteps again, accompanied by a cry of savage fury. Ritch's enhanced senses told him that Swilling was charging where he had been, not where he was now. He didn't have to move to keep from getting hit. Swilling charged again with equal futility. Whatever had changed his body must have also addled his mind.

Caprinium, has to be. A strength and a side effect--a power and an unintended disability. Like when Lockhart gave it to me and I came away with a wolfen mode and a maimed arm. And if caprinium is involved with Swilling, then Lockhart probably is as well...

...Which makes this worse than I had thought. He's a victim, but he's also a full-fledged monster.

"Hold up, Swilling!" a familiar voice intoned through the darkness, sounding as if it was coming through speakers. It reverberated through the empty room. "Hiding from your problems isn't going to help you, Mr. Ritch."

"Lockhart!" Ritch shouted. "Figures that you'd be behind anybody exposed to caprinium!"

"That's what I always liked about you, Ritch. Unlike some of our other subjects--unlike Mr. Swilling here--you've always been quite perceptive. Very good."

"And you've always been too cowardly to show yourself when I'm around!"

"Mere semantics, sir. What you label as cowardice, I call common sense. This is war, and a general cannot make a target of himself."

Sounds familiar, Ritch thought, remembering how they talked Mrs. Dell into this trip in the first place. "What do you want?"

"Of all our test subjects, you impress me like none other. Even at our last encounter, you cheated death. I want you back in the fold, back in our camp to help us fight against the living nightmare from the Other Side that threatens us all. So we did a little research into reports of wolf attacks that sounded like your modus operandi, and that's how we located and recruited Mr. Swilling here."

"Funny how your way of recruiting ruins lives!"

"The Other Side must be stopped! No matter what the cost, no matter how much collateral damage might be incurred along the way, this world—this dimension—has to be saved from the Other Side. New fighters have to be recruited and indoctrinated by any means with the caprinium. As for the ones like you who have turned their backs on our cause, you either need to come back into line or be eliminated."

The ones like me? I know about Boyle and his old National Guard unit. Have there been others?

"There's no way out for you," Lockhart continued. "Might as well face it and surrender now, or else I let Mr. Swilling get the revenge on you that he craves."

"I get revenge anyway! Him no surrender!" Swilling shouted, his voice trembling in anger. "Searcy said I could kill him! I kill!"

"Silence!" Lockhart retorted. "That is not your decision to make! I am in charge here!"

They're not on the same page, Ritch thought. *Maybe that can be useful.*

Swilling laughed, a combination of guffaws and piglike snorts. "Me Swilling already set explosives," he chortled. "Me Swilling trap him wolfman, hurt, and then blow to pieces! Her Searcy said I could!"

"Searcy! What did you tell him?" Lockhart demanded.

A female voice piped up. "I said you could kill him if we couldn't get him back on our side. Why can't the big bad wolf and the third little pig work together if we can get the wolf to agree?"

Ritch detected something off about the way she spoke. Her words were rushed, almost panicked—as if she had been caught in a lie and was trying to backtrack before she got caught. *So who did she lie to?* he wondered. *Lockhart, or Swilling…or both?*

His eyes were adjusting to the darkness now. Two figures were in the cavernous room with him. One was the mutated Swilling, and the other was a female standing up on a catwalk at least eight to ten feet above floor level. Lockhart himself was nowhere to be seen. No surprise there. Ritch knew from experience the scientist liked to operate from a distance. There were probably speakers and at least one hidden camera in here, perhaps even a body cam attached to either Searcy or Swilling.

And if my eyes are adjusting, theirs are too. Silence isn't going to be golden for too much longer.

"You lie to me!" Swilling cried. "You promise me revenge!"

"Actually, that sounds like an excellent idea," Lockhart said. "What will it be, Mr. Ritch? You come back to use the powers I gave you for my cause, or shall I let Mr. Swilling do as he will?"

"I do what I want now!" Swilling shouted. "I see him! I kill him!" He charged again, right at Ritch.

Ritch dodged again. Playing matador wasn't going to work much longer. He would have to fight to escape.

Don't see the man, see the monster. Innocent people have suffered and died because of him. Forget roast beef, this little piggy has issues. He must be stopped.

Swilling needed a second to right himself after his last failed attack. Ritch rushed at him, pouncing. At the last second, Swilling swung his arm. The swat deflected the wolfman into a metal pylon, stunning him for a second.

The pig was on him immediately. His acrid breath worked on Ritch like smelling salts. Reacting quickly, he kicked Swilling, catching him in his porcine snout and sending him staggering. Ritch scrambled to his feet and lunged, spearing his opponent while he was off-balance. The two hit the floor in a heap.

They wrestled, neither gaining an advantage. Ritch clutched one of Swilling's tusks in his good hand and struggled for control of it. He knew he could end the battle if he could just get his wolfen fangs into the pig-man's jugular, but Swilling was pushing back against his forehead. Strength against strength, they were almost evenly matched.

"You murdered my brothers!" Swilling snarled, his breath putrid. "I kill you!"

An idea came to Ritch, a risky one. He hated to let his mouth morph and give up his wolfen fangs even for a moment, but he had to speak.

"Not what they want," he rasped, keeping his voice low so that it might not carry too far.

Swilling's beady eyes widened. "Searcy promised…"

"That was a lie! She tricked you!" *Come on, please let this work!* "You heard her and the other man. They want me to live!"

"But…but…she said…"

"She lied. Told you what you wanted to hear so that you'd help her." *Just like you and your brothers would have lied a lot to get what you wanted,* Ritch wanted to add, but he held that back. This was dicey enough without drawing any more of Swilling's ire.

"Why she lie?" Swilling hadn't stopped struggling, but he was clearly shaken. Not enough to give Ritch the upper hand yet, but maybe an opening…

"Because she works for Dr. Lockhart. He's her boss, but he doesn't see people. He sees pawns. They're using you to get me back, so that they can use me too. Lockhart doesn't care about anything else…or anybody else." Then, for a little extra punch, he added, "In fact, they would rather have me than you, if it came down to it."

"Why you say that?"

Ritch snickered. "Use what brains you have left. They want us to fight for them. Which do you think would make a better fighter, a wolf or a fat pig?"

Swilling frowned and furrowed his brow, as if thinking was difficult. His lips moved slightly as he muttered to himself. Ritch waited expectantly, looking for an opening…

With a sudden burst of angry strength, Swilling shoved Ritch off him. Ritch scrambled to regain his footing, only to realize that his opponent's attention was focused upward, toward the catwalk.

"Searcy! Why you lie?"

Searcy hesitated for just a moment, just enough to incriminate herself. "What are you talking about?" she stammered.

"You said I could kill! He says you use me to get him! Which is it?"

Searcy recovered her composure quickly. "And you take the word of the freak that killed your brothers over me, the person who gave you the power to get your revenge? Without me, you're still sitting in that pathetic little bar, drinking your life away while everyone mocks you for your stories about him!"

Now Swilling trained his beady eyes on him again. "Searcy right! You ruin my life!"

"But who are you going to actually believe?" Ritch pressed. "Just because she gave you power doesn't mean she's telling you the truth! Her boss is the one who gave me my powers, so isn't it his fault your brothers aren't here anymore?"

Lockhart's voice came in over the speakers. "Searcy, get control of this situation before…"

Swilling yelled, a cry of feral rage. "Enough! Everyone shut up! Only one way to make sure liars die!" He pulled a device like a remote control out of his pocket. A detonator.

"Ham! No!" Searcy screamed.

Ritch scrambled for the bay door. He was still about ten strides away when the building rumbled all around him and the ceiling crashed down...

~~~~~

The voices sounded as if they were a million miles away as they cut through the darkness.

"... found him yet?"

"Here! Under here!"

"Boyle! Get all that off of him!"

"Yes ma'am, on it!"

Ritch was dimly aware of a heavy weight pushing down on him. Suddenly, to the sound of a massive grunt and creaking metal, it became a little less heavy, like some of the weight had been pulled off him.

Fighting against his splitting headache, he opened his eyes to see Boyle's distinctive boots. His comrade was using his enhanced size and strength to dig him out, to move the debris off him piece by piece.

"Swilling..." Ritch groaned, changing his mouth back to its normal shape.

"He's alive!" Boyle shouted, making no effort to hide his joy. The decibels felt like a baseball bat against Ritch's aching head, but he'd take it. Being alive with a headache beat the alternative.

"Oh, thank God!" Mrs. Dell's voice. A little farther away but coming closer.

"What did you do, Marshall?" Boyle asked. "Huff and puff and blow his house down?" He tried to joke but was not quite able to mask the concern in his voice.

"Swilling..." Ritch repeated, wondering if he was loud enough to be heard. "Find Swilling...looks like a pig..."

Another piece of debris was flung aside. "Uh, we've already found him," Boyle said, hesitation in his voice.

"He's crazy. Don't let him..."

"Uh, buddy," Boyle interrupted, lowering his voice. "I don't think you're gonna have to worry about letting him do anything anymore. Or about him doing anything at all. Know what I mean?"

"Yeah." *At least he won't be able to hurt anyone else.* "What about that woman? Is there a woman here?"

"I haven't seen anybody else but you, and I've been digging for a while. Have you seen one, Mrs. Dell?"

"No, I haven't," the old lady answered with obvious concern in her voice. "Why? Who was she?"

Ritch filled them in on the details as Boyle continued to clear debris off him. At last he was able to move. He tried to stand, only to feel his left
~~~~~

leg give way beneath him.

"Careful," Mrs. Dell warned. "It looks like it might be broken."

"Watch this." Ritch transformed himself back to human form. In the process, his leg moved back into its correct alignment. He switched to wolfen mode again and back to human, his leg staying whole. "One of the few side effects of what Lockhart did to me that I actually like," he explained. "Other than my arm, any injuries I take in one form heal up as soon as I morph to the other. It came in handy many times during my…well, previous occupation, before I met the two of y'all."

"It's weird that woman disappeared," Mrs. Dell said. "Just like how Val Owens disappeared after that business with the Mindbender."

"You think they're related?" Boyle inquired.

"I'd be very surprised if they weren't," the old lady replied. "We already know that she had access to caprinium. No telling what else she might have from the Other Side."

~~~~~

"Quite an escape you made there," Lockhart remarked over the Bluetooth connection.

"The Warp Tunnel is a wonderful thing," Searcy answered, careful to keep her tone neutral. "Can only open it so often because it takes so long to recharge, but still…"

"Interesting how you acquired one of those," Lockhart said. "Since that's what the Other Side uses to worm their way over here."

Did he suspect something? Maybe he meant for the comment to throw her, but she didn't tip her hand. "Not like it's the only piece of their technology that we've acquired. We have caprinium, don't we?"

"True." It was hard to tell if that appeased Lockhart or not, but he didn't push the issue. "Still, we've lost another recruit, and we still don't have Ritch back in the fold. Hardly a successful mission, Searcy…but I'm glad you lived to fight another day, so to speak."

"Me, too." *Although I doubt you'd be nearly so glad if you knew who I'm really working for…*

The End
~~~~~

BY THE LIGHT OF THE MOON
Deborah Cullins Smith

Indian Reservation For The Blackfeet Tribe In Montana
1912

The sound of running footsteps echoed in the little wooden church.

"Padre! She's gone! Abby is gone!"

The cries caused Father Andrew to wince. Another child — another innocent little girl.

How long, O Lord? His heart cried out silently, knowing that the answer would not be coming. He believed in the goodness of God, but how could He turn a blind eye to the evil in a man's heart? And what monster dwelled in their community that could take young girls from their families and never let them be found by their grieving parents? This was the fifth child to go missing this year.

The elderly caretaker, Sam, hurried toward the priest, his long gray braid swinging with every step. The young mother threw herself down at the altar, hands clasped together in supplication in front of her tear-stained face. Sam's native features would have seemed impassive to the casual observer, but Father Andrew knew him well enough to see the pain and anger in his eyes. Only he knew the depth of Sam's anger, shared in the confessional.

And maybe with Miss Lucille… Father Andrew thought.

"Padre?" His voice rasped with both age and anxiety. "Should I fetch the sheriff?"

"One moment, Sam," Father Andrew said, holding up a warning hand. "Maria, when did you notice Abby had disappeared? And have you checked with some of her friends. Perhaps she is visiting with one of them and —"

"No!" Maria's voice broke as she grasped his arm, pulling him to his knees beside her. "Do you think I would not check her friends before coming here? She's gone! She was supposed to spend the night with Marybelle Cornflower last night. When she didn't come home this morning, I went to their house to ask for her. They told me she never arrived last night! They thought I had said no, but she left in the afternoon. I wanted to be sure she made it there before dark. It's no longer safe to roam about on the Res after the sun goes down." Her cries became keening moans as her story poured from her like the tears that now streaked the wooden planks of the altar. "I remember the others, the ones that never came home. We've never found any part of those poor girls. Last month it was Noni Stormcloud, and now my Abby, my sweet Abigail. Father, what if I never see her again?"

"No, Maria. We must believe God will help us find her. Hang onto your faith." His large hands encompassed her small, work-worn fingers.

Maria's husband had been dead for ten years, victim of a mob of angry white men from the surrounding cattle ranches. He'd been wrongly accused of stealing calves, but by the time they found the real culprit behind the thievery, it was too late for Martin Two Feathers. Little had been done to the men who murdered an innocent man. That was justice in the West. When Indians died, no one looked too closely into the reasons. Or the perpetrators. Father Andrew's jaw clenched at the memory of Maria clutching three-year-old Abigail's hand beside the grave that held her husband's bloodless body.

God forgive me, but I cannot forget what those supposedly 'Christian' men did to an innocent man, just because he was an Indian. Father Andrew's heart cried out in rage, but he quelled his own anger to try to bring comfort to the grieving woman at his feet.

"Padre?" Sam whispered. His gnarled hand fell on the priest's shoulder, tentatively, hesitantly. Needing permission before entering the white man's world, even in a time of great need, Sam would not venture off the Res without being sent at the priest's behest.

"Yes, Sam," he sighed. "Maybe you had better go for the sheriff. You can take my horse."

As Sam moved swiftly to the exit, Father Andrew wondered just how useful the sheriff would be this time. If past performance was any clue, the sheriff wouldn't make much of an effort for one little Indian girl, even though she was the last relative this poor woman had left to cling to.

Lucille Tanner stood watching from the door to Father Andrew's office. Her face remained expressionless, but her gaze missed nothing. She was middle-aged, but one wouldn't guess it from her posture or her swift movements. Lucille had come to the small mission ten years ago. Her first interview with Father Andrew had made him wonder if she was applying for the position of housekeeper and cook, or if she was interviewing him before deciding to stay. But his first bite of her buttermilk biscuits had sealed the deal. When he overheard her comforting and counseling a young Indian girl who had run to the church for protection from an alcoholic father, he knew she'd been sent by a heavenly agent. Her compassion, as well as her command of Scriptures, were beyond anything he could have hoped for in a partner for the mission to the Res.

These disappearing girls had touched her heart, and the priest knew they troubled Lucille profoundly. She shared the grief of these mothers, and he knew instinctively that she champed at the bit to do something about it. He often wondered what she thought she could do against whatever ruffians were behind the crimes.

Father Andrew beckoned her with a nod of his head, and Lucille glided swiftly from the doorway to kneel on the other side of the weeping mother, folding her calico skirt beneath her knees. She gently wrapped one arm around the woman, and Maria leaned into her embrace, laying her head on Lucille's shoulder. They remained on their knees, praying at the altar, until the sheriff arrived, Sam following several paces behind him.

~~~~~

Father Andrew rose and met the sheriff at the entrance of the sanctuary. Walter Higgins was a wiry scrap of a man, short in stature but wearing his authority like a man twice his size. He moved with a swift intensity that left the county in no doubt about his willingness to bust a skull or two if the occasion demanded it. His intense green eyes burned beneath bushy gray eyebrows, and a weathered, creased face pronounced his advanced age and a life spent riding the Montana countryside dispensing his own brand of justice. He looked and acted like a throwback to the last century when lawmen like Wyatt Earp and Bat Masterson dispensed "justice," often brutally. He wore a brace of pistols strapped around his waist as religiously as he wore thick cowboy boots and a black Stetson with a wide brim to keep the sun from affecting his vision. Father Andrew had never seen him unarmed, even when attending worship services, which the sheriff rarely took the time to do.

The sheriff nodded brusquely. "Father."

"Thank you for coming," Father Andrew said, fully aware that this would be as brief an interview as the sheriff could manage.

"The mother is sure the girl ain't hidin' out somewhere with her friends?" His question riled the priest, the implication being that Indian girls were prone to misbehaving and were unworthy of his precious time.

"I would not have sent for you if I thought it was not a serious matter, Sheriff Higgins." Father Andrew took a deep breath, realizing how testy that comment had sounded. Sheriff Higgins' eyebrows shot up a notch.

"Don't be so tetchy, Rev'rend," he snapped.

"We've had four other little girls disappear in this community, sir, and you haven't found any of them 'misbehaving' as you put it," Father Andrew retorted. "Abigail Two Feathers is the fifth girl this year. This needs to stop. When are you going to take it seriously? Just because they live on the Res, you act like they don't matter. Well, they *do* matter—to their families, to this community, and to God." The last two words rang out and echoed in the rafters of the little church.

"I know they matter, Father, but if I don't know where to start lookin',
~~~~~

it's a little hard to find a little girl on several thousand miles of range and mountains. You know where to start, because I surely don't." Higgins' eyes snapped with sparks of anger.

Father Andrew lowered his voice. "I think you know just like every person on this Reservation knows—just who the most likely culprits are and where to find them. But they're white, so no one does anything to stop them from violence against Indians. And if Indians take any action, they're strung up or beaten to a bloody pulp for daring to raise a hand to a white man. How is that justice?"

"Rev'rend, I can have all the suspicions in the world, but without evidence, I can't make an arrest. And that goes for *any* man, be he white, red, black, or purple polkie-dots." The sheriff leaned closer as he finished his tirade, and though his voice remained low, his words still rang in the priest's ears.

The sheriff stalked away from the priest and approached the women at the altar. His conversation with Maria Two Feathers was as brief as Father Andrew had expected it to be. He watched, arms crossed defiantly, as Higgins patted Maria awkwardly on the shoulder, tipped his hat to both women, then marched back up the aisle.

"Rev'rend," he said curtly, jerking his head to nod, as he exited the little church building, and hauled himself back in the saddle.

Sam watched him leave, his gaze never leaving the dust kicked up by the sheriff's horse. "Father, I need to talk to someone. You mind if I'm gone for a little while?"

"Sam, please don't get your people all riled up. You know it will only lead to more bloodshed, and it won't be the men responsible who'll do the bleeding—"

"No, Father, it's not like that." Sam shook his head, though his gaze still remained on the sheriff's back. "I've got a friend who might know something. I just need to have a quick talk with him."

"If you're leaving the Res, Sam—"

"No, Padre. I'm heading that way." He nodded toward the pine-covered mountains a short distance to the west. "Not going to town at all. I promise."

"Sure, Sam," Father Andrew said, swallowing hard. "Just... be careful out there."

Sam shot the good father a wobbly half-smile and a nod. "I'll walk with God like you preach that we should."

Father Andrew sighed, then genuflected, his hands forming the sign of the cross. "Go with God, my son. Take the horse."

Sam shook his head. "Naw, you may need it, Father." He set off toward the mountains at a steady jog, his stride lengthening and his gait speeding up as he left the grounds of the church.

~~~~~

Sam made his way through the woods, climbing slowly higher. He breathed in the pine scent, constantly alert for the presence of animals. Most of them would shy away from a man, but bears were another matter. Sam reached a certain stand of trees with a fallen log between them. He paused to dig into the hollow of the log, and he pulled out a long package wrapped in a tattered blanket. Pulling the blanket around his shoulders against the chill of sunset, he picked up a well-kept bow and a quiver of arrows and continued up the mountain.

"Getting too old for this," he murmured to himself as he slid quietly through the trees. Hearing a rustle in the underbrush nearby, Sam paused and nocked an arrow. As a rabbit scurried away from him, he released the arrow and the small animal collapsed. Right through the head.

"You didn't suffer, little one," Sam murmured as he knelt beside the rabbit's body and removed his arrow. "Thank You, Great Father, for providing supper to nourish me on this mission." He cleaned the arrow on the edge of his blanket, then picked up the rabbit and continued on his way.

When the sun had almost gone down behind the mountain top, Sam stopped in a small clearing and built a fire. He pulled a knife from his boot and cleaned his kill, then skewered it on a small branch and roasted it over the fire. Crude, but it worked. He missed the fry bread and beef stew he was sure Miss Lucille was making right about now. Her biscuits were a little slice of heaven, but Sam had taught her how to make his mother's fry bread. It had always been a filling treat when he was a child, and Miss Lucille indulged him by making it often. He smiled at the thought of her. What a godsend she had been to the Mission.

Must be getting soft in my old age, he thought. There were more important things to deal with right now than longing for a warm meal. These "disappearances" needed to stop. Sam only trusted one man to have his back. He just hoped that man was still alive and in the area.

The rabbit was tough and had none of Miss Lucille's good herbs to flavor it, but it filled his belly. Sam added a few small branches to the fire, then wrapped himself more tightly in his blanket and curled up to sleep.

The snap of a twig woke him. The moon had moved in the sky, so Sam knew he had slept for some time. Moving slowly, he grasped his knife and turned to face the dark forest. Two glowing eyes met his gaze, blinked, then the shape of a large gray wolf appeared in the shadows. They stared at one another for the space of several heartbeats, then the wolf turned and loped into the woods. Sam sighed, releasing the breath he'd been holding. Slowly, he sat up, still staring intently into the woods. Another twig snapped and he reached for his bow.

"Ya' don't need that, Sam," called a voice from the dark. Seconds
~~~~~

later, a grizzled old man ambled out of the darkness and sank down beside Sam, holding out his hands to warm them over the coals of the fire. "Whatchya' doin' up here at this time of night, old friend?"

"Lookin' for you, amigo," Sam said, his eyes crinkling into a half-smile.

Sharp eyes stared from beneath bushy brows. "Ya' don't say," the old man murmured. "Trouble on the Res?"

Sam nodded slowly. "Missing girls, Henry. Five of 'em, the last one just today."

"How old are they?" Henry asked, his gaze fixed on the embers of the fire.

"Let's see." He paused to consider the girls, all of whom had been familiar to him. "I'd say between thirteen and fifteen years old. This last one was about twelve, but she looked older. Know what I mean?"

Henry nodded and sighed. "You figure it's white men, don't you? That's why you came to me instead of dealing with it yourself."

Sam's eyes misted over with unshed tears. "Yeah, you know how it goes. If we even try to search in the white man's world for those girls, the whole community will pay for it. Even if we prove we're right, they'll hurt our families and friends, just for making the accusation."

"Got any thoughts on who might be behind it?" Henry asked, his head swiveling to stare full into Sam's face.

"A few." He pursed his lips and refused to meet Henry's gaze for several minutes. "Probably better if you visit one of the watering holes in town and form your own opinion, though. The Shack, maybe."

Sam refused to say the name "Bigsby," even though the three brothers were notorious for misbehaving. Somehow there was never enough evidence to suit the sheriff when it came down to arresting the three piglets. They'd been problem children from their younger years, and now that they were in their late teens and early twenties, they were as wild as the mountain lions that plagued the Res.

The worst of the town's drunks and reprobates hung out at the Shack. It was located outside the town limits and sported nightly poker games that frequently ended in gun- or knife-fights. No respectable men ever stopped in there. The owner, Jasper Redding, kept women on the second floor and made his own rotgut whiskey in a still out in the barn behind the bar. The sheriff's opinion seemed to be that anyone who went to the Shack deserved anything that happened to them. He rarely investigated out there, and the bodies were buried with little ceremony in the pauper's plots not far from the bar.

Henry nodded. "I'll head down that way. You do realize I prob'ly won't find these girls though, don't ya?"

Sam sighed. "Yeah, I know. But maybe we can at least tell their families that it won't happen to anyone else. Yeah?"

"I'll get back whatever I can," he said. "Maybe I can sniff out something of their remains. At least enough to give the families some peace."

"This won't put you in danger, will it?" Sam's brow creased.

He laughed. "I'm always getting in trouble eventually, Sam. If I ruffle too many feathers, I'll just relocate. Maybe the other side of the Rockies. I haven't been to Denver in a spell."

"Don't want to see you leave us." Sam sighed. "I just didn't know where else to turn. Sheriff Higgins ain't gonna look too hard for our children."

"Well, let's see if I can find 'em for you." Henry clapped him on the shoulder and rose to his feet. "Might want to add a log or two to that fire. You can still catch a few hours of sleep before headin' back down the mountain." He stood for a moment, staring into the fire before facing the old Indian. "You wouldn't be suspecting those Bigsby boys, now would ya?"

Sam felt around, and his hands found a few twigs. "See you in church," he said, his measured gaze giving Henry the answer he needed.

"I'll meet you at the Mission when I'm done." Henry's footsteps faded into the woods.

Sam fed the fire, but sleep took some time coming to him. He stared into the flames and wondered what Henry would unearth in the white man's world.

Nothing good, for sure.

Finally he gave up on sleep, kicked dirt over the fire and stamped out the last of the embers before starting down the mountain by the light of a full moon.

Should be home by breakfast, he thought, smiling at the notion of Miss Lucille's fresh biscuits. He hadn't even lingered to tell Lucille what he was up to. He'd catch the sharp side of her tongue for that one, he was fairly certain. She rode herd on the young Father Andrew and Sam, as well as anyone else who might be staying at the parsonage, keeping them well-fed and their home tidy. She might have been middle-aged, but it didn't show in her snapping brown eyes. Her command of the Scriptures rivaled even the good Father's, and she fussed over them like a mother hen.

On his way down the mountain, he stowed the bow and arrow back in his log, along with the blanket. Sam shivered in the early morning chill. The sun was just beginning to rise beyond the horizon, and he paused to watch the splendor.

"Thank You, Great Father, for my good friend Henry. Watch over him as he does what he must do."

Yeah, Lucille might have some words for him over what he'd done tonight. She'd worry about Henry's involvement in the situation. But what else could he do?

~~~~~

Lucille bustled around the kitchen, pulling biscuits from the oven and frying bacon on the stovetop. Occasionally, she peered out the window, searching the mountain for signs of Sam returning from his "errand." She had a pretty good idea what had sent him up there, and it worried her. Old Henry rarely came down from his perch in the higher elevations, but when he did, there was always a specific reason.

"Lord, protect them both," she murmured as she set the table for Father Andrew and Sam, trusting that he wouldn't miss breakfast if he could help it.

Father Andrew greeted her warmly when he appeared moments later for breakfast, just as she set the biscuits on the table. She paused in her kitchen duties. One keen look at his tired face told Lucille that the priest had prayed all night. He blessed the breakfast as they bowed their heads. Then she pulled the bacon from the hot grease and cracked eggs into the fragrant pan as she continued to pray and watch out the window.

"No sign of Sam yet?" he asked gently.

"No, but it's early yet," she replied, filling his plate with hot eggs and bacon. "Barely sunrise."

Father Andrew had almost finished when Sam opened the back door.

"I smell biscuits!" His voice made Father Andrew snicker. Sam whipped off his hat and hung it on the peg by the door before entering the kitchen and heading for his seat at the table. Plate and silverware already waited for him, and Lucille had a cup of coffee in front of him before he had pulled his chair up to the table.

"Of course, you do," she said, giving him a light smack on the back of the head. "Although I can't say you deserve them after taking off without a word."

"Yes'm," he mumbled. "Shoulda' mentioned it at the church. Sorry 'bout that. But you were a little busy with Maria Two Feathers."

She rolled her eyes, then nodded in agreement.

She cracked three more eggs in the bacon grease while Sam took bacon and biscuits from the platters on the table. He slathered his biscuits in Lucille's blackberry jam while his eggs cooked. Father Andrew allowed him time to down three of the flaky biscuits and a full cup of coffee before he finally spoke.

"Do I really want to know what you've been up to?" he asked quietly.

"Probably better if you don't ask too many questions," Lucille said, sliding the eggs onto his plate. "The less you know, the better, Father."

Sam shared a quick glance with her, and knew she was fully aware of who he'd gone to see. But he didn't see reprimand in her eyes. She
~~~~~

understood. She had reservations, but she understood his reasons. And she wasn't going to fuss at him for it.

Father Andrew watched them both, then cleared his throat. "Just went into the woods to enjoy the first full moon, did you? Well, I suppose that's a good enough excuse. It was beautiful last night, wasn't it? Soon it'll be too cold to go up into the mountains for the night."

Lucille and Sam shared a smile. Father Andrew was getting better about knowing when he should close his eyes to his surroundings.

~~~~~

Henry strolled into the Shack, his long gray hair pulled back in a ponytail at the back of his neck. His brown pants and faded flannel shirt were wrinkled, and his black, short-brimmed hat rested on his head at a rakish angle.

"What'll you have, old timer?" the bartender asked. His eyes were narrowed, obviously expecting Henry to be a bum looking for a handout.

"Beer," Henry said, slapping a few coins on the counter. The bartender nodded, revising his hasty opinion as he scooped up the coins and set a tall mug of beer on the counter.

Henry took in his surroundings casually, noting the quiet poker game in the corner, and the girls just coming downstairs to get their lunch from the kitchen. They glanced his way, but he ignored them and they moved on, probably relieved that their services would not be required, if Henry had to guess. He nursed the beer, then ordered another one, just to have an excuse to stick around.

After about two hours, the doors burst open and three young men charged into the room, their entrance unruly and loud.

"Hey, Jasper! We're hungry! What you got cookin' back there?" The lad was tall and brawny, his bib overalls stained with dirt and grease and something that smelled rank.

"You been wallering with the hogs again, Thad?" Jasper said, his nose wrinkling with disgust.

"Hogs gotta be fed," the young man said defiantly. "Cain't help it if I get some slop on my britches from time to time. You gonna serve us or do we have to get ornery?"

"I'll serve you, but I can't say anyone else in here is gonna have much of an appetite with you stinkin' up my place," Jasper grumbled.

"You tell 'im," the second boy said, nudging Thad with his elbow.

"I just did, Ben!" Thad said, whacking the boy on the back of the head.

"Ow! No call to hit me!" Ben shouted, shoving Thad against the bar.

As Thad bounced away from the bar and came up with balled fists, the third young man stepped between them. "Y'all need to knock it off before Jasper throws us out of here. You know what he's told you about
~~~~~

fighting in his bar."

"I ain't takin' no sass from this little whippersnapper, Cal!" Thad roared. "You keep him away from me."

Henry kept his eyes on his beer, but the hair on the back of his neck stood at attention. These three bore watching. The Bigsbys? He hadn't seen them in many years. They were unkempt and brutish, just the type of men who might think that little girls made for good sport.

Cal herded his brothers to a table in the center of the room. Jasper came out of the kitchen with three big bowls of beef stew, a small loaf of bread, and beer to wash it down. The stew smelled good to Henry, but as the boys dug in and ate, he lost his appetite. They chewed noisily, and soon stew dripped down their beards and onto their clothing. Breadcrumbs flew from their mouths as they chattered boisterously. Henry felt his stomach turn. Jasper seemed to share his revulsion, because he shot them glances of pure venom as he wiped down the bar with a wash rag. Now and then, Henry saw him shake his head in disgust.

"Pigs," Jasper muttered under his breath.

Henry suppressed a smile. He wondered why Jasper didn't just ban them from coming in, but figured money was money. If the boys were paying customers, Jasper must be willing to put up with their disgusting habits. Personally, Henry would have preferred watching hogs eat. To call these boys pigs seemed to be unfair to the species.

"Did you hear her squeal when…" Thad's voice dropped too low to be heard, but Henry's attention snapped toward the table.

"I told you not to talk about that stuff when we can be overheard," Cal snapped, looking around the bar to see if anyone was listening to them. "You want to get us all in trouble?"

His voice was low, but Henry heard him clearly. He kept his eyes on his beer.

"Nobody in here listens to us," Ben said, his voice high-pitched and whiny. "Ain't got no call to get snappish about it."

"Yeah, you want to swing for them others?" Cal whispered, but his voice reached Henry's ears. His eyes narrowed.

Yup. I think I found what I'm looking for, Henry thought.

"Hurry up and finish. We need to get back to the house." Cal cut off further comments from Ben and Thad. They grumbled but finished their meals and paid Jasper. They left as rambunctiously as they had arrived, pushing and shoving each other, and cursing loud enough to raise the roof.

Jasper pocketed the money, shaking his head in disgust.

"They always like that?" Henry asked as Jasper came back to the bar after clearing away the debris from their meal.

"Yeah, every time. I never met three more worthless youngsters in all my life." Jasper put another beer in front of Henry. "That's for you having to put up with those piglets."

"Thank you," Henry said with a nod. "Much appreciated. Who are they, anyway?" Best if he didn't seem to know who they were. He had never come into the Shack before, so hopefully no one would recognize him from his visit every year or two to town.

"The Bigsby boys," Jasper said. "I call 'em the Piggy Bigsbys. Filthy dirty in body, mind, and soul, if you know what I mean. They're always braggin' about some mischief they've been up to. Don't know for sure what they was talkin' about today, and I don't want to know. But I can tell you one thing. Whatever they've been up to, I hope it catches up to 'em. I know this isn't what you'd call a respectable establishment, but I don't need them givin' the place a bad name."

Henry nodded in sympathy. He sipped his beer, then cocked his head.

"Now that the smell is better in here, have you still got some of that stew left?"

"Sure do," Jasper said with a smile, and he went to the kitchen to fetch a bowl for Henry.

As he paid for his meal, Henry murmured to Jasper, "If I was you, I think I'd be dropping a hint to the sheriff about those boys."

"What for?" Jasper asked.

"I hear there's some Indian girls missing from the Res. I don't know. Just seems like something those boys might know a thing or two about." Henry shrugged.

"Don't know if I want to get mixed up in it," Jasper said doubtfully.

Henry dropped a generous tip on the counter. "What if they was your girls?" He nodded toward the stairs. "You know they won't stick with Indian girls if they get a taste for unsavory practices."

Jasper looked at the tip, then back at Henry. "Might be right."

Henry smiled as he left the bar. *If I have my way, the sheriff won't have much to clean up when he gets around to investigating.*

~~~~~

The moon had begun to rise, full and bright, as an enormous gray wolf trotted across a field and into the woods a couple of miles from the bar. He sniffed at the ground, stopped, and his sharp eyes scanned his surroundings. Then with his nose to the ground, he loped further into a wooded area. Between tall pine trees stood a ramshackle cabin with a pig pen set next to it. The wolf paused and smelled the air around the enclosure where the pigs moved restlessly, aware of a predator.

Ducking behind a tree, the wolf morphed slowly into an old man with a gray ponytail. Henry stood upright, his eyes narrowed as he gazed at the cabin. Something besides the smell of swine emanated from the pig
~~~~~

pen. Something—or someone—else had bled in that pen. The wolf knew it. And now so did Henry.

Suddenly, he heard a shriek of pain, and Henry moved swiftly toward the window of the cabin. His jaw tightened as he saw two Indian girls in their teens, arms wrapped around each other, cowering away from the three Bigsby boys. They laughed as they pulled at the girls' clothes and taunted them with crude comments. Thad wielded a riding crop, and he struck at the girls as they tried in vain to evade his blows. Lash marks bled on the legs and arms of the poor girls as they cowered and cringed away from their captors.

Henry's blood surged and he felt himself changing, turning back into the wolf. He hit the door with the full force of his enormous body and it crashed inward. He lunged for Thad and his teeth tore at the brute's throat. Thad gurgled as the whip fell from his hands. Henry tasted blood in his mouth, and knew he'd taken the boy's life in a single blow. Uttering profane curses, Cal grabbed for a shotgun, but Henry leapt at him and bit down, feeling wrist bones break beneath his powerful jaws. Cal screamed and tried to pull his arm from the jaws of the wolf. Blood spurted from his artery, and his weeping melted into whimpers as the life began to drain away. The wolf shook his enormous head viciously, ripping at the mangled arm clamped in his teeth. With one last growl, he released it. Cal clutched his mangled limb to his chest as the blood soaked the front of his filthy shirt. Then his arm fell limply to the floor and the wolf turned to survey the room.

Ben backed into a corner, scrabbling away, his eyes never leaving the wolf who had turned burning, gold eyes toward him. Henry advanced slowly, menace in every step.

"I won't never do it again," Ben whined. "Don't hurt me, please don't hurt me. We was just havin' some fun. They's just Injun girls. Thad said it didn't matter."

"They. Matter." Henry's voice emanated from the wolf's mouth, and Ben's face drained of blood.

"He talked! That wolf spoke!" he screamed. "Demon wolf! Demon wolf! Stay away from me!" His voice trailed away into whimpers as spittle ran into his scraggly beard.

The wolf stared at Ben as he blubbered and peed his pants. He had lost the last of his marbles, and Henry couldn't bring himself to kill a witless boy.

He turned to the girls and his gaze softened. He whined softly and drew closer. When they saw he would not hurt them, they leaned into his fur and felt his tongue against their cheeks. He padded toward the door, then looked back at them, waiting for them to follow. Skirting away from Ben, who still blubbered incoherently in the corner, they followed the wolf out of the cabin and through the woods.

~~~~~

Lucille sat in the rocking chair on the porch. Sam sat on the steps. Both of them watched and waited. It was close to midnight before they saw a wolf leading two girls toward the church. They ran to meet the children and embraced the girls gratefully. They were too exhausted to even begin to tell what had happened. Lucille ushered them into the house where she had beds ready.

"We'll contact your families," she said. "Abigail, your mama has been so worried. We've been praying for you since she discovered you were missing."

Gently, she washed their faces and applied ointment to the whip marks on their arms and legs. In halting voices, they told her of their many injuries at the hands of the three brothers. Injuries she could do nothing about except hold the weeping girls and assure them that they were safe now. Noni Stormcloud had been missing for close to a month. Lucille was astonished that she was still alive but shuddered to think of all she had endured in that time period.

"You know, girls, it might be better if you didn't tell anyone else about the wolf who saved you," she said cautiously.

Noni and Abby stared at her with dark eyes. "He saved our lives," Abby whispered.

"And men might hunt him if we tell what we know," Noni added.

Lucille nodded slowly.

"Maybe we didn't see clearly what happened. We hid under the bed and couldn't see anything. But we heard the screams and knew when it was safe to come out."

Lucille's eyes clouded over with tears. "Thank you, my dears. May the God of all comfort give you a peaceful night's sleep." She rose from their bedsides. "Call out for me if you need anything in the night. But we'll try not to wake Father Andrew if at all possible. He didn't sleep at all last night because he was praying for your safe return."

"We will try," Noni promised solemnly.

When she had the girls calmed and bedded down beneath clean sheets, Lucille went out to the stable. Henry sat on a bale of hay, dressed in the clothes she had set out for him earlier in the afternoon. She had known he would need fresh clothes if he showed up in wolf form.

"Billy," she said, hugging him firmly, and calling him by the name she'd known him by many years before.

"Miss Mina!" He returned her hug.

"Outside this barn, you have to remember to call me Lucille," she said with a smile.

"You'll always be Miss Mina to me," the old man said, his eyes
~~~~~

crinkling into smile lines.

"And you'll always be Billy Bonney to me," Mina Harker said.

"Billy the Kid is dead, ma'am," Henry said with a twinkle in his eyes. "Didn't you hear the news?"

"Yes, I did, but I didn't believe a word of it." She huffed. "Anything that Pat Garrett said was bound to be one half lies and the other half exaggeration."

Henry laughed.

"Did you kill them, Billy?" Mina/Lucille asked, her voice becoming serious.

"Well, yes, ma'am, I killed two of them. One's still alive, but his cheese done slid off the cracker, if you get my drift. I don't think he'll be hurting any more little girls." Henry's eyes were sad as he told her how he'd found the men, and what he'd done when he got to the cabin.

Lucille patted him on the shoulder. "Jasper Redding is not a sterling citizen, but he'll tell the sheriff what you two discussed. And he's apt to remember you and wonder if you had anything to do with the mess at the Bigsby cabin. What are you going to do?"

Henry sighed. "Well, I'd say it's time to move on. At least I got to stay near you for quite a few years, Miss Mina. It's more than I had hoped for. But I'd better disappear. If they look into my past too close, they may figure out who I am—who I was at one time. Might be better if I don't let 'em open that can of worms. After all, Henry McCarty was my name back before I changed it to Billy Bonney. Not very many people know that, but they're bound to find someone who does."

"Where will you go?" Lucille asked.

"I've been thinking about the Rockies. Maybe somewhere close to Denver. I like to stay near mountains so I can let the wolf run, especially under a full moon." He smiled wistfully. "Keeps me from getting old to let the old guy out now and then. And sometimes the wolf comes in handy."

"Be careful, my friend. And may God go with you wherever you decide to settle."

"Same to you, Miss Mina. You're always in my prayers." Henry smiled at her. "I really do say my prayers, ma'am. You taught me that."

Sam appeared at the door. "Sun's coming up, Henry. You might want to make yourself scarce."

"I'm going," Henry said, hugging Lucille one last time. "Til we meet again, Miss M—Lucille." He caught himself in mid-sentence.

Sam and Lucille watched Henry amble across the field, heading for the mountains.

"If he heads south, he can follow the mountains a ways until he gets closer to Billings. Then he can pick up a train in the city and head for

Denver, or anywhere else he wants to go. Henry will be okay, Miss Lucille. He'll lay low and they'll never find him."

"I know, Sam, but I wish he could find a place in this world to settle down. He's been wandering all his life." Lucille hugged her shawl closer around her arms. "He's my friend. And he's done what I couldn't do."

"Why couldn't you handle this, ma'am?" Sam asked. He'd known Lucille for ten years, and in that time, he'd seen her in action. She was formidable against evil forces.

"Because they weren't vampires," she stated simply. "I have a mandate from God to destroy vampires wherever I find them, but He won't allow me to hunt humans. And I knew if I went looking, I'd find them and I'd want to kill the men who could hurt our little girls. The temptation would be too great. But the wolf could do it. Henry's done what I wanted to do. I just hope he doesn't end up paying for it."

Sam nodded somberly. "Maybe the Great Father will shield him from the eyes of the sheriff."

Lucille smiled wistfully. "We can pray for that, Sam."

~~~~~

The next afternoon, Sheriff Higgins appeared at the door to the church.

"I heard tell that you might have recovered two of the missing girls," he said, hooking his thumbs in his belt. "Any truth in that rumor?"

"Yes," Father Andrew said, "they showed up on our doorstep around midnight last night. We took care of them, then we contacted their families first thing this morning. They've both gone home now."

"Which girls?" Higgins asked.

"Abigail Two Feathers and Noni Stormcloud. Abby's mother came to get her, and Noni lives with her grandfather. He never thought he'd see her again. She's going to need a lot of time to heal. What those boys did to her…" Father Andrew's face clouded over with grief.

"So they told you who kidnapped them?" Higgins said grimly.

"Yes, they said it was the Bigsby boys. I've heard of them, but don't know them personally. They never attend church services," Father Andrew said wryly.

"Well, they won't be attending anything anymore. Thad and Cal were killed by a wild animal. As that idiot Ben is tellin' it, a wolf that talked to him killed 'em both. Ripped Thad's throat open and tore up Cal's wrist. Both of them were bled dry. Ben's lost what little mind the boy had to begin with—which wasn't much—and we're packing him off to a looney bin. He'll be locked up for the rest of his miserable life." Sheriff Higgins' voice was sarcastic. "And that's only because we don't hang idiots in this state. If it was up to me, I'd find a branch and hang that boy from it." He sighed.
~~~~~

Father Andrew stared at the sheriff. He didn't usually side with Indians in anything.

Higgins sighed at the priest's expression and finally explained his violent opinion. "We found some girls' clothing, a few pieces of beaded jewelry, and such in the cabin. When I asked Ben about those items, he said they belonged to some girls they'd 'taken.' He said when they were done 'playin' with 'em,' they'd fed the bodies to their pigs. We checked in the pigsty and found some bones. Doc Wells said they look to belong to girls. Not full-grown, but young girls. Fits with the ages of the missing kids from the Res. I'm going to have to see the families of those girls and show them the stuff we gathered from the cabin. See if they can identify their children's belongings. Rev'rend, I know we don't always get along, but I'm here to ask you to come with me to see these folks."

Father Andrew saw the pain in the sheriff's eyes. This had been terribly difficult for the man to ask. Humbling. Father Andrew nodded slowly. "I can do that, Sheriff. They'll need comfort from their priest with this type of news. And I do know all of these families well."

Lucille stepped forward just then. The sheriff was startled. He hadn't even noticed her in the pew near them, where she had been praying.

"May I come too?" she asked. "You might need a woman's touch with some of the mothers."

The sheriff nodded.

"Sheriff," she asked, "are you going to hunt for an animal?"

"Hunt for a talking wolf? Lady, you're as daft as that Bigsby kid! I don't know what killed those boys and I don't really care. From what I saw in that pigpen and in the cabin, I'd give the devil himself a medal for killing those two wild beasts." The sheriff turned and stomped toward the door. "I ain't wasting my time hunting for figments of a madman's imagination."

Lucille's eyes closed for a moment and her lips moved in a silent prayer before she followed the sheriff out of the church.

As he followed them out into the Montana sunshine, Father Andrew smiled softly, wondering just how they had been so fortunate to score such a wonderful housekeeper.

The End

HIGPINS
Jim Doran

Rebecca raced her ATV through the middle of nowhere, searching for a fabled species. Her vehicle bounced over the bumpy field with the peak of the Cordillera Vilcababna Norte in the distant west. Her transport's last jolt slammed her against the driver's side door.

That's it! I'm calling in.

Rebecca cut the engine and swiped away the map of the terrain on her vehicle's dashboard. She punched the keypad on her phone. When she finished entering the digits, the phone trilled. *Click.* Then, a smooth, automated voice answered her call.

"First line of security. Please state your name."

Rebecca cut the motor. "Rebecca Eidelweiss."

An image of Rebecca formed on her dashboard's screen. Short, cropped black hair, hazel eyes. She had the body structure of a modern woman—the perfect disguise.

The phone flashed, taking her picture. The image and the picture overlaid each other, and the view turned green. Sounds followed, beeps and blips meant to simulate an old computer. A computer hadn't made those noises in decades.

The next question interrupted the sounds. "Second line of security. Please state your identification."

Rebecca hummed a few bars of an old song. The music was her passkey.

Again, simulated machinery noises blared from her speakers. Rebecca returned to her map and expanded her destination. She flipped to the satellite view. What? The final coordinates ended at a mountain.

"Third line of security. Were you, Rebecca Eidelweiss, born in Naples, Italy?"

Always answer the third question incorrectly. Her department's protocol demanded it. A correct answer signals an alarm. The field agent is compromised.

"Yes."

A pause. No more irritating noises. And then the voice announced, "You are triple secure. Welcome, Rebecca Eidelweiss. How may I assist you?"

"Connect me with Marie at DEED."

"We're sorry. You must state a full name. And the term 'DEED' is unfamiliar."

Were they kidding? Now, I can't use the common acronym for my department?

Rebecca recalled reading a memo about updating security procedures. It mandated all employees state every person's and place's complete name.

She glared at her phone. "Connect me with Marie Usley, my handler, at the Department of Extraordinary Emigration and Delivery." *Or I will throw you six meters!*

The trilling noises returned, followed by Marie's high-pitched voice. "Hey, Rebecca. Why did you stop?"

She switched to video. "I'm in a nondescript field in Peru, and my map ends five kilometers from the base of a mountain. Something is wrong."

Marie's image formed on her viewscreen. Her profile information appeared as a list down the side of the screen—languages: four; security clearance level: five; species: dryad. Her brown braids matched her tan skin. Vertical lines ran down her face. "I was ordered to withhold information until you started on your mission. I was going to contact you when you arrived."

Withhold information were the last words a secret agent wanted to hear. "What's going on?"

Marie thumbed a braid, "A consultant will make contact at the mountain. One of my kind."

Rebecca gripped the steering wheel. "No way! The department knows I work alone. No consultant."

"Your records indicate you are delinquent on your sensitivity training."

"I fail it every year. The department forces me to watch those terrible videos. Why take the test?"

Rebecca knew the answer before her handler voiced it. "Higpins are one of the most misunderstood of all species. Humans have made legendary odes about gorgons, cyclops, giants, and all mythicals. Though ignorant of our existence, an average homo sapien would be in awe if they met any of our kind."

Rebecca made a hand-rolling gesture, indicating to Marie to make her point. "Precisely why we mythicals must remain hidden."

"But higpins are different," continued her braided coworker. "They're not threatening. You know the types of stories humans make about higpins."

Rebecca suppressed a chuckle. She didn't blame humans at all. While higpins were bipeds and had hands and feet, they also were born with snouts and twirly tails. Nobody could miss the resemblance to pigs. Of course, they'd make nursery rhymes out of them.

"The department wants the consultant to do the talking." Marie took a deep breath. "The home office is concerned about how you'll address them."

"I'll address the higpins with the utmost respect. Whether they're in the market or at home. Whether they're eating roast beef or none."

Marie clasped her palm over her mouth. Trying to keep a straight face, she spoke through her hand. "This is why the department's worried. Higpins can't take a joke. You're going to start an incident."

Yes, I probably will. "You sent me here to find a missing higpin before a human discovers it. Timing is crucial in missing-person cases. I can't have a consultant slowing me down."

Her handler raised an eyebrow, compressing a knothole on her skin. "She is one of my kind. I've heard of her, and she has impressive credentials. With the way she travels, she won't slow you down."

Rebecca pushed the drive button for the ATV. "I'll meet her, but I'll call you back if the situation is unacceptable."

~~~~~

The car bounced to a stop fifteen meters from the mountain's foot. Rebecca's stomach was as firm as iron, else she would've vomited upon exiting. She grabbed her backpack and hoofed over to the base. Her contact was late. More grist to her mill.

She leaned against the rocky surface and surveyed the terrain in the direction of the higpin village.

"I'm over here."

Few people could sneak up on Rebecca. She jumped and turned, crouching and holding her arms out. Her fists were in front of her face.

The woman had gray, shoulder-length locks, and a marble texture to her skin — a classic Grecian statue come to life. She wore umber-colored cargo pants and a tanned leather jacket.

Rebecca lowered her fists. "I expected a dryad."

"Well, you have me."

An oread.

Dryads were wood nymphs. This mythical was an oread, a mountain nymph. Marie was using the broader meaning of the words *my kind.* Oreads were rare. Rebecca had viewed only two in her life and never conversed with them.

Rebecca relaxed her posture. "I suppose I do."

"I'm Krsrt, but you may call me Krysta." She didn't offer her hand. "You're Rebecca?"

"Eidelweiss, yes. I didn't ask for a consultant."

Krysta retrieved a sheet of paper from her jacket. "I'm here on your
~~~~~

superiors' orders. They're worried you may say something you shouldn't. The higpins trust me. They won't talk to you."

Rebecca crossed her arms. "And what makes you an authority?"

Krysta reached into her cargo pants and produced a cell. She swiped it as she talked. "To the world, I'm a leading anthropologist with PhDs in anthropology, archeology, and history. I've written extensively on the origins of South American human tribes. During my research, I've visited dozens of mythical tribes as well."

Krysta held her phone screen to Rebecca, showing her a web page with the anthropologist's erudite credentials.

Rebecca scanned the text. "So, you're a bit of an authority."

Krysta returned the phone to her cargo pants. "What did you expect? I lie around naked all day on mountainsides?"

Nymphs are so grouchy.

Rebecca clicked a button on her key fob, and the car lights flashed. "This is a missing persons mission, not research. I've interrogated hundreds of people, mythicals and otherwise. Higpins aren't any different."

The oread marched forward. "Interrogating is your first mistake. The villagers aren't suspects. All evidence indicates the higpin in question left on her own."

Rebecca walked alongside her. "Do you know this higpin?"

Krysta continued her steady pace. "Her name is Fellie Mirk. She is a beautiful and kind botanist higpin. Smart, too. I haven't a clue why she would leave her village."

"Maybe she was murdered. Her house fell on her when the big, bad vuleryn blew it down."

Krysta turned and raised her index finger. "And this is why you don't talk. Your statement is highly offensive to a higpin."

Rebecca smirked. "They have no sense of humor."

~~~~~

The higpin village streets were paved with brick. A set of wind sails generated electricity for all the half-sized buildings. The architecture resembled European origins with its gothic arches and stones. The atmosphere evoked the pre-industrial age, clearly for show rather than function. The small town felt out of place in the rockier regions of Peru.

No one invited Rebecca or Krysta inside any of the buildings. Instead, a higpin trio met the two travelers in the middle of the main street. Though standing on two legs, the higpins' heads reached only to the base of the women's necks. The first was a female with long lashes and brunette tresses flowing past her shoulders. The second, a male with carrot-colored hair, bore a scar along his cheek. The third of three wore a straight, faded yellow wig parted down the middle. All had the snout-like noses native
~~~~~

to their kind.

As they approached, Rebecca leaned over to Krysta. "Is this the 'four legs good, two legs better' committee?"

Krysta glared at her.

The female higpin held up her hand. "No further."

Krysta and Rebecca stopped about five meters from the higpins. The secret agent wrinkled her nose. It smelled like a garbage dump here. How could the higpins not identify with their boarish ancestors?

Krysta interlocked her fingers and gave a short squeal. Rebecca bit her lip to keep from laughing but recognized it as a gesture of coming in peace. She mimicked the action.

The higpins didn't respond with a greeting. The brunette had a nasal voice to go with her snout. "Agent, why do you come here?"

I thought they weren't talking to me.

"I have a name." She gritted her teeth. "Rebecca Eidelweiss. I've come because you have a missing higpin. The mythical department is concerned she may intermingle with humans, exposing us all. All higpins must stay hidden from the world."

The redhead snorted. "All mythicals in this area have complied. The closest human habitation is over a hundred-fifty kilometers away."

Krysta laid a hand on Rebecca's shoulder to signal that she would lead the conversation. "If she was motivated, Fellie might make the journey. She is strong-willed."

"And why would she?" questioned the brunette.

She held her arms out. "We don't know. We seek your guidance on Fellie's last days here."

The golden-wigged higpin spoke. "Fellie was fascinated with botany and explored the farthest from the village. She would spend the entire day collecting and studying flora in her lab tent. But she wasn't careless. She was well-trained in keeping herself out of sight of anyone but a higpin."

Krysta clasped her hands together. "And one day, she didn't return from her excursion?"

"She spends many days in the field. More time in the last six months." The redhead grimaced. "She practically lives in the shadows of the mountains. However, she returns to the tribe to check in every two days."

"When did she last check in?"

"Six days ago," admitted the red-haired higpin.

Rebecca scowled. *Kidnapped, likely. And if her abductor was human, what a mess. These tiny higpins are lucky I'm here.*

Krysta asked the query in Rebecca's mind. "Did she leave any clues as to her whereabouts?"

The brunette pointed to the east. "She had been focused at the base of the Vilambra Mountain. We think she ascended it and is lost."

"Some of us," interrupted the blonde, "aren't so sure. Fellie is rebellious, questioning our ways. She may have left us permanently."

Rebecca wanted to pull on this thread more. "What do you mean 'rebellious'?"

Krysta's tensed body language showed she was annoyed Rebecca had spoken. The yellow-coiffed welcome committee member, however, answered her question.

"She questioned our laws concerning the vuleryns. She thought it cruel to kill a vuleryn without a trial."

Unjustified killing is cruel. Unfortunately, higpins and vuleryns have always hated each other. The two have endured centuries of fighting now.

Krysta's thumb rubbed her lip. "Have you seen a vuleryn around here recently? Is it possible one has killed Fellie?"

Again, she spoke aloud Rebecca's thoughts. Vuleryns were nomads. An individual from their tribe might have wandered into higpin territory. The redhead spoke for the group. "We haven't encountered a vuleryn here for decades. But if we did, we'd shoot it and hang its corpse in front of the town hall for all to view."

Rebecca's stomach turned.

Krysta said their farewells, and they retreated from the neighborhood.

When they were out of the inhabitants' boundaries, Rebecca broke the silence. "Not much to go on but a direction. Still, it's nice to see they are honoring old stories."

"What do you mean?"

Rebecca side-eyed her. "You didn't notice? One had a straw-colored wig, and the second's hair color reminded me of bark."

Krysta glared at her. "Don't—"

"And wouldn't you say the last had a muted red mop top? The shade of bricks, I would say."

Rebecca chuckled at her joke as they made their way to Vilambra Mountain.

~~~~~

They arrived after a two-hour trek through inclines, plains, and meadows. Rebecca received a geography lesson from Krysta the entire time. The oread steered the conversation off-topic whenever Rebecca tried to mention Fellie. The agent gave up on the third attempt.

Vilambra Mountain loomed above the pair at the base. A well-trod path ended about halfway to the top. The rest would be a slow climb. For Rebecca, not Krysta, of course. Her species could merge into mountains and ascend them as swiftly as an eagle launching itself into the air. Mountain nymphs could transmute clothing and technology into rock and
~~~~~

back again. No nudity — or loss of cell phone function — was necessary.

Krysta remarked, "You won't reach the summit until well into the night."

Rebecca eyed the land mass and then unslung and unzipped her bag. She rummaged inside and removed several articles. "Give me a few."

Five minutes later, Rebecca strapped on an assembled device over her shoulders. Poles extended upward, ending in small propellers. She selected a button, and an engine whirred on the square device on her back. Compressed air blasted from metal pipes at the bottom of the pack. The resultant force lifted Rebecca off the ground. "You were saying?"

Krysta touched her chin. "I wasn't aware the department had such advanced tech."

"This is an older model," replied Rebecca. "You really should interact more with us."

"How long will it take you to reach the top?"

Rebecca peered at the summit. "Ten minutes."

"See you up there." Krysta stepped into the rock face.

Rebecca turned a knob and shot upward like a carnival performer from a cannon. The wind was the most troublesome element when flying. Currents were unpredictable, and the gusts of air interfered near mountaintops. Yet, Rebecca had more than forty hours flying the propulsion pack, and her steady hand on the controls kept her from smashing into the mountainside.

Envying flying mythicals, Rebecca navigated the slope. Her species preferred having their feet on the ground, similar to cats. Learning to walk on two legs was hard enough as a child. Flying was disturbing.

Yet, Rebecca was a professional. She landed on a plateau, an expansive flat area connecting a series of mountains. A spring from higher ridges fed abundant pine trees and other foliage — a solitary, natural sanctuary. The surroundings recalled Hilton's *Lost Horizon*.

Someone tapped Rebecca on her shoulder as she unstrapped her device. Krysta, of course. She had heard her tread behind her. The nymph wouldn't surprise her this time.

The disassembly of her device was quicker than the construction. As she packed it away, Rebecca asked, "What are our chances she's here?"

The wind whipped at Krysta's marmoreal hair without moving it a centimeter. "I studied the mountain as I was ascending. Oreads can sense if a person climbed it recently."

Rebecca donned a heavy overcoat. "And has someone climbed it?"

Krysta raised two fingers. "Not only one."

With my luck, the second is a vuleryn.

The wolf wouldn't eat the higpin unless starving. It would be uncivilized. Yet, killing Fellie for sport was a possibility. Vuleryns still hunted for leisure despite their advances in culture and technology.

Krysta interrupted her thoughts. "Do you think Fellie's alive?"

A gust ruffled Rebecca's heavy coat. "If we wait too long, she won't be."

Without another word, they made their way across the plateau.

~~~~~

While journeying, the nymph knelt and placed her ear on the ground. She had done this before twice but stood and moved on without a word. On the third occurrence, she addressed Rebecca.

"I sense movement in a cave to the east."

They trekked through a line of trees to a rocky ridge with several caves. Krysta pointed at a cavern near the top, a twenty-foot climb.

"There."

Rebecca charged toward the cavern. "How does a higpin climb a rock face like this?"

"Perhaps she transforms into a human form, like you."

"Higpins can transform?" Rebecca reached the ridge.

"Never read *The Enchanted Pig* fairy tale, then? Only *The Three Little Pigs*? It's a shame our kind doesn't remember the more honorable stories."

Rebecca examined the rocks. "Wait. This outcropping is hiding a narrow gap. It's invisible to the eye until you're closer."

A narrow, rock-strewn trail made an incline curving around the mountain. She entered the path, shoulders brushing against the entrance.

"Let me reach the top first."

"Why?"

"I have a taser."

Rebecca unholstered her weapon and followed the road to—what she hoped was—the cave. Moving stealthily, she wound around the summit with a cavern wall on the outside. *This would be a good place for an ambush.*

She kept an eye skyward. Tight places or heights didn't bother her, but she worried about an attack from above. At this altitude, though? No way! Only—

When pigs fly.

Rebecca rounded the final bend and spied the cave's mouth. She fingered the trigger on her gun and advanced, pressing her body against the wall. Krysta emerged beside her and startled her.

Brandishing her taser, Rebecca whispered, "Do that again, and I'll shoot you."

"Are you going to announce yourself?"

She shook her head and then raced around the corner, keeping her back to the wall of the stony interior. Her species' vision was better in the dark. An occupant of the cave wailed. Someone in trouble! Rebecca focused on the source of the sound.
~~~~~

A toddler-sized body covered in fur was in a bed, crying out. Rebecca spied the pointed ears and snout of a vuleryn. It wore a snug, cotton onesie with a zipper and footies. A blanket-wrapped figure next to it uncovered itself, and Rebecca spied another vuleryn of similar age.

Rebecca pointed the weapon at the ceiling when a scream broke the cavern's stillness. A curtain against a wall parted, and a female higpin with short, blonde curls and a butcher's knife grunted as she sprinted across the floor at Rebecca. Instinct and training took over, and the agent swung her gun at the aggressor. The higpin raised the knife as a third body emerged from a wall. Krysta. The nymph leaped at the higpin and tackled her to the ground. The knife wielder held onto the blade.

Rebecca aimed. Krysta shouted, "No. Don't!"

The oread directed her command at Rebecca, but the higpin halted. She lowered the knife and examined the nymph. "Krysta?"

"Fellie." Krysta raised her hands. "We mean you no harm."

A third vuleryn had popped its head from beneath the covers of its bed. All three were wailing like tiny wolves baying at the moon. Fellie's gaze darted to the youngsters. "I won't let you take them."

Rebecca's attention shifted between the vuleryns and the higpin. What was Fellie's game? Kidnapping was a crime no matter what the society. Rebecca was determined to reunite those poor wolf-like tykes with their parents. She plotted a course to them, her finger rubbing the taser's trigger.

But a single word from one of the vuleryns changed everything. The little one's tear-filled eyes focused on Fellie.

"Mama!"

Mama?

Fellie dropped the knife and rushed over to the three vuleryns. Rebecca moved to intercept her until she spied all of them reaching and crying for Fellie. Then, the other two repeated the same word.

"Mama! Mama!"

Tears flowed from Fellie's eyes as she scooped and embraced all the tykes. Her stubby fingers stroked their fur. "It's all right. I have you. Everything's fine."

The three weren't a mixed breed. Rebecca had never come across the offspring of a vuleryn and a higpin, but she would expect more pink and less fur. No, they were pure wolf beings. What was happening here? And then she remembered what the "hair of straw" higpin had said: *She questioned our laws concerning vuleryns.*

Of course, she had. She was a mother of three little wolfies.

Rebecca positioned her gun near its holster. "We're here because you went missing. Please explain yourself."

Fellie's features relaxed at the news. "Let me calm them down first."

Krysta and Rebecca watched as Fellie soothed away the vuleryns' fears with caresses and kisses. She reassured them of her presence and to protect them until their cries became murmurs. Rebecca was impressed with the amount of love pouring out from the higpin. Biologically, Fellie couldn't be their mother, but in all other ways, she was.

The vuleryns gaped at the strangers until Krysta crouched down. "Do you want to see a trick? Watch me walk into the wall!"

The vuleryns regarded Krysta. She retreated from them and stepped into the far wall of the cave. She emerged, gentle as a deer steps out from behind a tree. "I won't hurt you."

Krysta's little act pacified the vuleryns. Rebecca was grateful for it. She wasn't an affectionate person.

Krysta asked, "Fellie, what is going on?"

The higpin eyed Rebecca. "The human leaves, Krysta. How dare you bring her here!"

Rebecca holstered her gun and removed her backpack. She unfastened her pants, dropping them. She stood in a short kirtle with a stretchy waistband. Without a word, horse legs emerged from her midsection, her waist expanded into a horse's body, and new equine legs grew to match the front two. "I'm not human."

The vuleryns made gurgling, delightful noises. They liked Rebecca's trick more than Krysta's. Fellie executed a slight bow to her.

"Sorry, centaur. I didn't recognize you as a mythical."

Rebecca cleared her throat. "I'm from the department of—"

Krysta interrupted her. "Her name is Rebecca. She's investigating your disappearance. She's not going to take you away."

Oh, yeah. I should've started with that.

"True," said Rebecca. "As long as your story checks out. Let's hear it."

Fellie took a deep breath. "I met Narkoff in the wild while he was searching for healing herbs. An avalanche killed his entire vuleryn tribe, including his wife. He had to choose between saving his spouse or his children, and his wife urged him to protect the babies."

Fellie regarded the children with fond eyes. "They were smaller, then. Infants. He was carrying them when he stumbled into my site. He wasn't aware I was in my tent, but I observed him. He talked lovingly to his children."

Rebecca shuffled, hooves clacking on the stone floor. "You didn't attack or kill him?"

"I don't murder people," said Fellie. "He was my enemy, but he was alone and being silly to his wee babes. So, I walked out and talked to him."

Krysta gasped. "Without a weapon? He might have hurt you, Fellie."

Fellie shrugged. "Yes, vuleryns are much larger than higpins, and we're supposed to be natural enemies. I didn't care. My curiosity was piqued, and I respected how he comforted his children. He was defensive of them when I addressed him.

"He told me about the avalanche, and I offered him food and supplies. He was wary but accepted them. I told him he was close to a higpin establishment and would have to leave. My information scared him, and he asked me where he should go. He trusted me to direct him to safety."

Fellie put her hand on her chest. "It was the first time I felt attracted to someone else."

An awkward silence descended on the cavern. Fellie blushed. "One day led to another. He returned every day. Months later, we went through the higpin mating ritual."

The oread gasped. "You married him."

"We also enacted the traditional vuleryn union. Did you know vuleryns are monogamous? I didn't." Fellie's eyes teared up. "What an honor. Anyway, I became his wife and mother to three beautiful children that day: Dimitri, Fyodor, and Petra."

Rebecca examined the cave. "What happened to your husband?"

Fellie twitched her snout. "Do you think we couldn't make it work? Why are you surprised? It's his turn to hunt. Next week, it will be mine. I must be extra careful. I mustn't allow the other higpins to spot me. If they find us, they'll kill my family."

Krysta eyed Rebecca. "As long as it's fine with her, I'll cover for you. I will return to your village and claim I found your dead body. I'll tell them that this mountain and the surrounding area are prone to landslides. The fib should keep them at bay."

Rebecca leaned against the wall. "The office must know the truth, but we'll keep it highly classified. They'll want me to assess the danger you're in. When the children grow up, do you think they'll still regard you as their mother?"

Fellie frowned. "I should be insulted, but my learning tells me children who develop their personalities away from social prejudice accept others. Hatred is culturally influenced. Love is wired into all of us."

Rebecca nodded, accepting the answer.

Fellie put her hands on her stomach. "Besides, they'll have brothers and sisters who won't resemble them either. I'll farrow in a half year."

For the first time, Krysta lit up with a smile. Rebecca blinked in amazement. The nymph stepped forward, extending her hands. "Congratulations, Fellie."

Fellie accepted Krysta's warm gesture. "We might have made it work hiding at the base of Vilambra Mountain if we hadn't expanded our family. But I loved Narkoff too much. We fled when I was sure."

"Naturally." Krysta pulled her into an embrace.

A tear slipped down Fellie's cheeks. "You two may wait for Narkoff and stay for supper."

~~~~~

Rebecca and Krysta strolled through the night toward Rebecca's car, bellies full after the late dinner. Spending the afternoon with the higpin-vuleryn couple, Rebecca intuited they had a deep and abiding relationship. Her department need not worry.

The nymph had indicated she would journey with her to her car and then return to the village. Krysta wasn't talkative. Normally, Rebecca was the taciturn member of a group. As they neared the car, she decided to lighten the conversation before they bid each other farewell.

"Peter for a wolf name? His brothers will tease him."

"His parents won't tell him the odious *Peter and the Wolf* tale or any other divisive fables. Fortunately, they won't have to endure hearing *The Three Little Pigs*."

Rebecca retrieved her fob. "What's with you hating *The Three Little Pigs* so much?"

Krysta stopped and glared at her. "You aren't aware of the legend behind that story, are you?"

Rebecca stopped outside of her car door. "Enlighten me."

Krysta straightened her shoulders. "The story has its origins in prehistoric times when we lived with humans. In one area, three tribes lived together: higpins, vuleryns, and humans. Somehow, a recipe for vuleryn stew became a delicacy for the human group. They increased their hunting of the poor wolves. Rumor was the higpins gave the human tribe the recipe to steer them to hunt vuleryns rather than their kind.

"In their panic, the vuleryns grew furious with the higpins. One day, a mob with torches invaded the higpins' neighborhood. They burned all their houses, mostly built of straw or wood. Naturally, those materials succumbed to the fire. The higpins had to retreat to caves with red-lined clay. Later, they mined the clay to form bricks to rebuild."

Rebecca narrowed her eyes. "I don't like where this is going."

Krysta ignored her comment. "During the assault, the vuleryns without torches brought bellows to spread the fire. Furthermore, those without torches or bellows did their part, too. They hated higpins so much that they got on their hands and knees and blew on the fire to spread it."

She sighed. "They huffed, and they puffed."

"Exactly."

Rebecca clicked her fob, and the ATV blinked its headlights. "I still like the story."

Krysta put her hands at her sides, indicating no farewell handshake. "I'm not suggesting we ban it. We are all aware that restricting literature
~~~~~

is both reactionary and unwise. But we should strive to understand the deeper meanings of older tales. They teach lessons, even the simplest stories."

Rebecca said, "Noted."

Krysta stepped back. "Good-bye, agent."

Without another word, the oread turned around and marched toward the village. Rebecca entered her car, watching her leave. She tapped her fingers on the steering wheel until Krysta was a shadow against the moon.

Rebecca hit the button on her phone to connect to the home office. Marie answered, "It's early, Rebecca."

"It's the middle of the night here. Your mountain cousins are quite a trip."

"They're stoic for sure. We tree-huggers are the best nymphs, you know."

Rebecca grinned. "Absolutely. Where should I book my next ticket?"

"They're hunting naiads in the Caspian Sea again. I would've thought they heeded your message the last time you were there, but they're back. Our friend in Oregon has ignored our commands to take down his website. Oh, and Mrs. Kralston of Nova Scotia is now terminal. You know what that means."

"Sign me up for the hunters. Maybe the Kralston case next as a breather between assignments."

"Hunters, check. And the report is due on *The Three Little Piggies* by midnight tonight. Don't make me hound you—"

Rebecca tuned out Marie after she mentioned the fable. Her handler's quip wouldn't have bothered her before. She gazed at Krysta's retreating figure, recalling her story.

Why can't we all get along?

And yet, the memory of a vuleryn father and a higpin mother tucking their children in together softened her features.

Maybe we could.

The End

ELEVATED RISKS
Etta-Tamara Wilson

Cyrus slid the last bag into the space in the back of his hatchback. It wasn't everything he wanted to bring, but it was everything he couldn't replace. The rest were in waterproof boxes in the second story alcove in the house. They would be fine weathering the storm there. Besides, he had to leave some space in the back for others. It was only polite. Speaking of which...

He slid the car door shut and turned around, looking toward the house next door. It was two stories, made of white brick, topped with red clay tiles and studded with far more windows than Cyrus thought was practical. Between the house, the massive garage and the ridiculously fancy pool in the backyard, the whole property just screamed, *I'm richer than you are*. It was just so unnecessary. But knowing the homeowner, it made sense.

Cyrus never imagined he'd end up as neighbors with his own cousin. Especially not the one he'd never really gotten along with very well. Cameron had always been a real fussy kid, refusing to play with the other children because they wanted to play a rougher game like chase or wrestling, or throwing fits if his clothes got wrinkled or dirty—a common occurrence, considering they grew up in a rural area of southern Missouri. He'd gotten better as he got older, but he was still a bit too obsessed with appearances for Cyrus's taste. Unfortunately, the guy had made a fair chunk of change with a few good choices and a lot of good luck in his career, and he decided a change of scenery had been in order. Imagine Cyrus's surprise when the lot next to his own sold and the buyer happened to be his cousin. He'd had no warning. But Cyrus always prided himself on rolling with the punches, and at least with this particular punch, he could squeal on Cameron to Grandma if he got obnoxious.

Cyrus took a few steps toward an open window in the front and raised both hands to his mouth. "I left a space open for your stuff. You got twenty minutes, and then we need to get out of here," he hollered. A loud bang echoed inside the house, accompanied by a muffled curse. A man in his late thirties stuck his disheveled head out the window and glared in Cyrus's direction.

"What's the big hurry? It's not like the hurricane is here already. It's not supposed to even hit until tomorrow."

Cyrus had to admit that it was hard to imagine a hurricane was incoming. The late afternoon sunlight was only just starting to fade, and the sky was a sort of washed-out blue, with small bands of wispy clouds here and there. It was pretty, but Cyrus had lived here long enough to know it for what it was. The earliest bands of the edge of the storm had arrived, the first indicators of the tempest that would arrive tomorrow night. It was time to leave.

"I don't know about you, but I don't fancy sleeping in the car. This entire side of the state of Florida is leaving in the next few hours. If we actually want to get a hotel room at our destination, we're going to have to leave now. Just think of it this way, we're skipping the traffic."

Cameron just rolled his eyes and pulled his head back through the window. His body faded into the gloom behind him. Cyrus brought his hands back up to his face. "Remember, only bring what you absolutely need. You only got the space the size of a suitcase to work with." A disgruntled sound of agreement filtered faintly through the window. Cyrus turned and sauntered down his driveway to the edge of the street, stopping at the mailbox and turning to gaze at the neighborhood around him.

It was an interesting place. Neighborhoods without homeowners' associations were impossible to find, so he'd hustled like mad to find one with an easy-going group. As long as people kept their paint from peeling and their yards under control, the board didn't give a fig about the house color or mailbox, or flowers, or even the style of house.

The board was made up of real independent types, and thankfully, that tendency stretched to their style of governance. For the price of the occasional conspiracy theory lecture, it was easy to live in the neighborhood. What little fees they collected from the members were used to pay one retired security guard named Smith. He didn't do much except walk the occasional patrol and sign for packages, but it wasn't like they had any real security issues. As long as he kept an eye on the community, everybody was happy.

The houses on the block were a whole smattering of different styles and ages. There were a bunch of ranches from the 1980s and '90s, a few contemporaries, a handful of mediterranean-style houses built in the last few years—like Cameron's house—and then there were the experimental ones. There was a massive Victorian down the street, remodeled to look like it fell out of a HG Wells novel, with bottle green walls, copper plate trim, and giant gears decorating the front. A strange box-shaped house from the late 1940s was constructed of nothing but blue enameled-steel plates. One old bungalow owned by an earth mother type had been recently stripped down and renovated with recycled materials. And then there was Cyrus's house. Too bad his cousin had finished building his own home before Cyrus broke ground, because if Cameron had seen what he was going to build, he might have picked a different neighborhood.

Cyrus turned around and looked back with pride at his house, the round white building rising from the terrain like a fairy hill. Despite most of the lots in this neighborhood being larger than those typically available in other neighborhoods, the fifty-foot concrete dome dwarfed the lot it was situated on. The bright Florida sunlight gleamed off the snowy stucco he'd applied to the outside, broken only by the occasional flash of light off small round windows that dotted the middle section of the building. The section closest to the ground **had several sets of glass** French doors.

Cyrus thought the building was beautiful. He had considered having the stucco painted a bright red, with white trim on the windows and doors. The idea of the building looking like a giant mushroom appealed to him. Cameron, of course, was horrified, and said he already thought it was ugly but that color scheme would be even worse. It led to an argument at that year's family reunion, stopped only by a grandmotherly intervention, so Cyrus put the plan on the back burner. But if Cameron really tempted him someday…

Across the street, two people sat side-by-side in lawn chairs, baking in the sun. Cyrus recognized one of them, a neighbor from a few doors down who liked to engage him in occasional verbal battles around their childhood regional differences, especially about food. His name was Ignazio, but everyone just called him Iggy. They were currently at odds about which city had superior food. Iggy was certain it was New York. Cyrus leaned more toward Chicago.

Iggy had moved in a few years ago, back when all the New Yorkers had moved into the area, and he stayed when many of the others moved on. The middle-aged man was currently shirtless and working on developing his nearly glow-in-the-dark pale chest into a pretty nasty sunburn. Slathered in less-than-effective sunscreen, he resembled a baked ham in tropical shorts and sunglasses.

Morisa, the free spirit in her late twenties who owned the recycled house, sat in the next chair in a pale green peasant dress made of crushed cotton. A floppy straw hat shielded her eyes, her attention focused on a battered paperback in her hands.

The sunbathers didn't look all that concerned with the weather. Normally, Cyrus would have moved on, but neither of them had been here for very long. Maybe they didn't know… He hustled across the street.

"Hey, guys? Do you see all those clouds up there?" He pointed up, and Morisa leaned back to stare at the wispy shreds of white dotting the sky. "That's the edge of the storm. The governor is gonna order everyone to leave by nightfall, I guarantee it. You'll have an easier time getting out if you leave before that."

Morisa dropped her book into her lap. "Oh dear. We have to leave?" She glanced at Iggy, eyes wide. "I don't have a car. It'll take me all day to arrange a rental. Should I try?"

Iggy shrugged. "You can if you want. I plan to stay here, whatever they say."

Cyrus frowned. "That's not a great idea. Hurricane Felan is already a Category 3, and it'll only get stronger as it gets closer."

"No one is chasing me off my property. That includes storms."

Cyrus shook his head. It was a bad idea, but Iggy was an adult. "So be it. But if it gets bad, my house is concrete and I've got a guest suite on the first floor you can access from outside. You can shelter there if you need to." He waited for Iggy to nod and turned to Morisa. "If you don't already have a car, I doubt any will be available for rent by now. Do you have anyone you can catch a ride with? Where would you be headed?"

Morisa twitched up her shoulder in a half-hearted shrug. "No, not really. I've only been here since April and hadn't thought about what to do for bad weather. We didn't get many bad storms in Portland."

Great. She was totally unprepared. He couldn't just leave her here; she'd never survive. Cyrus sighed.

"Well, if you're up for it, you can catch a ride with Cameron and me. I can clear a space in the back seat. You'll have to keep it down to one bag, though, since it'll have to sit in your lap. Go with only the essential, cannot-lose documents and a few changes of clothing, whatever you need for a couple of nights away from home. That okay?"

Morisa nodded her head so enthusiastically, he could almost hear her eyes rattle.

"Great. Go grab your bag. I'll go clear some space." He turned and hurried across the street and back up the driveway toward the parked car, ignoring the clatter as Morisa scrambled out of her chair and bolted for her house.

As he neared the car, a loud thump from the far side got his attention. Cyrus looked over at Cameron's house just in time to see a large bag sail through the open window and land with a crash next to another, bigger one on the lawn between the house and the driveway. Both bags were the same size as the available space in the car, and it didn't look like Cameron was done. A third and fourth bag followed in quick succession.

This better be stopped quickly, Cyrus thought, *before we end up trying to locate a U-Haul on short notice.*

"Hey, Cameron? I said only what you absolutely need."

The door next to the kitchen banged open and Cameron stormed out, holding a packed bag in each hand. He hurried over to the pile to hover protectively over it, setting both bags down next to it. His chest swelled up and he huffed, bright patches of pink appearing on both cheeks. His short, dark hair pointed in every which way, like he'd been in a wind tunnel or tried styling his hair with a vacuum cleaner. He'd never been very tall and only came up to Cyrus's chin — it was a family **trait,** as his father was only about five-foot-three physically, but seven feet tall in terms of attitude, and Cameron usually reminded Cyrus a bit of a storm-blown rooster. Although, if he got out in the sun for too long, his stocky build and tendency to turn red caused him to resemble more of an aggravated piglet.

"This *is* all that I need. Technically, I need even more stuff, but this is what I can get away with."

Cyrus had always thought of Cameron as a bit of an odd guy. Although he gave the physical appearance of a somewhat overdressed but fairly normal Midwesterner, on entering his house, that all changed. Cameron had always been a serious collector, and since he moved to **Florida,** he had haphazardly stuffed more collections and fancy trinkets into the house than anyone else Cyrus had ever seen.

He was rather touchy about it, too. Cyrus had called it a pigsty once and teased his cousin that he wasn't surprised if one day, the mess attracted the big bad wolf, looking for an easy pork chop dinner. Cameron had turned a remarkably unattractive shade of pink and ordered him out. Cyrus didn't go inside much anymore, but he did like to occasionally sneak in when Cameron was distracted and hide figurines of wolves among the clutter. Cameron hadn't said anything about them yet, so they evidently hadn't been found so far.

"All this stuff is necessary?" Cyrus bent over and opened one of the bigger bags. Inside was what looked to be a good portion of the contents of Cameron's wardrobe, including most of his designer sneakers. The nearest bag contained an assortment of fancy toiletries, a couple expensive watches in protective cases and a few choice pieces from Cameron's many collections wrapped in his fancy hand towels.

Cyrus looked up at him, one eyebrow quirked. "Really, Cameron?"

"What?" Cameron crossed his arms and pursed his lips. "You can't just run off unprepared. Just because we're running from the storm is no reason to look unkempt."

Cyrus tilted his head to one side and held up a small desktop art nouveau statue of a mermaid. Cameron twisted his hands together and glanced quickly toward the street, his blue-gray eyes taking on the same dull hue of the slowly darkening sky.

"We're going to be gone." His voice was hushed but pitched much higher than normal, straining against the heavy pressure of the building storm front. "Everyone we know is evacuating. If I leave the valuable stuff here, it might be gone when we get back. Or destroyed by the storm."

Cyrus sighed. He could understand the impulse. Still didn't mean they could take it, but he couldn't really blame Cameron for trying. He dropped the figure back into the bag and stood.

"I know. But if everyone is leaving because of a dangerous storm, I doubt too many thieves will be all that eager to run about stealing things. Plus, we'll be back before they could reasonably manage anything afterward. And as for things getting damaged…" He reached down and grabbed the bag full of trinkets.

"I'm sure the house will be fine. But if it'll make you feel better, we can put anything we don't take in my house. It's designed to stand up to storms bigger than this, so it'll all be fine. Besides, we need the space in the car. We've picked up a stray we have to take with us, and she'll need a place to sit. We'll just take the clothing and any important documents, Okay?" He waited for Cameron's reluctant nod, then transported most of the bags to his storage alcove. Only one bag of clothing went into the back of the car, much to Cameron's dismay.

True to his word, twenty minutes later, Cyrus had repacked the back seat to free up space and was rolling the car toward the street. Cameron sat in the passenger seat, a folder of important papers in his lap and a disappointed frown on his face. He huffed when Cyrus pulled up in front of Iggy and parked again. "We're taking him?"

"No. He's staying." Cyrus climbed out of the driver's seat and crossed in front of the car. "Hey… are you sure about this?"

Iggy nodded, his eyes closed as he continued to bake. "Yep. I got plenty of supplies. I'll be fine. I'll keep an eye on your houses for you. Have fun on the drive."

"If you say so." Cyrus dropped a key with a keyfob in the shape of a bronze palm tree in Iggy's lap. "Here's the key to my guest suite. The door is around back, marked with a palm tree just like the fob. There are some emergency supplies and bottled water in the closet in there if you need them."

Iggy scooped up the key. "Thanks."

Cyrus nodded. Morisa came puffing around the car at just that moment, arms wrapped tightly around a large backpack straining at the seams, her plump face a shiny pink from exertion. She was short, but she wasn't exactly the smallest woman he'd seen recently, her lack of height going instead to the padding she had gained widthwise. The bag was almost the same size as her in both directions. There was no way she'd be able to see around that thing while it sat in her lap, but he did have to hand it to her, technically, she'd done exactly as he said. He took the bag from her and was surprised when it nearly pulled him to the ground. How tightly had she packed this thing? Did she put bricks in it or what?

"Did you bring everything you need? Is your insurance paperwork in here?"

Morisa nodded. "I added everything from my documents folder, just in case."

"All right. Let's get going, then, before the big bad wolf of a storm catches us out in the open and devours us. After you." He opened the back door and waited for her to settle in, handed her the backpack-shaped boulder and closed her door. He nodded at Iggy as he walked back around to the driver's side door. "Good luck." At Iggy's lazy salute, he climbed in and started the car.

He carefully steered the car out of the neighborhood, looking back only once to see Iggy sitting in his chair on the edge of the road, surrounded by the eclectic mix of houses that made up what Cyrus thought of as the best neighborhood he'd ever lived in. He glanced up at the storm slowly building over the block, and just hoped it wasn't the last time he'd ever see home.

~~~~~

So, the storm hadn't destroyed everything, but there was a lot of damage. A few houses remained intact in the midst of the debris. The steel-plate house seemed to come out of it okay, although a number of plates now had cracks in them. The Victorian wasn't so lucky, as a tree seemed to have fallen through the side. Most of the ranches were roofless.

A few houses were practically gone. Morisa's little recycled bungalow was one of them. When they pulled up to her lot, the only thing left intact was the foundation, embedded with pieces of supports for the walls. The rest of the house had slouched sideways a few feet and rested in soggy piles partially overtaking the enormous garden in the backyard. Morisa made a quiet little sound, visibly deflating as she stared at the mess. Sitting in the back of the car in her loose-fitting sundress, staring at her destroyed house with wide eyes and slumped shoulders, she reminded him of that little depressed pig with the speech impediment in those old quaint British stories his grandmother had read them when they were children. Cyrus felt bad for her.

"It'll be okay. I've got plenty of rooms at my house. You can stay with me while you figure out what you want to do."

Morisa nodded. It took her a moment to make audible sounds. "... thank you."

"You had insurance, right?"

"Yes. The neighborhood association made me buy a rather expensive plan when I finished my bungalow."

"Okay, then it'll be fine. File a claim, and we'll see what you can do once it comes in."

He pulled away from the remains of the house to complete the short drive to his own property. As they crept down the street, he gazed around at the other houses as he tried his best to ignore the quiet sniffling coming
~~~~~

from the back seat. She deserved a moment to herself to adjust. It was only fair. He was pleased to see that Iggy's house was mostly intact, missing only a large patch of shingles. It boded well for the sturdier houses.

He would have thought of Cameron's house as pretty durable. His cousin had bragged about its construction often enough, after all. The fact that Cyrus could see the building's insides from the street made that description a bit overambitious, though. A portion of an unrelated roof was sticking out of the front wall, resulting in a fairly large hole directly into the kitchen. It wasn't a catastrophic injury to the house, since Cameron could live without a kitchen during the repairs, but it certainly wasn't a simple patch-job.

Cameron sat in the passenger seat, staring at the house, his mouth hanging open. He was silent. That was not a great sign, in Cyrus's experience. With Cameron, silence usually built up to a meltdown. He'd better get everyone inside before his cousin turned into a human firework.

He turned the car into his driveway, dodging fallen branches and an occasional bundle of torn shingles from his less-fortunate neighbors, easing to a stop as close to his own house as possible.

"Come on." He pulled on Cameron's sleeve, trying to distract him. "Let's all get settled in, and then we can go check out the damage."

He popped out of the driver's seat, turning to gaze at his own property. Overall, it looked fine. The building appeared intact, with the damage seemingly contained to a few scuffs to the stucco and a dire need to wash the windows. He'd have to look closer from the inside to be sure, though.

"Hey there!"

Iggy rounded the back of the building and approached the car. He wore a pair of shorts and sandals very similar to his attire when they left. Now they were joined by a threadbare white button up shirt that had definitely seen better days. The real distraction, though, was the massive blue-and-purple bruises stretching across his left arm and dotting his face.

"You're back! Welcome to paradise."

Morisa squeaked in dismay at the sight of the bruises, followed by another sniff. She took a quick step forward and threw her arms around the man's neck, burying her face in his shirt. She just hung there, quietly sniffling from time to time. Iggy wrapped an arm around her back in an awkward sort of hug and looked at Cyrus.

"So… I take it she saw what happened?"

Cyrus nodded. "Just before we pulled up."

"It went the minute the wind changed direction. It was quick, but made a heck of a racket."

"Did you hear it from your house? Are you okay? How much damage did you get, anyway? I saw that missing patch of roofing."

Morisa shivered. Iggy patted her back absently. "The house was fine when I last checked it. I lost all my trees, and the stupid things started smacking me back when I tried pulling them off my fence. The roof patch came off early, but it's the only **structural** damage I had. I just have to cover it until we can get the stuff to fix it. Speaking of which…"

He eased Morisa back squarely on her feet, patting her arms gently. Then he turned to gesture at the dome. "You said you had some supplies. Are any of those unclaimed tarps, by any chance? I don't have any, and we need to start covering the damaged spots."

Cyrus nodded. "Yeah, I've got a few. I've got to pull some out for Cameron, anyway." He gestured over his shoulder with his thumb, pointing vaguely at the perforated mediterranean behind him. "I can give you a couple for your bald patch. I just gotta get Morisa here inside, put her in the guest room. Do you need a room, or are you good?"

"Great! I'm good, I'm staying at my place. But thanks for the offer. Oh, here's your keys." Iggy dropped the palm-tree keychain into Cyrus's hand.

Cameron finally spoke. "This was supposed to be stormproof! They promised it was stormproof! Why did they charge me so much if it was gonna crumble in a stiff breeze?!"

Ah, there's Cameron's freakout, right on time. A closer look at the dome will have to wait a minute, Cyrus thought.

Cameron had abandoned his bag in the car and stumbled over to the hole in the side of his house. He shoved his arm halfway in to try to pull out the debris. Broken sheetrock swayed as he did so, held in place by frayed electrical wiring running through the broken section of wall. Cyrus hurried over to tug Cameron away from the wires, blessing his lucky stars that the power was clearly out for the duration. He did not look forward to explaining to his grandmother that she was one grandkid short because Cameron electrocuted himself while throwing a tantrum.

"Don't do that, we need to snap pics first so they can see how it is now to process the claim." He turned Cameron back toward the dome. "My place looks okay. I should have some tarps and tape in my supplies. Let's go get them and cover over the hole while we call the **insurance** company."

"You said the house would be fine. That's not fine."

Cyrus sighed. "I know. The storm was bigger than I thought. I'm sorry. But you do have insurance, so…." He smirked, pushing his reluctant cousin back toward his dome. "…you can rebuild it. You have the technology. Better than it was before. Better, stronger… and knowing you, covered in fancy decorative murals or something."

Cameron huffed. "You are such a nerd."

"A nerd with a dry, comfortable house full of supplies. Let's go sit in it."

"Fine. But I'm telling Grandma you lied."

"You do that."

~~~~~

The patch on Iggy's roof was indeed the only damage they found at his place, which was good, as most of the spare tarps were needed to try to patch Cameron's kitchen. It took two full days to tape everything down. It would have gone faster if he hadn't kept fussing about every little speck of damage he found. Cyrus thought Cameron was going to have a coronary when his cousin noticed the cracks on the countertop from a tree branch landing on it. Thankfully, the damage was mostly limited to the kitchen. He couldn't imagine how much of a fit his cousin would have had if more of the house, or the massive collections it contained, had been decimated by the storm.

Cyrus had managed to get in a quick inspection of the dome just before the sun set that first evening. A couple of windows were cracked and dirty, but all in all, it came out rather well. He'd chosen that style because they said it was storm-resistant, and he was glad to see the building was indeed as advertised. Even the lawn furniture and the back deck were mostly undamaged. It made all the difficulties he had, from arguments with family about the unusual design to his trouble finding a mortgage company to fund the thing, all worth it.

His supplies also came in handy with two unexpected houseguests. Three, if he included Iggy's tendency to come hang out every night. With all the power services out, they were limited to cold food, which was starting to wear on everyone. Cyrus had a plan for that.

Several days after the storm, he sat cross-legged in the backyard, quietly assembling electronic parts from a large box. He'd never put together a device quite like this one before, but if it got them lights and the ability to heat water and cook, he was gonna give it a good try. He would have appreciated better instructions, though.

Who wrote this manual, a dyslexic cryptographer with ADHD?

As Cyrus puzzled over the tiny picture next to the useless text, he heard a quiet crunch a few yards behind him. It had to be Morisa or Iggy. Cameron would have yelled rather than walk out across the yard. The ground was still too muddy for his cousin.

"What's up?"

"We have visitors."

Cyrus fumbled with the parts for a moment before dropping them gently back into the box. He turned toward the voice. Iggy stood on the edge of the yard, just past the end of the driveway, a slender man with salt-and-pepper hair and wearing a windbreaker positioned next to him. From the symbol on the breast of the jacket, he was from the insurance
~~~~~

company.

"Oh, yeah. The others are inside. Hold on right there, I'll get them." Cyrus skirted around the box and headed for the house, side-eying the man as he passed him. He was just slightly taller than Cameron, and from the expression on his face as he stepped back on the driveway and scraped the mud off his shoes, would be about as easy to deal with. Hopefully, that wouldn't impact the appraisals.

The ten minutes it took for Morisa and Cameron to assemble by the driveway clearly disagreed with the man, if the frown and rapid clicking of his pen were any indication. He eyed the group of homeowners.

"My name is Randell Dodd. I'm a field appraiser for Dolon Insurance, and I've been called in to assess your damages. We've got a lot of claims in this area and not a lot of time, so we'll do the appraisals in a line as a big group to speed things up, starting with the furthest one. That work for you?"

He didn't bother to wait for a response. After checking the map on his clipboard, he flipped to the last page. "So, we start with… Marisa? Marisa Larue?"

"Morisa." She held up her hand. "And all right. But there's not really much left to see."

"What? What do you mean by that?"

A quick jaunt down the road led them to Morisa's house. The sight left the inspector speechless for a moment. It looked even worse now than it had when they first assessed the property. The best Cyrus could say was that the concrete foundation was undamaged. Demolition would be fairly quick.

"What did you build with, originally? Cardboard? Straw?" Dodd began furiously scribbling notes on his clipboard. Cyrus craned his neck to see if he could read the page. He couldn't see much, but the form did include small copies of the photos they had sent when they filed the claims. He frowned as Dodd scrawled the words *insufficient materials?* beside a photo of Morisa's property.

Morisa pried a broken piece of siding out of the mud and turned it over in her hands. "The original building was made of wood frame and crumbling asphalt. We changed the outside to bamboo siding and reclaimed metal shingles, and then insulated it, repainted... We didn't do any structural changes, it was mostly all cosmetic and comfort adjustments." She sighed, tossing the piece back into the pile. "I don't understand. Was the frame bad? What did we miss?"

"Well, the storm could have just been too strong. Or your contractors could have damaged the walls enough that the roof couldn't withstand a Category 4 storm. It happens sometimes. Or it could have been pre-existing damage." Dodd made a final note on his clipboard. "They'll have to compare my notes with the original inspection report to decide which one is most likely. I'll send in my findings, but I must say that if I were you, I'd hope for the first theory to be true. The latter two are likely to get your claim denied."

Morisa made a quiet gasp and stared at the demolished bungalow, twisting her hands together repeatedly. Dodd clicked his pen and turned away from the property.

"Next!"

Iggy's place was a quick stop, no snide comments, just a quick look under the tarp and a brief note on the paper. Cameron's house, though, was anything but. Dodd marched straight up to the house and yanked the web of tarps away from the wall. His eyebrows rose at the size of the gap. "Did you try to make a drive-through?"

Cameron waved a hand at a nearby pile of debris from the mystery rooftop and assorted tree bits. "That thing certainly did. Took us two solid days to get it out of my kitchen. It ruined my countertops, too." He crossed his arms, his expression twisting. "Damned thing nearly took out the wall. It must have been going quite the speed."

"Possibly. But maybe not." Dodd stuck his hand into the hole and pulled on a chunk of the wall. It separated rather easily from the rest. "It doesn't look like the best of materials. Did you go for the cheap stuff when you built it? You might as well have used sticks!"

Cameron stared at the man with his mouth hanging open. His complexion rapidly darkened to a shade similar to Iggy's new tan. "I beg your pardon. I'll have you know, I used the finest available materials."

The inspector gave him an unimpressed look. "Did you?" He held up the chunk of wall. "So, does the poor quality of this material mean that you waited a week before you tarped the hole? Because this could potentially be the sign of some severe water damage. Or possibly cheap materials."

He dropped the wall remnants and wiped his hand off on his pants, then pulled out his pen and made a number of notes on another piece of paper. Cyrus couldn't see more than a screenshot of Cameron's house at the top of the page when he craned his neck. Dodd finished his notes and flipped the page over, putting the pen back in his breast pocket.

"I'll send in what I've found, and they'll likely have a lot of questions. Good luck with that."

He consulted the top page of the clipboard. "Okay, one last house to look at today, which is…" He glanced at the description of the covered house and then turned to Cyrus. "Considering you were working in the backyard, I assume you happen to be the owner of the dome house? Cyrus Brown?"

"That'd be me." He turned a half-step and gestured toward the house. "Follow me. There's not much to see, though." Cyrus led the group around the house, indicating the handful of broken windows.

Dodd frowned. "That's all? You do realize that if you find damage later and don't include it now, it's far less likely to be covered, right?"

"No worries. There's no other damage, I checked. My little patch of paradise is built to last." Cyrus smacked a hand on the sloped stucco wall.

"Well, I can file the report, but the house shape is particularly unusual. I'm sure that there's likely something broken that you don't know about yet. Don't be surprised if you get a lower amount than you expect."

Iggy scratched his nose and turned his face away from the group. "Aren't you just a bundle of joy," he muttered.

Cyrus didn't disagree. If the inspector claimed that none of them would get much, if anything, from the insurance claims, why had he bothered to come out at all? Why not just cut to the chase and deny them from the pictures they submitted? He sighed and gave Dodd his most neutral smile.

"Is there anything else we can do for you?"

Dodd closed his clipboard. "Not really. I'll go file these records and if they need further info, they'll call you." With that, he slung the clipboard back under his arm and walked briskly down the driveway toward his car. The quartet watched the man drive away, waiting until he disappeared from view to relax. Well, everyone but Cameron, who was far too immersed in his personal plans for setting the inspector on fire, using just the power of his indignation.

Morisa slumped a bit, sliding down to sit on the edge of the back patio. "What am I gonna do if they deny my claim? I spent everything I had on that renovation. And it could all go to waste because of damage done before I even got there?"

Iggy patted her shoulder. "Ignore the man, sweetheart. He didn't seem to have a single positive thing to say about anyone's property, so I doubt his opinions are very accurate. Besides, he gave me a bad vibe. Predatory but hidden, almost, like a wolf dressed in sheepskin. I'd not be surprised if we found out he'd been up to something recently."

"Agreed." Cyrus nodded. "He was a bit of a downer, and they seem to find problems in everything, no matter what happens in reality. We can only trust that things will work out and wait and see what happens. Luckily, he's not the last word in these cases. If his opinion makes things difficult, we'll call Senator Huntsman, have him come and handle the big bad wolf. Now..." He turned to look toward the box he'd been fiddling with before the inspections. "If we're gonna have hot water later, I better get a move on with those panels." He turned back toward the others. "I need to make sure we won't need any new parts or anything. We'll have quite a ways to go to get them if anything is broken."

Iggy helped Morisa to her feet. She smiled at both men. "I'll go take inventory of any supplies we need to replace, if you would like. If you have to go get anything, might as well make the trip count. Iggy can help me."

"Need a box lifter? Sure, I'll come chip in."

Cyrus nodded. "Sounds like a plan." He looked over at Cameron, who was still glaring at the empty stretch of road. If he didn't give his cousin a task, he'd be trying to immolate the inspector all day. There was one task, though, that might be right up his alley.

"Uh, Cameron... It would help a lot if you go tell the gate guard that the inspector has left. No one else is supposed to show up, so he should keep an eye out for any strangers. There might be looters around."

Cameron narrowed his eyes at his cousin. "You want me to go running off on one of your errands? Why should we bother Smith right now when he's likely to be busy?" He had a disgruntled expression for a moment, and then it cleared and a look of delight dawned across his face. Cyrus would bet all of his childhood comic collection that Cameron had just remembered that looters got arrested. And technically, the inspector was a stranger poking around properties he didn't have any connections to. Security would have a duty to investigate any stranger lurking about.

Cameron beamed at Cyrus. "I'd be more than happy to alert Smith, immediately." He hurried down the drive, on his way to the guard shack at the front of the development. Cyrus hoped Dodd had already left, or he was going to have a long day.

Nodding in dismissal to Morisa and Iggy, he walked over and seated himself on the ground next to the box. No sense in worrying about things when he had work to do. As Morisa and Iggy disappeared back inside, he reached into the box and pulled out the two panels and the unhelpful instruction manual. After a quick glance and a deep sigh, he resumed the frustrating attempt to assemble the infernal machine.

~~~~~

The wait had been long and boring, but necessary. Normally, Randell Dodd would have just turned in his carefully worded report and let the chips fall where they may. He couldn't risk it this time around. He'd been slogging his way through a lot of inspections daily for months, with dozens more since that stupid hurricane. The last few houses he'd inspected today could ruin it all.

Despite the handshake deal he'd struck with his supervisor at the company, it was never actually written down anywhere that he'd get a bonus for every claim he helped tank. Most of the claims were easy to sabotage with a carefully worded report sent to just the right agent back at the company, but the last set had a pair that would throw off the
~~~~~

average. Especially that weird concrete dome. He was too close to paying off his house to risk not getting that extra money this month because someone decided to live in a freaky mound in the middle of Florida. He wasn't gonna get the money any other way, not after that mark went on his record after Red complained about him giving her a wolf whistle during the company picnic last summer.

It had taken Randell forever after he left the property to get rid of an annoying security guard who had started pestering him. Luckily, he'd had to wait for nightfall anyway, so he had time. He ate dinner, a lovely shepherd's pie, slowly, to waste a couple of hours after signing out at work. He returned after dark to park down the street and stare at that giant wart on the landscape. Finally, it was late enough. There was still no power to this block yet—he'd checked—so they should have turned in for the night. Now he could act.

This wasn't the first time he'd done this, but it never got less nerve-wracking. It'd be difficult for him to explain why a sixty-year-old insurance adjuster was wandering around in the dark by himself, so he didn't want to get caught. Thankfully, this soon after the disaster, a lot of people weren't back yet, so there were less chances of that.

He pocketed the keys to his car, picked up the small bag of tools from the floorboard, and slipped out of the vehicle. He held his breath as he eased the door shut, waiting for an explosive burst of barking from the nearby houses, but the night stayed silent. People must have taken their dogs with them. Good, he disliked dogs. Noisy little monsters.

Randell loped up the street toward the dome, his bag under his arm. He looked at the dark streetlamps as he passed them. The lack of light would make it harder to see him, in the unlikely event that any of the homeowners looked out while he was busy. All he had to do was give the tomb of a house some sort of defect, something that would pass for storm damage but not be spotted for a few days. Just long enough to give his supervisor at the company enough time to crank down the claim amount. It seemed to Randell that fate itself was helping him out tonight. He grinned, his sharper-than-average canine teeth visible in the faint light of the crescent moon. He could almost feel the bonus cash in his hand already. It was as good as his.

He reached the house and slipped into the backyard. The building was silent and dark, and the yard itself was empty, save for a table-like structure toward the middle. A power cord protruded from a box attached to the side and stretched in the direction of the far side of the house.

Randell followed the cord, stopping when it disappeared into a large metal box next to a sizable concrete bubble that protruded slightly from the side of the house. Another cord ran from the back of the box and under a closed garage door that was sunk into the surface of the bubble. He tried peering inside a tiny gap in the side of the box but couldn't see any details. There were a bunch of stacked blocks, but he couldn't see what they were. He listened for a moment, but the contents made no noise. Neither did the space behind the door, whatever was in there.

Randell shrugged. It made no difference. Usually, in other houses he'd been to, he'd have assumed that a box like this shielded a temporary pool pump or a portable generator. This place didn't have a pool, so it wasn't a pump. If it were some sort of generator or something, it clearly was not running at the moment.

His eyes narrowed. It might not be working, but it did give him an idea. If he damaged the right part of this, it could look like damage caused by homeowner negligence. That'd kill the claim for sure.

Randell felt the smile stretch across his face as he set down his bag of tools. He rifled through it for a moment, then selected his best bolt cutter. He couldn't lose tonight. One quick cut and it'd all be over. Randell pulled out his glasses and slipped them on, the light of the moon glinting off of them in a flash as he bent his head to look carefully at the cable on the back of the box. He centered the cord in the jaws of the tool and clenched the tool shut.

<div align="center">~~~~~</div>

It'd been a long day, but everyone else had finally turned in for the night. Cyrus had a rare free moment and was trying to wind down for sleep with a book. It had just started getting good when the small reading light next to the head of his bed suddenly flashed like a strobe light for a moment, and then went out. Lovely, just when he managed to have a moment of peace, the lightbulb died. He sighed and climbed off the bed, crossing the room to turn on the bathroom light. Surprisingly, it didn't work either. Was the whole house out of power? The solar-powered generator was working fine earlier. Did he install the battery backup wrong?

He left his room and felt his way downstairs, using his phone for light while trying switches along the way. Nothing worked. He must have done it wrong, and the system finally ran out of stored power. As he passed the bedrooms, he heard the others snoring. Well, at least the outage hadn't disturbed them. He'd just go unplug the coffeemaker they'd prepped for morning and go back to bed. Restarting the system could wait until it was light out.

Cyrus had just yanked the cord of the appliance out of the wall when he saw a flash of light through the window in the kitchen door, accompanied a second later by a light knock. He crossed the kitchen as quietly as he could, opening the door to reveal the neighborhood security guard. A short, older man in a faded blue uniform, he was gripping a flashlight tightly in one hand and looked slightly spooked. Cyrus smiled reassuringly at him.

"Hey there, Smith. Is everything alright?"

Smith took a deep breath. "I was just starting my final rounds before taking off for the night, and when I got to this street, I saw a flash from around here and heard a loud crackle sound and some sort of large animal noise. I don't suppose you have a large dog? And maybe firecrackers?"

"Uh… no. No dog. And who would be lighting firecrackers at…" Cyrus checked his phone. "…1 a.m. in the middle of September?"

"That's what I was afraid of. Damn it, some animal must have gotten into the wiring or something." Smith rubbed a hand on the back of his neck. "I'm gonna have to check the back of your property."

"I'll go with you to get a look at any damage." Cyrus stepped through the door, closing it behind him. He waved a hand toward the curve of the dome. "After you."

"If you insist." Smith gave Cyrus a crooked smile, then stepped forward, swinging his light in an arch a few yards in front of them. "But do me a favor, would you? If a gator or something eats me, make the fight sound impressive when you talk to the reporter."

"Sure thing."

They had progressed halfway around the dome and neared the extension housing the garage when Smith stopped in his tracks, flashlight pausing on a smoking heap a few feet from the box housing the battery backup for the solar generator. It didn't look like an animal, unless it had gotten tangled in an awning or something. Smith held up his hand.

"Hang on a sec. Stay back, just in case."

"Okay. Don't get eaten."

Smith slowly inched up to the heap and bent down to check it. He straightened quickly, crossed himself in what looked to be an automatic gesture, and hurried over to Cyrus. "We need to go inside. I have to call 911."

"Okay." Cyrus turned and the two men hurried back to the kitchen door. "What was that?"

"Not an animal."

~~~~~

The chaos was not good on anyone's nerves so soon after the storm. The police swarmed the house after the call. Everyone in the neighborhood was investigated in connection to the death, even Iggy, before the police investigators found the charred bolt cutters in the bushes a little further away from the battery pack. From there, it wasn't hard for them to label Dodd's demise as a "death by misadventure," and the case was closed with no charges.

The insurance company conducted their own investigation, understandably concerned about the idea of someone connected to them
~~~~~

being killed on the site of a policyholder. Once the implications of vandalism came out, they expanded the investigation into Dodd's life and eventually uncovered the trail of money and fraudulent reports. In an effort to head off a scandal, all four neighbors got sizable checks, provided they stay away from the media if asked about Dodd's less-than-honorable side activities. Cyrus wasn't inclined to stay silent, but for the sake of Morisa and Cameron, he agreed.

It took time to get life back in order, but it did eventually calm down. Iggy and Cyrus got their minor damages fixed within a few months of the storm. Cameron, meanwhile, took advantage of the bigger check to include a new remodel of his kitchen during the repairs to his house. He once again had the fanciest granite countertops in the neighborhood, and shiny new appliances to boot. It took him forever to cook things in there. Poor guy could barely avoid burning water. He adored the new built-in shelves for his collections, though.

"So, does that mean he's bringing something inedible?" Iggy swirled his drink and frowned at the covered bowls of side dishes that littered the top of the new picnic table. The table was nestled between the twin tiny houses Morisa had built on her restored lot.

She'd painted the structures sky blue with trim in sunshine yellow and scattered tiny paintings of lightning bolts around the doors and windows. When asked, she told everyone it was in honor of the events that brought her the windfall she used to rebuild. Most people assumed she meant the hurricane. Privately, Iggy and Cyrus liked to refer to the houses as "Sparky 1 and 2."

"The poor dear." Morisa stepped out of the open door of one tiny house, a casserole dish carefully grasped in her hands. "If he needs some pointers, I'd be happy to help him out." She set the dish gently on the overstuffed table, sliding it over to settle with all the others.

"He might take you up on that. It'd get him brownie points at the next family reunion." Cyrus pointed at the dish she had just set down. "What was that?"

"Brownie surprise. Half my family is allergic to nuts, so we started looking for substitutes, and my sister swears by this one. I figured I'd try it tonight, as a treat."

"What's the surprise?"

"Ground beef. Can you imagine that? You can do the wildest things with food these days. I can't wait to try them." She straightened, smoothed the wrinkles out of her outfit—a pink sleeveless number with horizontal stripes—and beamed at Cyrus for a moment, her eyes stretching into crescents before partially disappearing as her smile shifted her cheeks upward. Cyrus was tempted to think of her as a living example of a smiling face emoji. She turned back to the house. "I'll go fetch the toppings for the main dish." She disappeared back through the doorway into the house. Cyrus stared at the newest dish, contemplating the sudden potential need for the discovery of an undisclosed chocolate allergy.

Iggy stared at the dish himself and shuddered, before looking back at Cyrus. "Is it possible for Cameron to just pick something up?" he asked, a hopeful expression filling his face, his eyebrows lifting.

Cyrus shrugged.

"He'll likely already have planned to bring some sort of purchased dessert. He used to attend all potlucks back in Missouri with something from the local bakery. Easier to hide his lack of cooking skills that way."

"Makes sense, if he can't actually cook. I'm glad I set up the grill myself. We'll at least have decent meats. Speaking of which..." Iggy put his drink on the table and walked over to check on the grill. Cyrus followed and peered around the bigger man.

"Excellent grill."

Iggy grinned. "Isn't it nice? Got it with part of my hush money from our encounter with the pre-fried big bad wolf. Cooks to perfection, runs on propane, and it's just big enough to hold the right amount of meat. It's the perfect tool to feed lots of little piggies like us."

"That's a lot of hot dogs on there."

"Best thing for our barbeque. The right hot dog, cooked properly and served with the *correct* accompaniments, is a delight to the taste buds."

Cyrus nodded. "Yes. The poppyseed bun and pickle spear are essential."

"Don't make me smack you."

The End

THE PROCTOR AND THE PIGS
Jordan Campbell

I have taught Elves and Faeries and Men. I have taught Dwarves and Gnomes and Goblins. I have taught Talking Beasts of every kind: Bear and Bull, Tortoise and Hare, Goat, Fox and even other Wolves. I have seen nigh on all that there is to see, learned all that there is to learn and yet…still my students find ways to surprise me, in ways both good and ill.

My name is Amadeus Lyall and when I was approached by His Majesty, Cole the Elder, to teach architecture at his academy, I thought that the ruler had lost his mind. Why me, of all people? I tried to turn down the offer, but His Majesty is nothing if not persistent and, like most Men, Cole the Elder is more stubborn than any Mule.

I still do not understand why Cole the Elder chose me, of all people, but he did and he is my sovereign, whatever else may be. My king is an idealist and I love him for it. There are far worse things a sovereign can be than too idealistic. The laws of physics, however, tend not to be as accommodating as His Majesty's philosophy. There is only one King who can rewrite the laws of physics, not that that hasn't stopped Cole from trying.

As for myself, I have seen many houses be built, only to then collapse due to structural instability.

But a soul is nothing if not creative, and I once taught a Man who designed a building in the shape of a pair of binoculars, of all things! After that experience, I doubted there was anything that could surprise me.

But that was before I met the Hoghauser triplets.

~~~~~

It was near the end of the year when I approached His Majesty. Cole the Elder was showing his age. His hair, once chestnut, was now snow white, though his face was ruddy and his cheeks rosy as ever. In one hand, he gripped a long pipe, pungent with tobacco. In the other, he fiddled with a scepter, though rare was the occasion that the merry man ever used it.

"My liege," I murmured, bowing down as low as I could. The tile and stone of the castle floor were cold against my paws, but the craftsmanship was fine.

"Arise, Amadeus, arise!" Cole the Elder boomed jovially. He puffed from his pipe and blew out a ring of gold smoke. "What brings you to my presence? Is it not near the end of the season for the Academy? Ought you
~~~~~

to be preparing your final examinations?"

"It is, my liege," I answered. "And I am nearly prepared…but there is something…I have concerns."

"What sort of concerns?" Cole the Elder's round face twisted into a pensive frown. "Amadeus, state it plainly."

That was easier said than done, for as much as I found Cole the Elder to be eccentric, I feared his disappointment. This was a man who ruled with absolute authority, yet it wasn't that I feared for my life being in his hands, but his chagrin. He dreamed of academies where a decade's worth of knowledge could be passed down in a year, where one professor could provide the knowledge of a dozen of his fellows.

"There are students," I said. "Three brothers…I have never met a set of brothers who argued as these have. The Hoghausers are beyond comprehension."

"Ha! Is that all?" Cole tilted his head back and laughed. "You make me laugh, Amadeus. There must be a score of a score of families who could say very much the same. Every set of siblings argues. That's been the way since time immemorial."

"Not like these three," I answered. "These three butt heads more frequently than any I have ever seen. The strife between them is like nothing I've seen and…it's something you have to see for yourself, for I have been driven to near exhaustion."

"You exaggerate, Amadeus." Cole the Elder shook his head. "You certainly don't appear to be exhausted to me."

"Would you like to see it for yourself, my liege, or are you content to stay on your throne and not budge an inch beyond what is necessary to indulge your smoking habit?"

The words were out of my mouth before I could stop myself. I prostrated myself lower to His Majesty and if need be, I'd roll onto my back and thrust out my belly, an act of absolute humility.

"What a lark! I accept! It's beyond time I take a more direct interest in the Academy and its courses anyhow. But first." Cole the Elder clapped his hands. "Music! I call for my three fiddlers, my three drummers, my three trumpeters! Ho ho!"

I straightened up and rose to my feet. I pressed a paw against my head as Cole the Elder led his musicians in a boisterous tune.

What had I gotten myself into?

~~~~~

The Royal Academy's grounds cover a wide stretch of land, over a hundred acres with stretches of woods and stretches of meadow. The castle itself was far enough in the distance that we could barely see it at this point. For all intents and purposes, the king and I were alone.

"What is it about these brothers that you find so vexing?" Cole the
~~~~~

Elder asked as we walked along the path.

"That's a fair question," I admitted. "Some of it's just their personalities bouncing against each other. The eldest triplet is named Hoagie, and he treats virtue as vice and vice as virtue. He celebrates sloth, disparages toil. He's the least favorite of my least favorite students."

"Surely, you exaggerate," Cole the Elder replied. "Come now, you've taught hundreds of students. He's the worst of the lot?"

"My liege, the oaths I took when I accepted your position mean I can turn away no student. You would not allow it. But more times than I can count, I have found myself to the point of absolute lunacy with Hoagie Hoghauser and his antics. He disregards instruction and information in favor of taking naps!"

"A sentiment I can have some respect for." He chortled. "I would think you would appreciate sleep, Amadeus. You've done tremendous work for me, but I think you'd do well to get some rest. Perhaps after this semester, you can take some time off and sleep for a season."

"I'm a Wolf, not a Bear," I muttered. "And more to the point, you're a Man. It takes the Fair Folk to force Man to sleep for a season…"

Over the course of my career, I have found ways to steady myself and keep my frustration at bay. Deep breathing exercises proved especially helpful. One of my students swore by them—she was older than most I taught and had more children than even I could count. But given she had been able to construct a house out of leather and cord and rubber—it actually resembled a large boot more than anything else—I found that her advice was not to be dismissed out of hand.

Inhale deeply, counting to twelve, hold the breath for twelve seconds, exhale for twelve seconds. Peculiar it may seem, but twelve worked well enough for me. Were there not twelve princesses who danced in the night, once upon a time? Were there not twelve Months who greeted lonely travelers? There is something special in twelve…

"What are you doing?"

"Breathing exercises," I replied. "They keep me sane…"

Cole the Elder raised an eyebrow curiously, but I appreciated that he didn't respond further than that and put his pipe back in his pocket.

We came upon the first house in due time. The sun was warm on our backs and the air was deep in my lungs.

The house itself was something of a bungalow: a single-story house, with no upper rooms built within the roof. That was not so surprising. Given their relatively straightforward design, many of my students through the years constructed bungalows for their final projects. But this was no ordinary bungalow. Ordinary was too polite a word…

"Is this…straw?" Cole the Elder asked.

"Technically, I believe it's hay," I corrected.

"There's a difference?"

I nodded, though what the difference was, I could not remember. Bales of hay, tightly bound with thin cord, stretched in a rough square of about twenty feet in all directions. But I saw no foundation, no framing to maintain the house's shape. The roof itself was straw, however, and my nose twinged.

"Hey, Teach! Who's your friend?"

I had forgotten just how far Hoagie Hoghauser's sloth extended. He could often not be bothered to refer to me by my name, much less my title—I was *Professor* Amadeus Lyall—but even I was surprised that he didn't seem to recognize his own king.

"I beg your pardon?" Cole the Elder asked.

I held up a paw, cutting off Cole the Elder before Hoagie could say something especially frustrating. I took a closer look at the house, to examine it in full. It did not take long. The hay bales were structured as a single square, with no inner walls to form rooms. This was little more complex than a building a child would construct out of blocks.

"Impressive, ain't it?" Hoagie gloated. "The finest work anyone has ever done, if I do say so myself!"

"Hoagie Hoghauser!" I shouted. I am a Wolf, but when the need calls for it, I can be louder than any Bear or Bull. It comes in handy when I need to intimidate students.

"That's my name, don't wear it out," Hoagie replied. "So I was thinking that we can replicate this structure, but in gold. You think I can get some leprechauns to work for cheap?"

"I beg your pardon," Cole the Elder repeated and his face was turning red, not with merriment but with fury. "The leprechauns are an independent people and if they are employed by you, you shall compensate them fairly, Swine!"

Rage bubbled inside my chest as Hoagie shrugged. How dare he show such contempt?

"You are an insult to this university, this kingdom, and to Talking Beasts in general!" I shouted. Out of the corner of my eye, I saw Cole the Elder looking both contemplative and outraged. "And for my part, this is the worst house that I have ever seen!"

"Then perhaps you're just an idiot," Hoagie sneered. "If you can't see that my bungalow is the best bungalow that has ever been, that probably just means you're a bad professor. I can't help it if you didn't teach me right."

"Raaaaahhhhhh!" I inhaled sharply and exhaled. My breathing exercises came back with a vengeance, and I huffed and I puffed and I huffed and I puffed. I exhaled sharply and my lungs blew out as strong as any gale. The bales of hay blew away, and the straw roof collapsed without the haphazard walls to support its weight.

"Uh…can I get an extension?"

The very nerve of such a question! I inhaled sharply again but my rage was such that no words came out. Instead, I exhaled…and the great gust of wind sent Hoagie Hoghauser flying, high into the air and into the distance.

~~~~~

"I did not kill him," I said before Cole the Elder could say anything. I bowed before my liege in humility. To kill another Talking Beast is no different from killing a Man in the eyes of His Majesty's court. "He's just somewhere far away…surely, there are others who would have done the same, had they been pushed hard enough."

"I never said that you did kill him," Cole the Elder replied. He frowned and his brow wrinkled. "But where was it he landed?"

That I could not answer. As it was, the grounds of His Majesty's academy were tremendous. This allowed my students to have respectable distance between their houses. Cole the Elder matched pace with me as we passed by three of my students' projects. They were relatively simple wooden constructs but were neither offensive nor particularly impressive, though one student did write along his doorframe *Seven In One Hand*. I made a few remarks and made a few notes, but there was little to dwell on. Whether that was or wasn't a good thing, I was not sure.

"You said that there were three Hoghauser brothers," Cole the Elder said. "Are we near the second?"

"We should be seeing him soon," I murmured. "I just hope that today is a good day for him."

"And is he as irksome as the first?"

"No, no," I said. "Club Hoghauser fancies himself erudite. He is convinced that ways that have long since fallen out of favor are superior to modern techniques. He is not lazy or unintelligent, but he lacks common sense. However remarkable historical feats of architecture are, Club lacks the ingenuity that would be necessary to replicate the triumphs of old. He also has certain…habits that…well, you shall see for yourself."

It was shortly after I said this that we came upon Club Hoghauser. Club Hoghauser sat on a stump, staring out onto the horizon. He didn't seem to be entirely aware of my presence, let alone that of the king's. He would not be the first of my students who was spellbound by the assignment and drawn on with exhaustion. But exhaustion did not appear to be what was motivating him.

His house was…truly, could it be called a house? I expected another bungalow or perhaps a hut, or even a cabin…this was something simpler.

In my years, there had been more than a few students who had attempted simple structures for their final projects, and they were not
~~~~~

always done in sloth, as Hoagie Hoghauser had done. Some students found temporary structures, based on the designs of various nomadic peoples throughout the world, to be rather fascinating in their immediacy and surprising sturdiness against the elements.

I tended to hold a dim view of such structures as final projects, given the relative lack of architecture applied, though I admit that this is biased, and I also acknowledge that I was generally able to discern the motivations of the students in question.

Club Hoghauser proved to be an exception on both counts. He was an enigma in his own right and as for the structure he had built…

"What exactly is this?" Cole the Elder asked. "This does not appear to be…it does not look bad necessarily…but it is…a hunting lodge, perhaps?"

This was neither a yurt nor a cabin nor a lodge. It was not a chum or a lavvu. Heavy wooden poles, pressed firmly into the earth, acted as support beams. But acting as the wall were a series of long, thin branches, not even planks of lumber, but actual branches.

"This is…a lean-to," I said. "You've constructed a lean-to for your final architecture project?"

Technically speaking, that wasn't true. A lean-to, from an architectural standpoint, had to be placed against an already existing structure, hence the name. A free-standing structure with at least one open wall was not a lean-to, even if colloquialisms called it such. This was…less than even that.

"It is most impressive, isn't it?" Club opened his eyes, basking in the glory of his own brilliance. "It's meant to represent our unity with nature."

"But what of the assignment?" I asked. "Where's the structural integrity? There's nothing in the way of a foundation here. There are missing walls…the roof is slanted but will not provide adequate shelter from the elements."

"I have to agree." Cole the Elder nodded at me. "This is not poorly constructed for what it is, but a house needs walls. It needs structure. If I were to lay siege to a structure such as this, it would be taken within a night. There's no way to store food stocks for winter. There's no protection against the elements."

"Isn't it better to be exposed to all that nature has to offer?" Club asked. He did not seem to notice that neither Cole nor I agreed with him.

The philosophical questions and musings on the nature of the universe were not what I was paid to teach. My annoyance and consternation flared as I attempted my breathing exercises to remain calm. I huffed and puffed and inhaled sharply, my chest swelling as I held my breath. I needed to keep my temper.

"Houses are a symbol of cultural decline, when you stop to think about it," Club continued. "How much do we lose when we coop ourselves in cages? Wood and stone and steel, shutting us off from air and grass and sky…really, to build a house is to cut one off from what's truly real."

"What's real?" Cole the Elder raised an eyebrow. "Son, there are thousands upon thousands of people who need their homes. To protect them from wind and rain and snow, to tighten their bonds together as families."

"Were I in your shoes, I would have it be that all houses, all buildings, be destroyed and we return to nature," Club proclaimed. "I am a Talking Beast, what do I need a house for?"

"Nay!" Cole the Elder protested. "I have a responsibility to protect my people! Talking Beast and Elf and Man! Houses enable that! Houses are homes!"

"Protect them?" Club retorted. "Or make them reliant on you, unable to manage anything on their own, cut off from reality while you play the part of a fat, music-loving tyrant?"

I exhaled, the force of my breath as strong as it'd been against Hoagie's sloth. The integrity of the lean-to was stronger than the straw and hay of the bungalow, but not by much. A moment later, perhaps less, the dust cleared and the sticks and branches that composed the majority of the lean-to had been cast into the air. Already, they gained distance and were little more than slivers against the blue sky.

"That's the spirit, Professor Lyall!" Club said, his smile radiating joy and exultation. "Destroy that which separates us from the glories of nature! Set your breath against those who oppress us most of all. Blow down the castle that merry old fool Cole lives in, and the people shall be all the more united without his decline dragging the rest of us down."

"How dare you!" Cole the Elder shouted and my blood turned to ice as I realized my student had just given perhaps the most disrespectful remarks imaginable. "Amadeus, place him in detention, forever!"

"Raaaah!"

In my haste and panic, I inhaled again, much more rapidly, and I did not wait to exhale. My breathing exercises were intended to keep me calm and abate my temper. It did not work out. Club barely had time for his expression to change as my huffing and puffing blew him out of the clearing and high into the air.

"I don't know if I care one way or the other where he lands," Cole the Elder said sternly. "Let's keep moving."

~~~~~

I did not stop to see where Club landed — I did not kill or eat him, to be sure. But now, I was genuinely angry and no amount of breathing exercises could mitigate my rage. To have not just one but two students
~~~~~

perform in such a haphazard manner was incredibly frustrating.

But there were yet more students to instruct, more houses to examine and my role as a professor was not yet over. How much longer I would work, after the display the two Hoghausers had given, I couldn't be sure. I walked through the meadow, my paws pressing hard against the earthen path, until I came to the area where Hero Hoghauser was supposed to be working.

"Well, would you look at that!" Cole the Elder said, his round countenance turning into a more cheerful form. "He's working away!"

And working he was indeed. Before me was a house that had to be thrice the size of Hoagie's straw bungalow, but it was constructed entirely of brick. Several different types of brick, actually: Slabs of burnt clay bricks lay on a pallet, next to a wheelbarrow, and had been used to construct several walls; concrete bricks composed an outer wall surrounding the house; sand lime bricks lay on a second pallet, no doubt used to construct load-bearing walls inside the building; engineering bricks to compose the basement; firebricks to form a chimney.

Hero Hoghauser leaned against one pallet of bricks and a basin he'd been using to mix the mortar. He exhaled and wiped his brow with a handkerchief, looking utterly exhausted.

"Professor Lyall," Hero wheezed. "I have faith that this house will prove satisfactory…I hope it meets your standards…I would love to hear what you have to say…my goodness! Your Majesty, Cole! King Cole, it is an honor, a privilege…"

Leave it to Hero to be as verbose as Club, but as I took in the house, I was increasingly impressed. It was a single story, but it was longer and wider than most of the houses I had seen so far. The brickwork was nothing short of immaculate.

I looked inside the house as well, to better examine the construction. Solid beams of wood intersected with the inner walls of bricks. The fireplace and mantel stood steady and stable, and a crackling fire nestled within it, a large cauldron bubbling inside it. The house was largely unfurnished, but it was finished to a degree that I rarely saw among my students. I was impressed and delighted.

"This is one of the finest houses I've seen in my many years." I smiled at Hero and out of the corner of my eye, I saw Cole the Elder rub his belly and chortle. "You should be proud."

"It's a start," Hero said, shrugging, "but there's plenty more for me to work on. There's a patio to build, the basement isn't insulated, the roof needs to be re-shingled, the attic needs some touching up…and that's not factoring in the wiring or the plumbing."

I'd have to leave Hero to his ramblings—it was my job to instruct students on house construction, but the inner workings of a particular house were not of my concern, truth be told. I gave the house another onceover, my gaze following the walls where raised flower beds had been built. Hero's devotion to not only constructing a house, but a *home*, had led him to plant wolfsbane…which I was desperately allergic to.

"Amadeus!" Cole the Elder called. "Are you all right?"

It was not intentional, far from it. I had no quarrel with Hero Hoghauser, but then again, my lungs and nose had minds of their own. I huffed and I puffed and I chuffed. I had to resist the urge to sneeze, but however much I wanted to avoid it, I could not.

I sneezed a far greater sneeze and exhaled harsher than any Wolf ever sneezed and exhaled before. The force from my lungs would have been enough to obliterate the "houses" that Club and Hoagie had constructed a dozen times over…but then, Hero's house was far, far more powerful than that.

As the gale force winds left my lungs, I rubbed my eyes and clutched my nose. Gradually, my vision returned and I found myself up on the roof of Hero's house. Somehow, I had sneezed myself atop it, but there did not appear to be any structural damage.

I raised myself to my full height, but as I did so, my nose caught a great whiff of the steam and smoke coming from the chimney. My nose, already long irritated, twisted, and I huffed and puffed once again. I stumbled backward and the next thing I knew, I was falling down a rather narrow tunnel…the chimney itself! And then the next thing I became aware of was a tremendous heat and a great splash and a terrible scream.

~~~~~

Cole the Elder was at my bedside when I woke up in the infirmary of his palace, three days later. I feared reprisal, but His Majesty proved to be gracious. I would take sabbatical and then work with him to reconfigure his policies with regard to education. Hero Hoghauser visited as well, frantic with apology, as he blamed himself for the accident. He calmed down, though, when he learned that he had passed the course with distinction.

~~~~~

Oh yes, I had nearly forgotten. As it happens, Hoagie and Club Hoghauser eventually landed from being blown away…onto a different house constructed by another one of my students for that semester. Where they had built their houses of straw and sticks, this student had constructed her house of gingerbread, of all things! I never had the chance to grade it, because Hoagie and Club Hoghauser fell to their own baser instincts and *ate* the house down to its very foundation, along with every piece of furniture within.

I didn't witness the aftermath for myself, but reportedly, the brothers were reduced to repeating the same phrase, "Whee, whee, whee," all the way home.

The End

BRINGING DOWN THE HOUSE
Kathleen Bird

David twirled the stick in his right hand while his left knee bobbed up and down to the never-ending rhythm in his head. The movement helped. One of the lights in the coffee house was out today, making the stage area a bit dimmer and more to his liking. He appreciated the ambiance more. Made him focus on the music better.

He hummed one of their newest tunes quietly, careful not to be too loud for fear of bringing down the teasing of the other band members on his head. He was the rhythm section for a reason, they always said. Singing was not his forte. Whatever. Didn't bother him.

"What's the hold up?" David finally snapped at the guitarist who was plugging in his amp.

The young man looked up from the tangle of cords in his hands and shrugged. Hunter was the quiet sort, but he'd been coming out of his shell a bit more lately. Maybe it was that girl who'd been hanging around at their gigs the last couple months. She wasn't the only new addition to their regular audience, but she was the only one who hung around afterwards to drink an excessive amount of coffee with a certain guitarist. David grinned, but his bandmate had already returned to the cords and cables he had to unknot.

"Sorry, sorry, sorry," came the familiar voice of Taylor as he barreled through the door of the coffeehouse. His feet were moving too fast for his white cane, and he came dangerously close to crashing into a chair pulled back too far from a table. Quickly, he righted himself and forcibly slowed his steps to avoid any other collisions as he approached the stage area. They performed here so regularly he almost didn't need his cane, but it seemed as much a part of him as an extra appendage. David thought he would look rather odd without it.

Taylor was more than just their lead vocalist; he also wrote all their original pieces and arranged their cover tunes. Recently, they'd been gaining some popularity outside of their sleepy little college town, so with some help from his sister, Taylor had also taken on the role of marketer and promoter. Made sense since he was the only member of the band not enrolled at the local college. He'd graduated with an associate's in business last year, around the same time he started the band in the first place.

"Guys, I have amazing news." Taylor's excitement interrupted the train of David's thoughts, and he even managed to stop spinning the drumstick for a moment to listen more attentively.

"What is it?" Hunter asked, finally clicking his cord into place with an unappealing screech of feedback that had all three of them covering their ears.

"Hunter!"

"Sorry! It was an accident, David!"

The ringing in his ears didn't care if it was an accident, and he frowned as he kept his left hand pressed against his ear just in case there was a second occurrence.

Taylor held out his hand in a pacifying gesture, and the two young men refrained from bickering further. "Just listen to me a minute, will you? The Purcell Sisters are coming to our show tonight!"

David glanced at Hunter to see if he knew what the big deal was and got another shrug in response.

"I take it from your silence that neither of you have any idea what I'm talking about?" Taylor tipped his head in both of their directions in that odd way of his, looking at them without being able to see them. David was amazed how accurate he typically was with the direction of his body language. Maybe if he was blind, he'd get better at understanding other people's body language also. Well, then again, Taylor couldn't *see* other people's body language, so how was he so good at imitating it? That probably wasn't something David could ask him. He started spinning his drumstick again.

Hunter went ahead and asked the question Taylor was obviously waiting for. "Who are the Purcell Sisters?"

"The Purcell Sisters," Taylor fired back with a huge smile on his face, "are one of the most popular music review accounts on social media right now. They went viral a couple of months ago, and it actually took. They've got sponsorships and connections with record companies who use them to scout for talent. It's a dream come true for a little band like us! And they will be sitting in those seats tonight listening to us." He swung his arm backward to motion at the assorted chairs, tables, and couches that cluttered the rest of the coffee shop and accidentally connected with the microphone stand. Thankfully, Taylor's quick reflexes kept it from crashing completely to the ground, and David let out a sigh of relief. It would come out of their tip money if they broke something.

Hunter smiled and started plucking at the strings of his guitar nervously. "Do you think they'll give us a good review?"

"Of course they will," Taylor said confidently. He tilted his chin up and stood a bit straighter as he continued talking. "We've really been improving the last few months. And I've been following the kind of music they've been reviewing recently. We're sure to be right up their alley."

Something interrupted Taylor's pep talk at that point. David could see the slight furrow in his friend's brow as something passed through his consciousness like a raincloud. "But?" he questioned as his knee continued bouncing nervously.

"But," Taylor replied hesitantly, "there's one tiny potential problem, barely worth mentioning, honestly."

"And yet you are," Hunter said with a suspicious glint in his eyes.

Taylor sighed and gestured for a chair. He hadn't noticed at first, but David now saw that the young man was slightly out of breath. Had he run all the way from his house? David dropped his stick and grabbed a folding chair that had been sitting in the corner. He pushed it open and set it next to Taylor before putting a hand on his arm to let him know which direction to expect it. Taylor's hand found the chair before his cane did, and he slumped into the seat.

"Well, the way things work is the girls show up at a gig, shoot some photos, videos, live commentary, ambiance shots and whatnot. Then they each give a rating, basically thumbs up or thumbs down kinda thing."

"You said Purcell sisters," David interrupted. "How many of them are there?"

"Three," Taylor said as he showed the appropriate number of fingers. "Identical triplets, actually. They each share their own thoughts and then give the group a rating of one to three stars based on the number of up votes they got."

"So, who are some of the groups that have gotten a three-star rating?" Hunter asked as he worked on tuning his guitar. The random notes were slightly distracting to the conversation, but David understood they were running short on time here.

Taylor let out a nervous chuckle. "Um, none?"

"None?" both of the other band members responded in shock.

"Yeah, so it turns out one of the girls is a real stickler. She's always got some sort of complaint that keeps her from recommending a group for one reason or another."

"What makes you think we're going to be any different?" Hunter laughed as he finally set his guitar down and crossed his arms. "What do we have that all those other bands didn't?"

"I don't know, I guess I just believe in us," Taylor said with a shrug. "Even if we can't get a three-star rating, we'll be sure to get a two-star. One of the girls is easily impressed. She pretty much always gives a group her vote, and the other sister is hit and miss but reasonable. We'll get her vote for sure, I think."

"We're not exactly going to stand out if we get a two-star rating like everybody else," David muttered, now wondering what all the fuss was about if nothing was going to come of it.

"Don't get huffy," Taylor snipped back, because *of course* he'd heard the muttered comment. "This is still a great opportunity for us! Getting our name out there more, drawing in a bigger crowd. I'm sure the coffee shop appreciates the extra business too, you know. Maybe I can get us a lower fee for renting the space." He finished his little speech with a shrug and waited for their responses.

Hunter picked at a few more strings before nodding in satisfaction and setting the guitar in its stand. "I'm cool with whatever. We just perform like normal, right? They aren't going to expect us to do interviews or anything, right?"

The door to the coffee shop opened and closed just then, and the two sighted members of the band glanced over to see if they recognized the customers. Taylor's girlfriend, Annaliese, waved cheerfully even though Taylor didn't respond. She was half-dragging her friend, Drema, who looked like she'd just finished an all-night cram session without even a cat nap. The two girls went directly to the counter to order, and Taylor cleared his throat to recapture their attention.

"Annaliese, I take it? She said she'd get here early to snag a good seat."

"Yeah," David said, nervously picking up his stick to start spinning it again. The movement helped his heart to slow a bit.

"To your question, Hunter," Taylor continued. "No, they kinda prefer it if the artists don't interact with them at all. I mean, don't be awkward but don't go out of your way to talk to them. Just play it cool." He tilted his head in David's direction at the last comment.

"I can be cool!"

"Sure thing," Hunter said with a chuckle.

"No, really. I can be cool. Just watch," he argued, feeling like he needed to defend himself against the subtle teasing. Inwardly, he knew that his friends meant well, and he knew that he was kind of socially awkward at times. But how hard could it be to *not* talk to someone? He just had to stay on the stage the whole time and ignore any strange girls. No problem. Stay in his space, and they would stay in theirs. No issue.

There were a few more customers coming in by now, including a few of their regular audience members. Hunter's girl showed up and ordered two large coffees for herself. There was a boy and girl with matching blue highlights that liked to cuddle on the couch while they watched the show. An older couple sat in the back, and she pulled out her knitting. Taylor had talked to them one time, and it turned out the husband was really a fan of theirs. The wife said they were a bit loud for her taste, but the mint tea was worth the trip.

As the seats started to fill up, David ignored Hunter and Taylor quietly chatting about the set list. He didn't need a heads up on their choices, so they just called it out as they transitioned. He had all the tunes memorized, and sometimes he even felt comfortable enough to improv the occasional drum solo. Probably not tonight though, with a group of critics in the audience. That probably wouldn't be cool. Unless they were drum fans. Then it might be the thing that would make them stand out. Maybe he should ask Taylor what he thought about that.

Just then, he noticed a rather distinctive group of women strut into the coffee house. They were all dressed in pink from head to toe, and even their blond hair had pink stripes dyed in. Two of the girls were chatting with each other and laughing while the third one scrolled furiously through her phone on a mission. The shortest one, who had her curly hair pulled back in pigtails, glanced at the stage and blew him a kiss as she giggled. David stopped staring and returned his attention to reviewing the rhythms in his head with his eyes locked on his bouncing leg instead.

"You ready for this?" Hunter asked gently as he stepped into place on David's right. "You seem a little off tonight."

"Not off. Just fine," he said quickly as he closed his eyes briefly to take a deep breath, hold it, and release it a few seconds later as he opened his eyes. Taylor would be introducing them to the crowd soon, and he needed to listen for the first song to be called.

His fingers drummed on the sticks as he made the mistake of glancing out into the audience one last time. Normally nothing would throw him off, but those three unfamiliar faces at the table just in front of the stage were completely distracting. The short blond gave him another air kiss and a little wave when their eyes met, and he choked on his saliva in response. David couldn't hear her giggle, but he could see it as she poked her sister in the ribs and started whispering in her ear. The third girl still hadn't looked up from her phone. Maybe she was livestreaming? But they hadn't started playing yet. Why would she be recording already?

"Focus, David!"

He heard Hunter's harsh whisper as he strummed the opening cord, and David's mind came crashing back to reality. Taylor's introduction had already started, but thankfully he'd tuned back in with just enough time to hear him call out the name of the first number. It was a cover tune, not particularly exciting but a crowd-pleaser. He clicked his sticks to count them in, and they were off to the races.

When they were playing, David's mind could finally stop racing a mile a minute, and he was able to remain completely in the moment. The drums became like a second heartbeat that rumbled inside him, keeping time with every hit of his sticks on the cymbals or the drumheads. Their first song was over quickly, but they rolled right into the second piece, which was another upbeat cover from a popular pop band. Usually, they saved their original stuff until later on in the set, which was fine with David. He liked the pumped up feeling that came from the crowd clapping along with familiar lyrics or singing off-key when they got particularly excited. It really got the blood rushing to his head.

They wrapped up the second song, which was usually where Taylor opted to take a break and chat with his girlfriend. David just wished the music could go on without ever stopping. The crowd tonight was pretty responsive and that cute new girl with the pigtails was cheering loudly as she snapped pictures with her cell. She smiled at him and winked when their eyes met again. He frowned, confused why this rando girl was so obviously trying to flirt with him. Normally, he wasn't exactly flirting material.

"David, you want me to grab you anything?" Hunter asked as he set his guitar back in its stand. Taylor had already disappeared to meet up with Annaliese for a few minutes.

"Nah, I'm fine. Besides, looks like you've got someone waiting for you," he added with a nod toward the brunette downing her second coffee as she tugged at the strings on her bright red sweatshirt. Hunter blushed but nodded and disappeared into the crowd with their fearless leader.

David was perfectly content to sit here behind the drum set until they started up again. Besides, he was supposed to be avoiding the social media girls, according to Taylor's instructions.

Unfortunately, they didn't seem to have gotten the memo. The girl who'd been eyeing him was beckoning him to come to their table, but he pretended not to understand. He closed his eyes and ran through one of their original numbers in his head since it wasn't as familiar as the cover tunes.

"Hey! Are you ignoring me?"

His eyes burst open, and he glared at the young woman staring at him just off the stage area with her hands on her hips.

"Uh, not on purpose," he said with a shrug.

"Come and talk to us," she pleaded, her bright blue eyes blinking at him with an innocent stare. "My sisters and I just *love* your band already. You can tell us all about it."

"I'm not supposed to talk to you," he muttered, questioning Taylor's instructions, given how determined this young lady seemed.

She blew a raspberry at him and then laughed. "Pish, posh. That's Klarissa's rule, and I think it's silly. Besides," she lowered her voice conspiratorially as she winked at him again, "you're cute!"

David cleared his throat awkwardly and glanced out at the crowd to see if his band members were going to rescue him any time soon. They were both engrossed in conversation and completely unaware of what was going on with him.

"I guess I can say hi," he finally said, standing up carefully as he set his sticks on the seat.

He slowly followed her to the table where her sisters were sitting. The girl in the middle was stirring her coffee with a cinnamon stick while she watched him approach, and the other sister was still glued to her phone.

His tour guide grabbed his hand and dragged him the rest of the way as she started her introductions. "Hey, yeah, so I'm Kelly, and this is my sister, Katrina," pigtail girl said as the cinnamon stick girl gave a weak wave in response. "And that stick in the mud is Klarissa."

"You know I don't talk to the band members," phone girl, whose name was apparently Klarissa, said without looking up.

"Doesn't mean that *I* can't," Kelly said before sticking her tongue out at her sister.

Her pigtails bounced as she moved, and he noticed that she wore the most pink of any of the sisters, from her pink sweater dress to her pink high heels that looked like lethal weapons. The neon shade was almost blinding to his somewhat sensitive eyes. But before he could come up with an excuse to leave, the girl was dragging him into the seat next to her.

"Soooooo, what's it like being a drummer in an awesome band?"

"Are we awesome?"

Kelly giggled, and Katrina rolled her eyes. "Like duh, of course! I've already given you my thumbs up review," Kelly said as she flashed him a double thumbs up for emphasis. "I've got a sense about these things. So, I knew you guys were the real deal right from the start." She smiled at him, and he hesitantly returned it with one of his own.

"What's your name, by the way?" Katrina finally said with a casual level of interest as she took a sip of her coffee.

"David," he said, giving her his second hesitant smile of the evening. She didn't return it.

"Are you hungry, David?" Kelly said as she dug through her pink shoulder bag and pulled out a Tupperware container. "I always bring my own snacks to these things. You never know what the venue will have, you know?" She tugged the lid off the container and shoved it at him. "Here, try one! I made them myself."

He glanced down at the oddly shaped little candies that looked like a bunch of melted pretzels piled together. "What is it?"

"They're haystacks! It's like a candy and a snack all combined into one. Little salty. Little sweet. Come on, just try one. You don't have any allergies or anything, right?"

"Uh, no, I guess I don't," he said as he looked around to see if Taylor or Hunter were returning to the stage. Surely it had been five minutes by now. Since they were still talking with their girlfriends, he decided it wouldn't hurt to try one just to be polite. Gingerly, he picked up one little haystack and resisted the urge to sniff it before shoving it in his mouth whole. There certainly was some sort of crunchy, salty flavor but mixed with butterscotch and maybe peanut butter? His teeth gnashed through the horrendous taste as soon as possible and gulped to rid his mouth of the unpleasantness.

"So? What did you think?" Kelly said brightly, with those blue eyes of her shining expectantly at him.

He'd never been much for tact. "That is quite possibly the most disgusting thing I've ever tasted."

Her face fell flatter than a pancake, and he could have sworn there were tears in the corners of her eyes. It was like he'd blown her house down with his words, and immediately he regretted having ever left the stage. He should have listened to Taylor, who actually knew something about girls and having a girlfriend. Like maybe he shouldn't insult their homemade snacks.

The only encouragement David got was a stifled chuckle from Katrina and what almost appeared like a smile from Klarissa, which immediately disappeared as soon as he looked at her fully. Kelly, on the other hand, was shoving her Tupperware, phone, and assorted other accessories back into her shoulder bag.

"Well, I won't stay where I'm not appreciated!"

"Wait, I'm sorry!" he said frantically as he jumped up from the table. Terror at the thought of wrecking this review that Taylor was so excited for pulsed through him. "Maybe I should try another one?"

"Nope, not a chance," she said, shoving past him as she flipped her pigtails in his face. "Your loss, David!"

"Are you going to retract your review?" he asked hurriedly in a whisper, hoping that they weren't making a scene as he followed her to the door.

She stopped and spun to face him with her hands on her hips and those blue eyes glaring at him. "Of course not. I still like your band, even if you have bad taste."

"Oh," he said sheepishly, running a hand through his messy hair as he looked at the ground. "Um, I really am sorry about what I said."

Kelly sighed and let her posture relax a bit. "It's fine, David. Really. But you should be a bit more careful about what you say to people you've only just met. You were a bit..."

"Huffy?" he muttered, remembering his bandmate's earlier warnings about his attitude.

He cautiously glanced up to meet her eyes one last time and was relieved to find forgiveness in them. "Yeah, huffy sounds about right. You should work on that, okay?"

"Sure," he said, shoving his hands in his pockets to keep them from shaking.

"Looks like your band's getting ready to start up again. Bring down the house for me, eh?"

He gave her a crooked smile that made her giggle. "Yeah, I can do that."

Kelly disappeared out the coffee shop door, and he made a beeline for the stage just as Hunter and Taylor were returning. He noticed their worried looks at Kelly's absence and the remaining two sisters looking rather disinterested.

"What'd you do, David?"

"I didn't do anything! They dragged me into their nonsense," he snipped back at Hunter before remembering Kelly's reminder about his words. He took a deep breath and tried again. "I promise, we're fine. Kelly already gave us her thumbs up, so we've got one star under our belt."

"Kelly?" Taylor said with a teasing grin as he reached for the microphone. "On a first name basis with the social media stars *that you weren't supposed to talk to?*"

David shrugged. "Apparently, Klarissa is the only one who cares about that." He took his place behind the drum set and tapped his sticks briefly to resettle himself.

Both of the other band members gave him confused looks, but there was no more time to waste. Their little break was eating into their performance time, and they still had a full set list to get through. Taylor greeted the crowd again, which was pretty much the same minus Kelly and the older couple who'd already left. Annaliese and her friends cheered loudly, which made Hunter blush and Taylor grin like a maniac.

They dove into one of their original pieces, a song about rain and coffee and first love that David didn't really understand. He switched over to his brushes for this tune to give the drums a softer sound. That was the best part about slow or sad songs since he liked to experiment with different types of sticks. His professors over at the college were impressed with how easily he transitioned between them, and it was a point of pride for David at this point. Taylor always made sure to incorporate at least a couple different styles into their set list so that he could show off. It was really nice of him and a great way to make their band stand out from the crowd.

His thoughts drifted off as the song came to a close and they transitioned to something a bit louder but still mellow. David grabbed his rods and tapped out the rhythms to accompany Hunter's guitar solos in this song. This had been a pretty collaborative piece between the three of them, and it was the one that Hunter especially was most proud of. David enjoyed the excuse to use yet another type of stick, and it was fun to see just how quiet he could play to keep from overpowering his band mates. It required a lot of concentration, which was just the way he liked things.

The crowd erupted into cheering when they finished, which felt like cannons firing to David's ears, given how quiet their last two songs had been. Taylor took a couple of minutes to explain the origins of the two songs since they were original, and that coffee-hyped brunette cheered loudly when Hunter's guitar solos were recognized. But David's attention was focused on the remaining two blond heads at the table near the stage.

Katrina, sister number two, was still stirring what remained of her coffee with a half-eaten cinnamon stick. But instead of the disinterest she'd shown earlier, she looked intrigued. Her pink glasses obscured the same blue eyes as her sisters, but he noticed a similar expressiveness to Kelly. Instead of pigtails, her hair was pulled back in one long ponytail with the streaks of pink clearly visible throughout. Her outfit was also a bit more subtle than her sister's, with a mixture of pink and gray in her skirt and blouse. He smiled at her, hoping that she wasn't irritated by his earlier blunder.

Her face clouded momentarily before returning to a puzzled state, and he knew that he needed to do something quickly.

"Taylor," he whispered fiercely, hoping his friend could hear him over the applause.

Thankfully, his supersonic hearing did the trick. "What, David?" Taylor whispered back without turning around as he put his hand over the microphone.

"Can we take a break?"

"We just took a break."

"Can we take another one?"

Taylor finally turned to face behind him as the applause settled down, confusion wrinkling his eyebrows. "Why?"

"Because," David muttered, unwilling to explain any further. He was not going to screw things up for his band. He was going to fix things.

"It's cool," Hunter said, stepping in to save him. "I need to use the bathroom real quick anyway."

Taylor glanced suspiciously between them but nodded. "Fine, but this is a *real* five-minute break this time. No delays!"

He announced the short pause to the crowd and then stepped away from the microphone. David jumped up from the drum set quickly and started to head down to the sisters' table, but Taylor reached out to grab his arm as he passed by.

"Remember, be cool, okay?" Taylor pleaded, and David felt renewed determination to fix whatever he might have already messed up. "This review could mean a lot for our band."

"I know that. I've got this, Taylor. I promise."

Taylor released his arm and stepped aside, grabbing his cane to move it out of the way as well. David took the couple of steps remaining to reach the girls' table and plopped down into the seat Kelly had vacated.

"So," he said cheerily, "what did you think?"

Klarissa gave him a glare that would melt Antarctica before returning to her phone. He cleared his throat and turned a slightly less confident smile to Katrina. "Um, what about you?"

The young woman shifted in her seat to lean back from the table and cross her arms. "And what makes you think I'll tell you my real thoughts after the way you chased my sister out of here?"

"Uh..." His brain fired randomly, trying desperately to come up with some sort of response.

Then Katrina laughed so hard she snorted and quickly covered her mouth with a hand. "S-sorry about that," she said as she tried to suppress the laughter further. "It was actually really hilarious to see you talk to Kelly that way. No one ever tells her the truth about those haystacks. I have no idea why she likes them!"

He nodded, relief sweeping over him. "They were so gross."

Katrina nodded emphatically and then drank the last of her coffee, chomping on the cinnamon stick once she finished. "Seriously, where did these guys find you?"

"I go to the college with Hunter."

"What's your major?"

"Music performance, same as him."

"Really?" she said, leaning forward with interest. "Is that where you learned to use all those different playing techniques? I loved what you did with the brushes in that first piece. Really jazzed it up."

He perked up, proud that someone noticed his efforts. There were times when being the percussion section felt like being the wallpaper background to the rest of the band. "Yeah, I mean, I started playing when I was a kid, so I'd been experimenting back in high school. But, for sure the profs here helped me improve. And, I mean, I practice a lot too. Sometimes too much if you listen to my roommates. They, uh, kinda hid my sticks for a while during midterms."

The snorting giggles started up again, and Katrina laughed so hard it drew her sister's ire. David straightened up when Klarissa shot him another glare, but Katrina saved him from saying anything stupid.

"You're not what I expected when I heard about this band. That's for sure. I mean, a blind guy who writes songs and his two college buddies? I figured all you'd play is 80s cover tunes. But you're a whole lot more than that, aren't you?"

He puffed out his chest a bit with pride. "Yeah, I like to think so."

Katrina gave him a genuine smile and reached out to pat his hand.

"You've got my vote, David. I'll post my review once I get home. I'm in college too, you know? This is just a side gig. I've got to get home and finish a paper before midnight." She pulled out a couple small bills and dropped them on the table as a tip for the staff before grabbing her phone and standing up.

"Thanks so much!" he said as he offered his hand for her to shake. She took it with one more little giggle and a glance at her sister.

"She's the one you've got to convince yet, David. My sister's got a brick wall built around her that no one's been able to break down so far."

Klarissa rolled her eyes without looking at her departing sister.

Taylor was starting to talk into the microphone again, so David returned to the stage without attempting to speak to the third sister. He returned Katrina's wave as she slipped out the door, and Hunter gave him a thumbs up excitedly. They still had about four songs to play, a mixture of covers and upbeat originals, so hopefully something in the mix would trip Klarissa's trigger. David wondered what she could possibly be looking for that no band had managed to receive her stamp of approval so far.

They liked to end their set on a high note, so they were back to the high energy songs that David liked best. He ended up having a few solos of his own sprinkled throughout that had him grinning like a wolf and breathing hard by the time they wrapped up. The audience had matched their energy with cheers and applause far louder than normal, and it wasn't just because Annaliese and her crew were hyping them up. It was almost like everyone in the coffee shop were connected by their music, living and singing and breathing together as one. It was a crazy feeling that most of their gigs didn't achieve, but as Taylor closed out with their thanks and shoutouts, David could tell the whole band was beaming with pride. The crowd even gave them a standing ovation, including the baristas who'd heard them play a bazillion times.

Yet there was one notable exception. Klarissa, whose eyes had yet to leave her phone, remained seated without clapping, and her stubborn refusal to show even a hint of interest crashed through his happy mood like a brick. David glanced at Hunter, who didn't seem bothered by the remaining Purcell. He was grinning at his girl and waving at the crowd like they were at a parade. Of course, Taylor couldn't see Klarissa's disinterest, so he was also responding to the overwhelming celebratory vibes of the rest of the audience.

Only David noticed that they were most likely still one star short of a perfect review, and he was worried it was his fault. Klarissa was the one who'd cared about not talking to the band members, and he had broken her cardinal rule twice. Once unintentionally, of course, but once purposefully. Maybe that had biased her against them? He felt the residual energy of such a great performance bursting through him, and he forced himself to take a couple of deep breaths to calm his jittery limbs. He needed to pack up his kit and clear the stage area with the rest of his band.

But his irritation kept rising the more he tried to push it down inside. How could she not appreciate *anything* they'd done? How rude to come and watch a band but never even glance up from your screen. What made her qualified to give music reviews anyway? David felt the anger building up inside him, and it was going to blow up soon if he couldn't find a way to calm down. He slammed the last of his sticks into his bag and zipped it shut before looking around for his bandmates. Perhaps they would be able to soothe his bruised ego.

Unfortunately for him, they were engrossed in conversation with their friends and girlfriends at the back table once more. David's shoulders slumped at the loneliness that threatened to grip him at being excluded from their post-performance conversation. He knew it wasn't intentional, and he often did wander back to join them once he'd packed up; but tonight, there was an annoying blond demanding his attention instead.

Flinging the bag over his shoulder and cinching the strap to make it secure, David made his plan of attack. He was going to stay cool. He wasn't going to mess things up further for his friends and his band. But he was going to have a few words with Klarissa and finally pull her attention away from her phone for more than a millisecond.

Taking a deep breath, which ultimately did nothing for his surging emotions, he stepped away from the stage area and crossed to her table. She pointedly ignored him, typing furiously away on her phone without acknowledging his presence. Her loose, short blond hair obscured her face, but he could see tension in the rest of her body from the way she sat stiffly in the straight-backed chair. It contrasted with her relaxed clothing choices, an oversized light pink sweater and a pair of jeans with some light pink sneakers peeking out underneath the table. She looked stressed.

A pinprick of sympathy tried to keep his anger in check, but David was too far gone to keep from exploding at this point.

"What exactly is your problem?" he snapped, voice so low it almost came out sounding like a growl as he glared at the top of her head. So much for not being huffy.

The movement of her fingers stopped, and her whole body became still for a second or two. Then slowly, she lifted her head and tucked part of her hair behind her ear with one hand. Her blue eyes blinked slowly, and he felt like he'd been punched in the gut. Klarissa still looked like her sisters, with the hair streaked with pink and those same expressive eyes. But there was also something deeper in them, something he'd never seen in another person. The same energy that pulsed through him when he played the drums seemed like it was simmering just behind those eyes, and it momentarily took his breath away.

She didn't speak, just stared at him with her phone still in her hand. He waited for her to scold him, tease him, or send him away. But she didn't. Klarissa's eyes just roamed over every inch of his face like he was the most interesting piece of art she'd ever witnessed. He felt heat rising within him, and David was sure that the tips of his ears were turning red with embarrassment.

"I like you," she said tersely before returning her attention to her phone.

"Excuse me?" he stuttered, completely flabbergasted at such a response.

Klarissa looked up at him again and repeated the statement. "I like you."

He slumped into one of the empty chairs at her table, setting his bag on the floor beside him as he took in her words. "You like me?"

"Yes."

"You mean, you like the band?"

She tilted her head to one side and furrowed her brow in thought without looking at him. "Yes, I do like the band. Your music selection was varied and excellent. There were a few pitch issues and a couple of moments where you were out of sync with the other members, presumably due to your excitement to get to a particular section, but otherwise it was a stellar performance."

He nodded at her assessment, remembering exactly the sections she was talking about.

Then Klarissa turned to face him and set down her phone on the table, finally fully engaged in the conversation. "But I also mean that I like *you*. You intrigue me, David."

"Me?" he asked with an awkward chuckle. "What's intriguing about me?"

"Your nonconformity to social norms, for one thing," she said with a smile. "You were given one instruction: to not speak with me or my sisters, which you repeatedly ignored. You ignored Kelly's flirtatious advances and didn't give her false compliments, for another."

"Those haystacks were really gross," he muttered.

"I agree completely," Klarissa said with a slight laugh. Then she continued her explanation by saying, "And I saw that you took direction, both from Kelly and your friends in regard to your attitude and actions. I like that in a person, a willingness to learn from your mistakes."

"Oh," David said, feeling that embarrassment return to the pit of his stomach. "I-I just hate messing things up."

"So do I," she said gently before pointing at her phone. "That's why I take copious notes at these events of everything I'm observing and hearing about the band, the surroundings, and especially the people performing. Most people get annoyed with my apparent lack of attention, but very few of them bother to confront me about it."

Now he felt even more embarrassed. He'd nearly blown his top at her for ignoring them when she was just appreciating the performance in her own way. "S-sorry about that," he muttered.

"Not at all, it was refreshing to see how much you care about your music and your friends to try to ensure a good review."

He offered her the same crooked grin that had gotten Kelly laughing earlier. "So, did I succeed?"

"You blew me away," Klarissa said as she smiled back at him, and David swore he fell in love right then and there. Finally, Taylor's weird coffee and rain song made sense.

"David!" he heard Taylor call from the back of the coffee shop. The group had vacated their table and were making their way to the door. "We're gonna grab dinner. Wanna join us?"

It only took a second to make up his mind. "Come join us?" he asked Klarissa excitedly. "We're probably going to Taylor's favorite Thai place."

She smiled, grabbed her phone, and shoved it in her purse before standing. "I'd love to. I'll eat anything but pork."

David grabbed her hand and dragged her toward his friends, who were all staring at him in surprise. He was probably the last person they'd expect to make a new friend so quickly.

"Sounds like a date to me!" he said, tossing another smile in her direction.

The End

TRUE LOVE'S ~~KISS~~ PIGS
An Enchanted Castle Archives story
Michelle L. Levigne

"We have a problem," Zella announced from the third-floor landing of the castle's central staircase.

"The family curse is acting up, and now isn't a good time to visit Dormie?" 'Na paused with her foot on the bottom step of the staircase and hoped the relief she felt didn't make her face glow.

The first item on the list of tasks to prepare for her and Ambrose's wedding was to decide who to ask to be their attendants. Making the requests through the mirror web could be problematic, because there were always rogue mirrors listening in and spreading gossip. On her parents' advice, 'Na and Ambrose were planning a long round of visits to friends, to ask them in person.

Dormie was a friend from 'Na and Zella's childhood, when they had participated in a distance education program conducted through the mirror web. 'Na and Zella had kept in contact with just over half of them. Chances were good that most would be too busy with quests or magical problems to attend, so 'Na didn't feel quite as much trepidation over asking all her school friends to be her attendants, even though the thought of a dozen bridesmaids made her feel rather doomed. She much preferred to just have Zella as her maid of honor, along with Princess Phibbia and Garnet, queen of the werewolves as her bridesmaids. However, there were social expectations to satisfy. The wedding of the daughter of the lord and lady of the enchanted castle was doomed to be the social event of the decade. If 'Na didn't ask at least a dozen daughters of powerful families to be her attendants, then twice as many scheming ambassadors and prime ministers would maneuver their princesses and other high-ranking snobby girls into the wedding party. 'Na was inviting her friends if only in self-defense.

Although, she had to admit, the thought of the dismay and chagrin suffered by the girls who had been so nasty to her and Zella, when they found they weren't invited, was rather entertaining ...

"If only it were that simple," Zella said. She hopped up on the banister and slid down to the landing between the third and second floors. "Although I wouldn't wish that problem on Dormie for anything. Sorry, but we didn't get that far. She was busy telling me about Circe-Beth."

"What new fibs is she telling now?" 'Na cringed and braced for the sound of Smedley letting out a roar from his nest in the highest tower of the castle. He had always gone outside or fled to the roof of the castle when 'Na had had her classes in the mirror web because Circe-Beth's voice hurt his ears. Just the mention of her name had been enough to send him running when they were all children.

"She has become a practitioner of a new, insanity-inducing magic. It tries to control the minds of huge crowds of people at the same time, using decorations and color coordination and food, and sometimes even dictating what type of clothes they wear. The simplistic name is 'event planning.' That sounds so innocent, doesn't it?" Zella closed her eyes and shuddered. "The truly wretched part is that she is announcing to everyone that she is in charge of your wedding."

That was it. That was the other shoe of doom poised to fall on her. Although, when it came to Circe-Beth and her overbearing ways, it was more like an entire dressing room of shoes being emptied out on her head.

"How did she ever learn I'm getting married? We haven't even made the formal announcement yet." 'Na leaned against the banister for support. This was already worse than all the ridiculous horror stories of the fuss and chaos and mayhem when her parents had gotten married.

"Eyesallova sends her apologies, but she was so excited, she told some of her closest friends, and now she thinks some of the mirror web security spells were compromised," Zella said, and slid down the next banister to the second-floor landing.

"Ya think?"

"I told Dormie that, of course, whatever she's heard is complete rubbish, and she would be among the first to know when you did become betrothed. I also asked her to keep an ear out for whatever Circe-Beth is up to." She hopped onto the next banister to slide down. "Well, look on the bright side. At least we've had some warning."

"When it comes to Circe-Beth, three months advance warning sometimes isn't enough!"

~~~~~

Dormie proved herself a good friend, despite the havoc the resurgence of the family curse was playing on her father's small mountain kingdom. She notified the rest of the circle of friends from their distance-learning class and asked them to be on the alert for Circe-Beth's newest schemes. By dinner time, horror stories were spilling through Eyesallova. The tamest ones detailed the mess Circe-Beth had made of several small festivals and weddings in the estates adjacent to the island where she had lived all her life.

A cascade of disasters in the days leading up to the first wedding she
~~~~~

managed had triggered one of Circe-Beth's legendary temper tantrums. Her family possessed a magical talent to turn people into animals. However, Circe-Beth's talent was limited to pigs, and she often lost control and aim when she was in a royal snit. That was the main reason why she had grown up in a tower on an isolated island, with only her mirror, Jallosy, for company.

The groom had been out of the country on military service and arrived two days before the wedding. Circe-Beth didn't know he was the groom and claimed love at first sight. She insisted he be her escort to the wedding. Then she made several jests in bad taste about outshining the bride. The groom made the mistake of stating no one could be more beautiful than the bride. Circe-Beth turned him into a boar, then added a boar hunt to the pre-wedding festivities. She accused the bride of setting out to humiliate her when she learned the boar's identity.

The planners of the other festivals and weddings refused to let Circe-Beth be involved. The events were destroyed when the majority of important guests and officials turned into pigs and stampeded through the food and decorations.

Zella and 'Na spent more than an hour reading transcripts of all the reports their schoolmates had sent them.

It got worse. Much worse.

Circe-Beth had appointed herself 'Na's maid of honor, as well as event planner. She had already sent out invitations to the wedding, with instructions for how guests should dress and what gifts to bring. Dolphus, prime minister of Cammerlang, made the mistake of pointing out that there was something very wrong with a wedding invitation that didn't list a date or the name of the groom. Circe-Beth tried to turn his entire castle's inhabitants into pigs. She hit a snag when the barrel full of enchanted apples destined for the castle fell off the wagon carrying it. The next four teams of horses that passed that spot stopped to eat the apples. Since Circe-Beth's limited talent was turning *people* into pigs, the horses flipped back and forth between horses and pigs while running amok for the next three days.

Lady Ashlyn joined the girls in the mirror room to get an update on the effort to track Circe-Beth's activities so she and Zared could counter them. She sighed with a sad little laugh and settled on the bench next to 'Na.

"I'm sorry, dearest. I hope you understand that I only want to protect you," Ashlyn said. "Have you considered eloping?"

"Could I?" For a few moments, 'Na felt almost seasick with the rapid rise and fall of hope. She had rather enjoyed the anticipation of seeing envy on the faces of all the stuck-up princesses and duchesses who looked down on her because she wasn't a "proper castle maiden," when they got a good look at Ambrose. And she didn't want to disappoint the housekeeping breezes, who had been running at near-hurricane speed ever since Ambrose put the betrothal band on her wrist. Every time she peeked into the workroom, the breezes and the castle's invisible seamstresses had designed a new wedding gown for her, each confection more elaborate than the last. She wanted to see what she would look like in one of those dresses, and dreaded it at the same time, because how would she be able to move?

Besides, the chances were overwhelming that someone would sabotage the wedding festivities or try to insert a curse of some kind into the vowing ceremony. Most likely a king who refused to take a dozen versions of "No!" for an answer.

"The castle won't let me," she finally said, if only to stop the visions of disaster from spinning through her head. "A big, fancy wedding is just as necessary for the morale of the castle itself as it is to humiliate the arrogant schemers who keep trying to make all of us their pawns."

Still, she had been so close to escape. Maybe there was a way around this impending disaster. She just had to think harder.

"I don't envy you at all," Zella murmured.

"Then you don't care that Zerocs was giving my betrothal band a very serious look?" 'Na muffled a burst of laughter when her friend's face lit up, and turned an incredibly bright shade of pink, generating enough heat to be felt from three paces away.

"I'm sorry." Ashlyn gave them an apologetic look. "I recommend some defensive measures. Pick your wedding attendants, register them formally with the Enchanter's Court, and put a seal on them. Then, no matter who Circe-Beth chooses, the list won't change. The seal proves she has no authority, and she can just humiliate herself to her heart's content."

~~~~~

'Na almost laughed at the relief that came from having to pick a small wedding party, for the sake of speed. She chose Zella, Phibbia, and Garnet, and Ambrose chose Prince Ruprick, Zerocs, and Rolf, the new werewolf chieftain. However, now King Ruprick knew about the betrothal. Ambrose and Phibbia both sent messages warning that the king was in a gleeful mood, plotting to take over the wedding festivities to put the enchanted castle's residents in his debt in some way.

"Well, that might be an interesting battle," Zared commented, after receiving the warnings. "Circe-Beth versus King Ruprick. I wonder who would win, in taking over the wedding planning?"

"That's not really so funny, Papa," 'Na said, though she did appreciate him trying to make light of what threatened to be an exasperating situation.

~~~~~

Three days later, Eyesallova summoned 'Na to the mirror room.

"You'll want to sit down for this," the mirror warned, as 'Na came through the door. "I just received this from a friend who oversees the security in Artisia."

Her surface cleared, while 'Na was still trying to remember why that name sounded familiar. A choked little chuckle escaped her when she looked down at her clenched hands and saw her betrothal band; braided strands of gold and silver, coated with blue and green gemstone dust. Ambrose had gone to Artisia, an artisan colony that resided inside a time pocket, to purchase her betrothal band. She had never really cared about jewelry before, but the fact that he had bought it before that sad incident with the invisible intruder made the band all the more precious to her. He had been planning to ask to marry her and hadn't been tricked into it through jealousy. Although, yes, the fact he wanted to marry her to protect her from more idiots like Dolor was rather romantic.

The image on Eyesallova's surface showed an artisan shop, full of all sorts of jewelry made of metal, ivory, and stone. The artist was a gnome with lavender skin and tall, pointy ears, so small he sat on a stool next to his crystal anvil and wove thin strands of silver into a mesh ball. The door of the shop slammed open. 'Na caught her breath when she recognized the young woman who swept through the door. That perky little nose kept twitching back and forth, flattening into a wriggling, wet pig snout and then going perky-pointed again. Circe-Beth hadn't changed. Still wearing multiple layers of pastel gauze. And who nowadays wore that tall, pointy hat that nearly bent double with the weight of all the fluttery veils hanging from it?

No sound came with the image Eyesallova showed her, but 'Na didn't need it. Circe-Beth sneered at the little gnome artisan and made her demand. The gnome shook his head. Circe-Beth's eyes sparked with irritation. The gnome snapped his fingers and a scroll appeared from thin air and unrolled. He pointed at several lines. Circe-Beth clenched her fists and shook her head and her nose stayed a piggy snout for a good twenty seconds as she shouted and steam came out of her ears. Her face turned red and her gauzy dress shifted from pastels to crimson. She pointed one thick finger at the gnome. He ducked.

The image vanished from the mirror.

"She turned him into a pig, didn't she?" 'Na said. "What did she want? Is the artisan all right?"

"They're still turning him back. That wretched girl has learned some control over her pig spells. Only true love's kiss can break the spell without her permission."

"And?" she prodded, when the mirror hesitated.

"Circe-Beth was ordering your marriage bands. That scroll he was holding was the order from Ambrose, which he is nearly finished filling. My friend kept watch on her once she stormed out of the shop and recorded quite a few threats against you and anyone who helps you plan your wedding without her. She seems to think that you owe her."

"I owe her a hundred-years nap for all the trouble she gave me and our classmates when we were children!" 'Na rubbed her temples with her fists, to fight off the approaching headache. "You know what's really wretched? If we hadn't sealed the names of our attendants and the date of the wedding, Ambrose and I could elope tonight, and avoid all this trouble."

"I suggest you bring your wedding party together for self-defense. I'm calling Rathelshiffen castle and summoning Ambrose," Eyesallova said.

"Thank you."

To 'Na's dismay, she'd barely finished explaining this new problem to Ambrose when King Ruprick flung back the privacy curtain around the mirror alcove. She'd once thought of Prince Ruprick as somewhat doughy, unfinished. Learning to stand up for himself and breaking the frog curse on Princess Phibbia had done a great deal to "bake" the heir of Raffelshiffen into a likeable, honorable man. King Ruprick was a nasty reminder of the scheming, self-deluded boor his son might have become.

Ambrose cringed as the king flung a beefy arm around his shoulders and grinned through the mirror at 'Na.

"I'm delighted to finally start repaying, in small part, the huge debt I owe your parents, my dear girl," the king began, and shook Ambrose for punctuation every fifth or sixth word. "Allow me to facilitate your escape. I can clear out an entire castle for your convenience, somewhere to hide for a month or two. Time enough to get used to married life, and give a black eye to all those nose-in-the-airs who make life so miserable for the rest of us, eh?"

"Thank you, Majesty," Ambrose said, while she tried to frame a polite refusal that wouldn't have the king declaring Ambrose a traitor and thrown into the deepest, darkest dungeon. "That is most generous of you. However, we don't want to bring down on you and the kingdom the problems this will cause. Circe-Beth of Aeaea Island is a vicious enchantress. You are too valuable an ally to the enchanted castle to endanger you this way."

"Hmm, yes, naturally." The king's scowl wasn't as manic with fury as it could have been, meaning Ambrose was safe. For now.

"If you don't mind, Majesty, could we consult with Ruprick and Phibbia? They are endangered, as our attendants," 'Na said.

"Much appreciated." The king tugged aside the curtain to shout for servants to bring his son and daughter-by-law to the mirror alcove immediately. He stepped out past the curtain but stayed so close that the lamp in the hallway cast his silhouette on the curtain. Meaning he listened as the four made their plans to gather the wedding party into the castle for safekeeping.

'Na just knew that would turn into another problem, but what could she do? In a choice between the trouble King Ruprick could make, and the nasty tricks Circe-Beth had played all during their school years … quite frankly, she would choose Ruprick any day.

If only she could trick Circe-Beth into turning herself into a pig. With the "true love's kiss" codicil part of her magic now, who would kiss Circe-Beth? That would solve all her problems.

Or would it?

She had too much else to think about right now. As soon as the mirror connection with Ambrose closed, she thanked Eyesallova and ran down to the library to tell Zella what they had decided to do. While Zella went to contact Zerocs, 'Na went to her room to pack. They would meet Zerocs at the portal on the edge of the Snarl River, then ride to meet Ambrose, Ruprick and Phibbia, who would go the long way around to the werewolf village, to gather up Rolf. By then, Eyesallova should have Garnet's location tracked down. The new werewolf queen was currently traveling the world, gathering up werewolves living in hiding, to bring them to safety in the enchanted forest. Then the wedding party would return to the safety of the enchanted castle.

~~~~~

Herkimer, the oldest moat monster, had a toothache. His moans had started up shortly after 'Na left the night before, and by dawn he was banging his head against the wall of the castle, demanding help. Zared put on his oldest clothes, full of patches and places where the acid from the creatures' coughing fits and tears had bleached the cloth interesting shades of poisonous green-white. Then he armed himself with several pikes and thick leather gloves with metal rings for reinforcement and waded into the moat, to the place where the shallows suddenly dropped down to the abyss where the moat monsters lived.

Half the job of tending the monsters was coaxing them into resting in the shallows so Zared could inspect their tentacles and multiple eyes and dig out material that got caught between their teeth as tall as his arm. He got along with them well enough, but he always suspected the creatures tolerated him more than they liked him.

He wished 'Na were here. She could even understand the squeals and moans the moat monsters used to communicate. She had loved swimming with the creatures when she was little. They had clowned to entertain her, to the point that some officious visitors to the castle had deluded themselves into thinking the moat monsters were friendly. That was their
~~~~~

mistake. Zared pitied the moat monsters, deprived of a well-earned snack, whenever he had to rescue someone from their own arrogant stupidity.

'Na could have gotten Herkimer to tell her exactly where the problem was. Zared would have to dig around in that mouth big enough to swallow three of him, to find the bad tooth. If it even was a toothache. It could be something else bothering the big slippery, multiple-tentacled, multi-eyed monster.

He waded into the moat, holding a pike in each hand, just as an enormous wave of water rose up from around the bend where the moat somewhat haphazardly surrounded the castle. The next moment, an equally enormous wall of writhing tentacles rose up with a splash that drenched Zared and sent him staggering backward. He sputtered and wiped moat weeds and water out of his face. Herkimer squealed and wheezed laughter. Before Zared could decide whether to play along and treat this as a joke, or threaten the monster with a pike, Herkimer opened his mouth.

"Ouch." Zared shook his head. No need to go digging. Rocks as big as his fist were packed in between two front teeth, with moat weed and what looked like a few tree branches jammed in on top of it. "We'll have you fixed up in just a few minutes, big fellow." He patted Herkimer's lip and hefted the first pike, bent, and got to work digging out the branches on top of the jammed mess.

The process always took some time, because moat monsters oozed a thick substance in their mouths like the nacre of oysters. It effectively cemented rocks and moat weed together. Zared didn't mind. He would much rather deal with this mess than be in the mirror room, helping Eyesallova and Ashlyn diplomatically respond to all the inquiries from people who had heard about 'Na's betrothal and wanted to be part of the wedding or get some benefit from the festivities. Already, eight merchants had tried to present bills for food and decorations Circe-Beth had ordered for the wedding.

He wished 'Na hadn't reported the plot of some of her classmates to enclose Circe-Beth's tower in a glass dome that wouldn't open for one hundred years. That was probably why the arrogant little snot insisted she and 'Na were best friends. She magnanimously "forgave" 'Na whenever she denied that friendship. What did she think she would gain by taking over the wedding, and displacing Zella as maid of honor?

"That is simply disgusting," an icy sort of female voice announced, punctuated with a sigh, maybe half an hour into his struggle with the teeth. "We can't have that thing hanging around and frightening the guests. The colors are all wrong."

"Excuse me?" Zared didn't turn to look, having used the tone of voice that had made armed bandits go pale and tremble until they dropped some of their weapons. That voice irritated him even more than the stench of Herkimer's mouth. He pushed extra hard, sending a tree limb flying, to land with a squelching sound on the big bumpy tongue. He freed the moat weed, held his breath, and gathered up handfuls to toss into the water behind him. Then he turned to see what the intruder looked like. Hopefully fleeing.

The face and expression that went with the voice were just as cold, although beautiful, in a crystalline sort of way. The young woman's upper lip curved up like she couldn't decide if it was ladylike to puke or just pinch her nose.

"Your job, whoever you are, is to cage that ugly thing and keep it out of the sight of the guests. It doesn't make noises, does it? That can't be permitted." She waved an elegantly thin hand, making the multiple, diaphanous layers of her sleeve wave in that just-so way that only existed through carefully calculated magic.

"No." Zared grinned and didn't wait for her astonished, offended dismay to sweep across her face. Turning back to Herkimer, he got to work on the next impacted layer between the moat monster's teeth.

"Who do you think you are, you useless, filthy—"

"I don't *think*. I *know*. And the moat monsters," he declared, acting on a burst of inspiration that he knew would make Ashlyn and 'Na laugh, "are part of the wedding."

"No!" She stomped up behind him, so close to the edge of the moat he heard her pointy-toed shoes squelch in the wet ground. "I will not permit it."

"It's not up to you." He dug deeper between Herkimer's teeth. The pike broke. He let go with a shrug. Pikes didn't survive very long when used as dental tools. Fist-sized rocks crumbled from the impacted lump. He tossed aside the broken pike and reached for the second.

"You are dismissed! Leave now!" the young woman shrieked.

"Dismissed from what—" he grunted and pushed harder, and the last of the rocks fell out, "—exactly?"

"Your service here!" She waved her hands, taking in the sprawling walls of the castle that spread out on either side of the drawbridge and main gates.

"That's not up to you." He grunted and scraped out more rocks and rotting moat weed. "Herky, old boy, you need to stop feeding off the bottom of the moat. Too much vegetation in your diet will lead to another explosion inside your cave. The girls won't like that."

Herkimer let out a groaning warble of agreement and apology. The young woman huffed furiously, her voice rising three octaves in three seconds, and turned, aiming for the drawbridge.

"You have no idea who you are talking to, do you, you filthy, disrespectful—"

"Don't take another step," Zared snapped, using that tone of voice that had been known to knock enemy soldiers off their feet. He was slightly impressed when this icy little bit of arrogance just stumbled but continued heading for the gate. He sighed. "Don't let her in, please," he called, and turned back to finishing with Herkimer. The shriek of dismay that followed nearly covered the scream of iron on iron as the portcullis slammed down, blocking the gate and access to the drawbridge.

"I don't believe this," she fumed, her breaths pulsing like a dramatic, overweight steam dragon. "This is unacceptable. You will report to Lord Zared and Lady Ashlyn that their event planner has arrived and refuses to step foot inside the castle until someone with some authority has an appropriate apology prepared. I will be waiting in that entirely inadequate meadow over there." She fluttered her fingers in the direction of the deer meadow. "We're going to have to chop down at least three acres of that ugly forest to make room for the dancing pavilions and the musicians' tents and the ladies tents and build—"

"No." He slapped the upper ridge of Herkimer's blubbery lip. "All done. Be a little more careful with your eating, will you, old boy?" He closed his eyes and held his breath, and deliberately didn't warn the snotty young woman, whom he now identified as Circe-Beth.

Herkimer let out a groaning wail and flipped over onto his side, rolling off the shelf and diving straight down to the depths of the moat. Just like the enchanted castle had built multiple subterranean layers to accommodate all the magical artifacts brought there for safekeeping, it had also expanded the moat to accommodate its monsters. Herkimer and his little herd of moat mares were more than triple the normal size for moat monsters, thanks to all the magic seeping into the water. Some accommodations were necessary. The castle had taken advantage of some dimensional magic akin to the spells that created time pockets, to essentially give the creatures unlimited room for recreational activities.

The effect of the moat monster diving meant an enormous displacement of water. Zared stood still as muddy, weed-festooned water splashed over him. Circe-Beth made the mistake of letting out another shriek of outrage just as the water hit her in the face. Zared pretended his ears were full of water until she got to her feet and staggered away. The last he heard from her, she was shouting for someone to draw her a bath.

Memories of the miserable time Circe-Beth had created for 'Na and her friends in the distance school drowned any sense of sympathy or guilt. He whistled the notes that summoned several housekeeping breezes. One immediately wrapped around him, drawing away the water. The others, he asked to interfere with Circe-Beth's people setting up camp. Including preventing them finding enough water for a bath. Then he picked up the pikes and headed to the drawbridge gate. It slid upward in smooth silence when he was ten steps away.

"Thank you." He raked his fingers through his damp hair and let out a groan. Clearly, this was becoming a bigger problem than his family had anticipated. Circe-Beth couldn't be dealt with like others in the past, whom he and Ashlyn had simply ignored until they blew up like an enormous balloon and exploded in an embarrassing way, providing their own punishment. The question was how this young woman was going to retaliate.

~~~~~

Her parents warned her, so 'Na was ready when she returned to the enchanted castle with Ambrose and their wedding party. Despite the interference of the housekeeping breezes, Circe-Beth's entourage managed to set up her camp.

The deer meadow was on the west side of the castle, so 'Na and Ambrose and their friends came the long way around and approached by the road on the east. They didn't even need to employ an emergency invisibility spell to prevent Circe-Beth seeing them and getting between them and the castle gates.

Then Eyesallova received warning that King Ruprick was on his way, coming from the west with an enormous entourage. Despite Ashlyn and Zared refusing every service and gift he wanted to bestow on them, he was determined to provide for the entire wedding festivities, since they wouldn't let him host the ceremony at his castle. For the first time in her life, 'Na was glad King Ruprick was coming to the enchanted castle. She couldn't wait for the clash between him and Circe-Beth. Although, when she stopped to think about it for a few moments, the fallout and destruction might actually threaten the foundations of the enchanted castle.

When the mirrors that monitored traffic through the enchanted forest notified them that King Ruprick's caravan of wagons was close enough to be seen, everyone climbed up to the west tower to watch the encounter. Circe-Beth's entourage had spread out to fill the deer meadow, with a dozen tents and twice as many wagons. Several of them seemed to hold nothing but cages. Lady Ashlyn inquired of the magic mirror, Spyder, who monitored the deer meadow. Moments later, the hand mirror Hazel showed them multiple shifting images of the contents of the cages. They appeared to be butterflies and several different species of songbirds. All of them glowed and sparkled, in colors nature never gave them.

'Na fought a shiver of apprehension. Circe-Beth had been obsessed with the proper "look" for royal maidens when they were classmates. Songbirds and butterflies were essential accessories for a princess, she insisted. She always had a snit when someone reminded her she wasn't a
~~~~~

princess. Her response was always, "Not yet." 'Na and her friends had conspired to send letters of warning to every kingdom with a widowed king or an eligible prince. It was the right thing to do.

Watching Circe-Beth's preparations for King Ruprick's arrival was difficult when limited to several hand mirrors. Zerocs cast a temporary display spell in a wall of mist twenty feet wide and ten high, so they could all watch the events in the meadow in comfort. He apologized several times for not being able to add sound to the images. 'Na and Zella didn't need to hear Circe-Beth's voice when she was in one of her, "but I'm doing this to help you, I know best, don't be ridiculous," moods. Her voice always seemed to rise several notes every time someone said no to her. It was a given that King Ruprick would refuse to relinquish his plans to control 'Na and Ambrose's wedding.

"If we're lucky, her voice will rise so high only dogs can hear her," Prince Ruprick offered. That got chuckles from most of them. Even from Rolf and Garnet, who had triply sharp hearing, even when they weren't in wolf shape.

"Has to be magic," Zella muttered as Circe-Beth made her grand entrance, stepping out of her glittery, gauzy pavilion to climb right into a carriage that looked like it was made of diamonds, pulled by four lavender unicorns. "No one can have that kind of figure without a lot of under-layer support and learning how to get by without air."

"I have to wonder how she gets all those little birds and butterflies to stay fluttering around her like that," Garnet said with a chuckle. "Do you think she covered herself with honey?"

"Oh, please, don't," Princess Phibbia said on a little gasp. She covered her mouth, and for a few seconds 'Na thought she turned a pale shade of green. After fumbling with a little scent box she wore strapped to her wrist, her color returned to normal. "Sorry," she said, ending with a sigh of relief. "The mention of any food seems to make me queasy."

"While we're here," Zella said, "we'll find you a charm to take care of your problem."

Phibbia was pregnant. She had told the women of the wedding party but hadn't told either her husband or his father just yet. She suspected the king would in effect make her a prisoner in the palace, surrounded by multiple healers and enchanters. The longer she could go without anyone realizing the heir to the throne was coming, the happier she would be. Personally, 'Na thought it wasn't pregnancy that made her friend ill, but the impending arrival of another Ruprick. She had already said a dozen prayers, begging A'theosius that Phibbia would have a daughter. The royal family of Rathelshiffen could use all the common sense they could get their hands on.

King Ruprick's caravan emerged from the trees. Circe-Beth's carriage moved out to intercept it. Even from half a mile away, anyone could have picked the king out of the crowd. 'Na wondered if his crown had a spell to make it reflect beams of light in every direction, or did he just have a staff of servants devoted to keeping it polished like a mirror?

For a moment it looked like a pincer movement, with all the spun sugar and glitter that hid the nasty magic of an event planner on one side, and King Ruprick and an entire battalion of courtiers and wagons on the other. Fortunately, 'Na and her wedding party were nowhere within reach, but safe inside the castle, with the drawbridge pulled up and the moat monsters on alert.

"I just had an awful thought," Ambrose said. He swallowed hard, loudly, and tried to force a smile. Only one side of his mouth managed it. "What if they team up, instead of battling to the death?"

"You do have to wonder why she's still hanging around," Zared said. "After I insulted her and we locked the castle doors, you'd think she'd be stomping away, shrieking about how mean everyone is to her, like she did when you were children."

"Being an event planner is just another tactic to put herself at the center of everything," Ashlyn said.

A new thought paralyzed 'Na for a few heartbeats. What if being the center of attention wasn't Circe-Beth's goal at all, but just a tactic for something bigger? Something nastier?

"Definitely, she's been waiting all this time to punish the rest of us for not letting her control every part of our lives when we were classmates," Zella said, when 'Na voiced her idea.

No one responded, mesmerized like a crowd anticipating some horrific disaster, as they watched Circe-Beth's carriage run circles around King Ruprick, separating him from his guards. Her mouth fluttered so fast her lips were a blur. Despite the lack of sound attached to the magnified image, the trilling giggles and the windchime notes of her voice carried clearly to those in the tower, watching.

"Oh, that's not smart at all," Phibbia murmured, when King Ruprick reached out and caught hold of Circe-Beth's hand, which waved about in that irritating way she had had since they were classmates. 'Na had always believed Circe-Beth was trying to hypnotize everyone around her with those constantly circling hand movements.

King Ruprick leaned down from his horse so far, magic definitely had to be involved to keep him from falling into the carriage. Circe-Beth's giggles trilled up and down three octaves as the king of Rathelshiffen kissed her hand. And her wrist, and up her arm.

'Na wasn't sure who she wanted to curl up and die first from that disgusting moment of contact. No woman who wanted to retain her sanity allowed King Ruprick to put his lips anywhere on her. She had heard that the late Queen Astonie had done a fair job of reforming her husband, but she had died under the weight of an untold number of curses levied against the royal family long before her task had reached success. Phibbia was protected by all the codicils of the magic involved when Prince Ruprick freed her from the frog curse. Quite a few blessings came from him finally acting like a hero. Phibbia just might accomplish the reformations and cleansings the kingdom needed.

Circe-Beth seemed to escape contact with King Ruprick without any damage, more's the pity. Her carriage turned, and the king turned his mount to follow her. King Ruprick was talking almost non-stop.

"Oh, that doesn't look good," Prince Ruprick said. "My father has that look in his eye. He's plotting something."

"Let's hope it's something to take advantage of Circe-Beth and leave her holding the bag when the scheme fails," Zared said.

"Let's hope he's not planning on giving you a stepmother at long last," Ashlyn added.

Ruprick went whiter than snow and wobbled on his feet. Rolf and Ambrose hurried to catch him just as his knees started to fold. The wedding party got him down the stairs out of the tower and into one of the guest rooms. Ashlyn and Zared left the tower as well, and 'Na hoped her parents were coming up with a new plan to deal with their unwanted party planners.

They left Phibbia and the breezes to tend to the prince. Hazel notified them that Zared had ordered the drawbridge lowered and the portcullis raised, and requested 'Na and her friends join them. The king and Circe-Beth were approaching the gates.

"They're not going to let her into the castle, are they?" Zella said.

"No." 'Na hoped her parents had something nastily brilliant planned. "Once she gets inside, we'll never get her out."

"Like sand mites," Garnet muttered. "If you're ever offered a chance to become something furry and fanged, don't do it near any deserts."

Rolf shuddered all over and made a deep, growling sort of whimper. Ambrose and Zerocs muffled laughter. The six fell in step and marched out the main doors of the castle, to face this newest plot or attack or whatever was about to happen.

Zared and Ashlyn were waiting in the castle courtyard when they stepped outside. 'Na wondered what her parents were up to, because they weren't dressed as lord and lady of the castle, prepared to overwhelm and impress their unwanted visitors. They were dressed more appropriately for travel, rather than an ordinary day of tending to all the tasks required for controlling all the rogue magic that filled the enchanted castle.

They didn't have time to confer over a plan as the eight of them hurried across the courtyard to the castle gates and across the drawbridge, keeping the oncoming horde from crossing it into the castle.

"You!" Circe-Beth's face shifted so fast from glittery, flirty delight to fury, 'Na was surprised it didn't crack. She yanked on the reins and the unicorns skidded to a stop. The carriage rode up on the backside of the rear pair of unicorns. She pointed one finger at Zared, who stood arm-in-arm with Ashlyn. "I told you that you were dismissed. What are you doing still hanging around? No, don't bother making your ridiculous, lying excuses. Go fetch the lord and lady and then take yourself off for parts unknown!"

How, 'Na wondered, did Circe-Beth manage to make her voice go so high and shrill without breaking glass for miles around?

"No," Zared said, and chuckled.

"Girl, you are an idiot," King Ruprick said, and shook his head.

"Bella, what is wrong with you that you allow such disobedient servants to pollute your home?" Circe-Beth wailed, using her "why am I the only sane person here?" tone of voice.

"First of all," 'Na said, "my name is not Bella. It has never been Bella. I've lost count of how many times I've told you."

"But best friends always have pet names for each other," she insisted, and her eyes filled with huge, rainbow-streaked tears. "Bella is ever so much prettier than Belladonna. What horrid person decided to saddle you with that name?"

"I'm not going to waste my breath fighting with you about how we are not and never have been best friends." She stomped forward, wishing she wore the sword that had let her grow to twenty feet tall, dressed in magic-enhanced armor. "Don't even start," she snapped, when Circe-Beth opened her mouth to argue. "Second, you weren't talking to a servant. These are my parents, Lady Ashlyn, the Beastly Beauty, and Lord Zared, the Disenchanted Prince."

"No. They cannot possibly—" Circe-Beth lost her voice, though her mouth kept moving. She pressed the back of her hand to her forehead and collapsed into the seat of her carriage.

No one moved. Not even her entourage raced to ease her distress. Someone chuckled. Her nose widened and flattened into a piggy snout for several heartbeats. Fury twisted her face as she struggled to sit up again. She took a deep breath, and in the silence of that moment, the creaking of her corset sounded like a casket full of curses swinging open.

"Now that's just not fair!" Circe-Beth wailed. "You should have introduced yourself! That's simply cruel!"

'Na came near laughing, to see how her hair stayed perfect, not a strand out of place, no matter how quickly she whipped her ridiculous pointed hat and all those veils around. Who expended that much magic on their appearance at all times?

"Oooh! I don't know why I keep forgiving you! You were the most selfish, the most—the most—the most piggish girl I ever had the miserable misfortune to ever know!" Circe-Beth shrieked, her tones rising to sound like shattered glass.

"Piggish? You should know," Garnet snarled, her eyes turning red and her lips pulling back to reveal lots of sharp teeth. "Did anyone ever tell you what a werewolf queen is given when she's feeling especially … hmmm … upset with liars and schemers and shrieking little twits who wouldn't know reality if it stomped them into a puddle on the ground?"

Circe-Beth blanched. Garnet took one long step forward for each word she said next.

"I just love … roast pork!" She drew the last word out into a howl.

Circe-Beth shrieked and snatched up the reins. The unicorns pivoted on their hind legs and darted away, nearly tipping the carriage on its side as it turned sharply. Garnet leaped, landing on all fours in the exact spot where Circe-Beth had been sitting just two heartbeats ago. She stayed down, her head tipped back and letting out a howl that shattered immediately into laughter. 'Na clung to Ambrose, laughing.

"Well, that was interesting," King Ruprick remarked. "Who was that glittery little ninny?"

"You don't want to know," Zared said. "Just saying her name can give her the ability to spy on you and bend your will to her service."

"You don't say?" His eyes narrowed as he turned to look in the direction Circe-Beth had gone.

'Na could almost hear his thoughts, calculating if the tradeoff was worthwhile, to gain that kind of power and turn it to his own uses.

~~~~~

The housekeeping breezes took over, guiding the king's entourage across the drawbridge and into the courtyard. There was no remedy for it now, they would have to host King Ruprick and find some way to convince him not to provide for the wedding feast. 'Na and Zella and Garnet retreated to the guest wing to check on Ruprick, and sneak Phibbia the charms Zella had promised. They were surprised, then briefly worried to find Phibbia in bed and Ruprick sitting by her side, holding her hand and looking charmingly flustered and adoring.

Clearly, she had finally told him about the coming baby.

The prince hugged Zella, when she produced the charms. Then 'Na informed him that his father was staying overnight, and they needed his help in discouraging the king from taking over the wedding. The most amazing transformation swept over the prince. He stood up straight and drew his shoulders back, tugged down his jacket, and squared his jaw.

"It's about time I grew up, don't you agree? Sweetheart, I know you're in better hands with your friends than with a bumbler like me. Do
~~~~~

you mind very much if I go try to talk some sense into my father?" He bent down and caught up Phibbia's hand and pressed it to his heart.

Sometimes, 'Na regretted not having been friends with Ruprick before this. She could never have fallen for him, even if she hadn't met Ambrose, but he was slowly growing into everything a prince should be. She was glad for Phibbia.

"Go be a hero, my darling," Phibbia whispered. She blushed prettily when Ruprick pressed a kiss to her palm and gently put her hand down at her side before turning sharply on his heel and striding out of the room.

"That was … interesting," Zella said. She chuckled. "You're doing a good job with him."

"I thought he'd never leave," Phibbia said, her voice much stronger. She sat up, swung her legs over the side of the bed, and held out her hand. "Charms, please. I have a lot of work to do over the next seven months, and I'll need all the help I can get. I am not bringing my child into the mess that Rathelshiffen is right now. The people think the king is a tyrant? They haven't met a mother-to-be with a mission!"

The four girls burst out laughing.

~~~~~

Dinner that evening was more entertaining than 'Na could have imagined, with King Ruprick in the castle. He was so delighted with the news of his coming grandchild, he roared and blustered until he nearly lost his voice. He wrapped an arm around his son, giving him a rough kind of celebratory shake multiple times. Until 'Na feared the prince's head would snap off his neck. Yet when Phibbia came down to the dining room, the king suddenly went gentle, his movements slow, his voice soft. A half-dozen times during dinner, he lost his train of thought and just trailed off, to turn to watch his daughter-by-law with a shining, awestruck gaze. 'Na wondered how he had been when his wife was pregnant with Prince Ruprick. Now, the tales of how he had changed so drastically after she died made a sort of sense.

Yet a few times, she felt thoroughly chilled, wondering what sort of plans for conquest were sprouting in King Ruprick's mind. Plans to turn his grandchild into ruler of the entire continent? Phibbia had better take advantage of the softer, gentler, malleable king from the very start, to protect her child and the kingdom. She had a huge task ahead of her.

'Na silently pledged all the resources of the enchanted castle to help her friend. And promised that her children would stand with the heir of Rathelshiffen against any ridiculous …

"Are you all right?" Ambrose whispered, and caught hold of 'Na's hand under the table. "You made a strange noise, and you're pale."

"I'll tell you later," she whispered back, and squeezed his hand hard. Her cheeks warmed and her heart resumed its proper rhythm. A chuckle
~~~~~

caught in her throat as she imagined Ambrose's reaction to what she had just been thinking. Had she actually looked ahead, thinking of their children? An image of a handful of children running around the castle popped into her mind. She pushed the image away before she looked too closely, to see how many looked like her or like Ambrose. *Please, A'theosius,* she prayed quickly. *Please don't let me suddenly have a gift of prophecy, with all the other problems attacking us.*

~~~~~

Eyesallova reported that some of the watchful mirrors scattered through the forest surrounding the castle were having their perceptions fuddled. Most likely Circe-Beth's mirror, Jallosy, was interfering. While it was admirable that a mirror could be so loyal, in this case, it was a problem when that loyalty focused on someone as narcissistic as Circe-Beth. She had a reputation for rewriting reality to suit herself. Eyesallova feared the rumors were true that Jallosy had cracked. What a cracked mirror would and could do was frightening. Especially when serving a selfish little opportunistic twit who practiced the strange new, mind-controlling magic, event planning.

The fuddling interfered with keeping watch on Circe-Beth, to prevent a surprise attack on the castle. 'Na had a vision of the castle being overwhelmed by a tidal wave of pigs, after Circe-Beth ensorcelled every werewolf, vampire, or unlucky travelers, and sent them to hurtle themselves into the moat and over the walls.

Garnet and Rolf volunteered to go on a spying mission. Ashlyn consulted several books dealing with healing and protecting magic mirrors, and they took two pouches of magic sand to sprinkle any fuddled mirrors they found, to end Jallosy's interference.

"Would this do any good if we threw some at Jallosy?" Rolf asked.

"Depending on how warped she has become under Circe-Beth's interference," Eyesallova said, "she could either shatter irreparably, or be healed and rebel outright. Either outcome would be good for the world in general, but no one wishes any mirror to shatter, no matter how sick."

'Na went outside with Garnet and Rolf. They shifted to wolf-shape and leaped over the garden wall. She stayed out there to think in the quiet. Lately, quiet and solitude were rare commodities in the enchanted castle.

When she came back indoors, she heard King Ruprick's voice from all the way up in the guest wing. He was entirely too jolly. Was he going to sing and tell jokes all night? Who had the brilliant idea to put the guest wing just down another corridor from the wing where her family lived? While it was nice knowing Ambrose was just a hallway away when he stayed in the castle, and Zerocs was conveniently close for midnight consultations with Zella over brilliant ideas for new magic spells, having other guests so close could be rather inconvenient. To add insult to injury,
~~~~~

the housekeeping breezes hadn't put King Ruprick in the sage wing guest quarters this time, like they usually did. What was up with that? He couldn't possibly have started to reform, just because he was going to be a grandfather. Could he?

"I'm sorry," Prince Ruprick said, leaning out of the intersecting corridor between the family wing and guest wing, just as 'Na stepped out of the gallery. "He got hold of some bottles of wine and a song book and found the room with the musical instruments that play themselves. He's having an incredibly good time." He winced as his father's voice rang out in a long note that threatened to rise up an entire octave. "I didn't want to stop him, because it's so rare to see him so happy."

"Who's in there with him?" 'Na thought she could make out at least two male voices. "Is that Ambrose?"

"And Zerocs." The prince shrugged. "Your father managed to escape before the wine arrived."

"How did you?"

"Phibbia wasn't feeling well. She asked me to sing her to sleep. I think she was protecting me. I don't know how I got so lucky to marry her." He blushed, which 'Na found charming. "I really don't want to go back in there, but I should protect Ambrose."

"I'll ask the breezes to bring in some new wine with a strong sleeping draught. That should take care of the noise problem so both of you can get some sleep," she offered.

"Would you? I know I'm a coward —"

"You're a wounded veteran in the war to restrain your father. Don't be ashamed."

It was definite. She did like Ruprick more, every time she encountered him. She bade him goodnight and peered down the corridor to the guest wing as the prince toddled off to his and Phibbia's suite. Light spilled into the corridor through the open door of King Ruprick's suite. The music changed into something bouncy and the king's rattling bass voice roared out in a solo. 'Na stepped down the corridor, led by her curiosity. Didn't Ambrose and Zerocs know the song?

"Hey! Hey, don't go to sleep! We're just getting started," King Ruprick cried. "Why's the room spinning around?"

A thud echoed down the corridor. The music faded away. 'Na grinned, relieved. Well, she wouldn't have to ask the housekeeping breezes to dose that wine, to put them to sleep.

"Wait a minute …" A chill raced up her back and made her hair prickle. A few moments of thought, and she raced down the corridor to her parents' suite.

Zared opened the door and stepped out when she was halfway down the corridor. He grinned at her. "What did you do to get them to quiet down?"

"I didn't—did you dose their wine?" That chill got stronger when her father shook his head. "Then who told the breezes to give the king that wine?"

"Are you thinking what I'm thinking?" Ashlyn said, as she joined them in the doorway.

They found Ambrose, Zerocs, and King Ruprick sprawled on the floor in the sitting room of the king's suite. They were all snoring with strange snuffling noises, interspersed with grunts, and their faces looked rather puffy. The self-playing musical instruments hovered in a corner, looking rather forlorn with no one to listen to them. Ashlyn caught them before they started in with a new song. She sent them back to the music room while Zared examined the three men.

'Na found the crate just inside the half-open door of the bedroom. Circe-Beth's signature pink, lavender, and mint green gauze provided padding for four wine bottles. One sealed bottle was still in the crate. A tag attached to the outside of the crate read, "For the bride and groom, to show I have no hard feelings. That's what best friends do, they forgive each other. Do drink a toast to our mended friendship, and all the fun we will have planning your nuptials."

Ashlyn found an open bottle and sniffed it. "It's a very fruity, sweet wine. Definitely something added to it."

"Mama!" 'Na yelped, and dashed forward, to yank the bottle from her mother's hand before Ashlyn got it to her lips.

Ashlyn's eyes widened and she paled as she looked at the bottle. She set it down on the table and backed away. "I know better ... but I had the most insatiable urge to drink..."

"Well, now we know why Ambrose and Zerocs didn't have the sense to stop at one glass," Zared said.

"Circe-Beth must have given him that wine while they were talking. Ruprick kept the wine instead of handing it over to you, as she intended," Ashlyn said.

She called the breezes to come clean up the toppled chairs and spilled wine and scattered dishes from the king's celebration. She called in the suit of armor at the intersection of hallways to take the bottles and crate and the remainder of the wine to her workroom. In the morning, she and Zared would try to decipher what sort of nasty magic Circe-Beth had tried to inflict on 'Na and Ambrose. Several suits of armor came in to put the three snoring, snuffling men to bed. Zella checked the workroom Zerocs used when he was visiting the castle, to find the general defensive cure-all he was developing. Although he had admitted it was nowhere near perfected yet, maybe it would counteract whatever nasty effects were hidden in the wine. Within minutes of getting the potion down Ambrose's throat, 'Na thought the puffiness of his face had decreased, and his snores didn't sound quite so squealy. Once again, Zerocs' experimenting and constant tweaking of tried-and-true spells had come in handy.

Garnet and Rolf returned during the cleanup and reported that they had found and treated four magic mirrors but weren't able to get close to Jallosy. They had watched Circe-Beth pace circles into the carpeting of her tent, muttering "I'll show you," and "I'll have the last laugh," and "True love's kiss will command." They didn't like the manic odor emanating from the tent and left when it was clear they weren't going to hear anything new.

'Na sat up for another hour after going to bed, gnawing on her former classmate's words. She didn't like the comment about true love's kiss. She and Ambrose both had ample proof that true love's kiss did work wonders. Even if it didn't always act quickly. It was just like Circe-Beth to take something with a firm foundation in the oldest magic and try to warp it to suit her desires.

~~~~~

'Na woke to squeals coming down the hall from the guest wing, and then doors thudding and furniture banging. Then the clatter of suits of armor waking up all around the castle. What need had brought the armor off their pedestals this time? She strained her ears, trying to understand what was happening. Were those squeals … pig squeals?

"Circe-Beth," she growled, and leaped out of bed. Her mind raced, trying to understand how Zerocs' cure-all had failed. She snarled, thinking of all the times she had tried to be a good girl and not steal all sorts of nasty, broken spells to use against Circe-Beth when they had been classmates.

Fury wasn't doing her any good. She had to get dressed, find Ambrose, and kiss him to counteract Circe-Beth's latest nasty trick as soon as possible. There was no telling what vicious, complicated magic she had added to her standard turn-them-into-pigs spell, but it had to be strong, if it resisted Zerocs' cure-all.

A surge of nausea made her stumble as she thought past the momentary distastefulness of kissing a pig to rescue Ambrose. Zella could rescue Zerocs, but who could they find to kiss King Ruprick and break the curse on him?

"Well, Circe-Beth might have actually done something kind for a change," she muttered as she snatched up her boots and headed for her bedroom door. Phibbia would have an easier time reforming Rathelshiffen, with no interference from her father-by-law.

Hopping on one foot as she pulled a boot on the other foot, she hurtled out into the hall. She reached the intersection where the hall from the gallery divided to go to the family's wing and the guest wing. Three
~~~~~

pigs hurtled down the hall from the guest wing. They bumped into each other and slammed into walls, squealing the entire time. Each was enormous, their ears higher than 'Na's waist. Eight suits of armor chased them, swinging nets woven of chains. She darted back into a doorway, just in time to escape being bowled over as the pigs tumbled past her, heading for the gallery and the central staircase.

"Please tell me I'm dreaming," Zared said, leaning out the door of his and Ashlyn's suite at the other end of the hall. 'Na could only glare at her father. He chuckled and ducked back into the room.

"They don't smell like pigs," Garnet said, trotting down the corridor after the pigs. She bent over, sniffing at the carpet, and went on all fours for a few steps.

"They're not." 'Na turned and headed for the gallery. "Not for long, anyway."

Zella stumbled out of her suite, struggling to braid her hair, which was twitching and visibly growing. A sure sign of her hair preparing to defend her against inimical magic. What else did Circe-Beth have ready to pounce on them? Zella opened her mouth to speak, stopped by the banging of three enormous pigs hitting the main doors.

'Na caught her breath, realizing the disaster that could have ensued if the castle had let the three pigs escape. Out into the courtyard. Across the drawbridge. And then scattering into the enchanted forest.

Or worse, and more likely, straight into whatever trap Circe-Beth had waiting. If she would organize a boar hunt when a faithful groom rejected her advances, what would she do to the men her school days rivals loved?

"Thank you," 'Na called to the castle as she hurtled down the central staircase, with Zella, her parents, Garnet and Rolf right behind her.

The sounds of big bodies hitting the doors, the swish-clatter of chain nets swinging through the air, the thud of metal feet on the flagstones, and the infuriated squeals of pigs echoed through the heart of the castle.

"The library!" Zella shrieked and vaulted over the railing of the second-floor landing. She landed crooked, and 'Na swore she heard a cracking sound that she hoped was the flagstone pavement and not her friend's ankles or feet. Zella hobbled to the doors of the library, waving her arms.

Then 'Na saw what her friend had seen. One of the pigs was trying to get to the open library doors. He kept getting stopped by a suit of armor lumbering into his path or a swinging net coming too close to enclosing him, so he had to leap away, but he was definitely getting closer to the library doors with every dodge.

The library doors slammed shut with a loud gasping groan from Zella, and an echoing, disappointed squeal coming from the pig. She slid down to the floor, her back against the doors, and gave a shaking sort of grin.

Why would a pig want to get into the library?

"That's Zerocs!" 'Na called down to her friend. "He's probably thought of something in his workroom." Not that she had much hope of it working, when his cure-all last night hadn't helped.

Or maybe it had helped, and this mess was an improvement over what Circe-Beth tried to do?

Another pig let out a shrieking sort of trumpeting call that 'Na could have sworn sounded like "This way," and darted out from under a swinging net, straight at the suit of armor aiming for him. He hit the armor, knocking it flat. The other two pigs copied him, attacking the suits of armor they had been avoiding just moments before. Snagging the chain metal nets in their massive jaws, they darted away. Straight at the company standing at the base of the stairs.

Zared let out a shout, grabbing 'Na and Ashlyn with an arm around each of their waists and leaping aside. Garnet yelped like a paw had been stepped on. She and Rolf separated and vaulted over the railings to get out of the way.

The pigs ran back up the staircase, clattering and banging and squealing.

Then 'Na noticed something. Circe-Beth was playing nasty. "They're exactly identical. The same black patch over the left eye, the same brown splotch on the right ear and down to the shoulder. The same splotches on their backsides. They're even the same size. How can we tell them apart to rescue them?"

Her stomach twisted and she was glad she hadn't had breakfast yet. The mental image of kissing King Ruprick by accident threatened to put her off food for the rest of the day.

"Where are they going?" Ashlyn started up the stairs after the pigs.

"Let us," Rolf said. He and Garnet leaped up the stairs, going onto all fours, and in two heartbeats had shifted to wolf. They streaked up the stairs, and in moments more pig squeals and shrieks resounded through the castle, accompanied by the banging of doors against walls.

"That sounds like they're on the third floor already," Zared said, as 'Na helped Zella to her feet.

"It sounds like they've gotten into the mirror room," Ashlyn said.

More squeals came to them, muffled now, and a few more bangs. Fortunately, Zella was able to walk without help, though she did favor her right foot a little as they started up the stairs. 'Na wrapped an arm around her waist to help her and they followed her parents up at a slightly slower pace.

"They went straight through to the balcony and down into the gardens," Garnet reported, when they reached the last flight of steps up to the third floor.

"Excuse me?" Prince Ruprick called, hurrying across the gallery to join them. "I can't find my father anywhere. He should be roaring about the noise by now."

"He's been turned into a pig," Zared said.

Prince Ruprick didn't seem surprised or upset by the news.

Eyesallova reported that a hazing spell kept her from identifying the man inside each pig. That wouldn't have helped anyway, because she confirmed they were identical. What mattered more right now was ensuring the pigs didn't find a way out of the castle gardens.

The gardens in the enchanted castle were much larger inside than they appeared from the outside. Space had a tendency to warp, the deeper someone wandered, or in this case, raced through the gardens. That had been great fun when 'Na was a child, accompanied by a dozen statues and Smedley the dragon, because the gardens considered her a friend. Frightened, bespelled, angry pigs wouldn't be treated as friends. Especially if their hooves and tusks dug up flowerbeds and turf and tore down vines and trees. The castle might decide to open a door that had never been there before, just to get the vandalizing nuisances out.

The way the pigs were running around, they weren't just terrified but had a very slippery grasp on their humanity. Then 'Na remembered something even worse. Just before their class disbanded, Circe-Beth had proudly announced that she had added a codicil to the pig spell. The longer someone remained a pig, the better the chances he would stay that way, and entirely lose all sense of self.

The seven gathered on the balcony, looking down into the garden, where the three pigs wove in and out of sight in a dizzying race among the foliage. By a huge stroke of mercy, the statues weren't chasing them, but how long would that last? When a new chase began, disaster could only follow. Heavy on destruction.

"What do we do?" Ruprick said. He looked remarkably calm for someone who had just had the responsibility for a rather large kingdom dropped on his shoulders because his father had been turned into a pig.

"She was muttering about true love's kiss," Ashlyn reminded them.

"That's fine for you, but … well, I do get along better with my father since I brought Phibbia home, but …" The prince sighed.

"True love isn't limited to romantic love," Zared said. "There's nothing stronger than the adoration of a child. If you can wait a few years, maybe there will be some strong affection between Ruprick and his grandchild, and that will do the trick?"

"A few years?" He shuddered. "Can you imagine how he'll be if he has to be a pig for a few years? We'd be better off leaving him that way permanently."

"It wouldn't be that much of a change," Zella muttered. 'Na muffled a chuckle into a snort. She glanced at Ruprick, relieved to see him fighting not to grin.

"We have a problem!" Eyesallova called from the mirror room behind them.

Zared and Ashlyn went inside, leaving 'Na, Zella, Garnet, Rolf and Ruprick watching the pigs, who didn't seem to be calming down.

"Smell something?" Rolf said. His face elongated, turning furry, until a wolf snout twitched and his long tongue hung out.

"Nasty magic at work," Garnet said. She nodded to 'Na, then leaped over the balcony railing, shifting entirely to wolf before her four feet hit the ground. Rolf shifted and followed her, and they headed off across the gardens, toward the lowest point in the surrounding wall.

"I have a bad feeling about that," Zella said, pointing at that spot.

'Na swallowed hard, feeling a zinging of magic in the air. And if she wasn't hallucinating, a blurring, like water haze in the air, covered the wall. That had to be Circe-Beth. Why was she attacking the wall?

"More trouble," Ashlyn said. She and Zared returned to the balcony with a large, sturdy hand mirror that swirled with blues and greens and peacock feathers. Eyesallova had transferred into the mirror to join them. Words spilled across the surface of the mirror.

Dare you trust true love's kiss?
Beware the cure becomes the curse.
First comes the kiss, and then true love.
Only one kiss for each, and the kiss will bind forever.
Choose carefully. The bond cannot be broken.

"That warped little..." Eyesallova growled. The image on her surface churned and dimmed, then exploded in a burst of angry red sparks. "I thought I felt Jallosy's touch."

"Take it from me, mirror magic is the worst, most twisted kind of magic," Zared said.

"Meaning?" Zella said.

"Everything that goes through a magic mirror gets reversed. That nasty little twit has found a way to turn true love's kiss inside out and backwards," the mirror said.

"But what does she want?" Ruprick said. "Why turn my father into a pig? I mean, yes, it's appropriate, but why Ambrose and Zerocs?"

"To get revenge on us. To take what we have," Zella said. "My interpretation? We only get one kiss each, and whichever pig we kiss to turn back into a man, we're bound to him. Maybe even trapped into some horrid, inside out version of true love."

"Can't," 'Na said, listening to that instinct that her many teachers had praised. She hoped her understanding about magic wasn't failing her now. "I can't imagine Circe-Beth allowing us to be happy with whoever we're bound to, through the kiss. A kiss that causes true love? More like infatuation, but with holes in it, so we know we've been tricked, we know we're being coerced."

"And she has to know that we love them fiercely enough, we can't leave them trapped as pigs forever," Zella said.

"Even at the cost of not being together?" Ruprick said. "It might be a greater mercy to let them stay pigs and forget they were ever men, than to be turned back into men and bound to a maiden they don't truly love."

"Either way, we lose," 'Na said. "So we have to identify which pig is which man. And do it before they forget who they are."

"We have to catch them, first," Zared said.

A clatter arose from the gardens. A sound like dozens of marble statues colliding. 'Na didn't want to look. She could guess what had happened. She looked anyway as she leaped down the steps to the gardens.

The garden wall had fallen.

A streak of white and brown wove through the chaos of stones and dust. A second streak followed it. Then a third.

The pigs were escaping.

"Stop them! Don't let them leave!" 'Na shouted, and a dozen statues looked out from the little summer house where they gathered every morning to breakfast on dew. She pointed to the gap in the wall.

Please, A'theosius, help us. Guide our hearts, 'Na prayed in endless repetition as she raced across the garden, straining her eyes for sight of a pig.

Not just a pig, any pig, but the pig who was still Ambrose inside.

Before he reached that gap in the wall.

Zella was just a few steps behind her. She could move incredibly fast, which was always a surprise to anyone who only knew her as the castle's librarian. Dealing with magic books all day required sharp reflexes and incredible muscle tone, either chasing down books that tried to reshelve themselves or start battles with books that once belonged to rivals of their previous owners, or dodging books that demanded her attention, or climbing ladders multiple times in an hour.

Circe-Beth strode through the dissipating cloud of dust from the shattered wall. She waved her hands, shooting off pink sparks that streaked through the air, straight at the pigs.

"Cheater," 'Na growled.

A streak of red crossed her path. Garnet-wolf intercepted a pig that trundled out of a clump of bushes, nose wriggling, making all sorts of grunts and squeals and snorts. It turned, heading straight for 'Na.

"Ambrose?" She leaped over a chunk of stone that had rolled away from the wall. "Ambrose, it's 'Na. Wait!"

The pig was covered with streaks of stone dust and scratches, and the tiny little eyes nearly hidden in rolls of fat had a definite reddish tint. 'Na fought down a shiver of revulsion at the thought of kissing that. She hoped she and Ambrose would be able to laugh about this someday.

Squeals rose up from far to the right, around a bulge in the castle wall. Two more pigs trotted out, chased by Rolf. A shriek escaped Circe-Beth. A whirlwind of stone dust spun around her as she lifted into the air, to fly straight toward the pigs. She flew over them and slammed into Rolf.

He leaped aside at the last minute and she hit the ground with a massive belly-flop that startled an ooph-gasp-belch out of her. The two pigs split up. Rolf ran after one.

Circe-Beth flew after the other, giggling—no, more accurately, cackling—with her arms stretched out before her, fingers curved into claws. The gleeful expression lighting her face darkened into a scowl as her path crossed 'Na's and their gazes met. She bared her teeth and yanked a ring off her hand and tossed it at the pig 'Na chased. It turned into a sparkling, gauzy net in mid-air and shot after the pig.

"Ambrose, run!" 'Na shouted, and changed course, fully intending to collide with Circe-Beth.

Circe-Beth shrieked and spun around in mid-air like a roast on a spit, hands curving into claws again, aiming at 'Na. She totally ignored Zella, who was now behind her. The two pigs darted toward a small grove of whispering flute trees.

"Baahnsigh!" Zella hollered and brought her hands together as she leaped onto Circe-Beth. Her rings clashed with a sound like a thousand gongs, sending out visible sound waves that flung Circe-Beth to the ground.

There were distinct advantages to being courted by an inventor wizard. Gifts of prototypes of all sorts of bizarre spells and charms was just one of them.

Zella landed on her knees on Circe-Beth's back cutting off her cackles with a loud ooph-belch sound. She bounced twice before getting to her feet.

What she did to their nemesis after that, 'Na didn't know. She followed the pigs into the grove.

"Ambrose?" 'Na aimed herself at a moving splotch of white among the shadows. "It's 'Na. Please come to me? I can free you from the spell. But hurry?"

Squeals and grunts answered her. White moved on the right of her. More white on the left. White directly in front of her.

All three pigs came tearing out of the shadows, heading straight toward her. 'Na choked, realizing just how big they were. She had a sudden vision of Ambrose knocking her down in his eagerness for the cure.

"Ambrose, slow down!"

All three pigs slowed.

"Zerocs, go to Zella." She pointed back behind herself, where she heard feet coming through the trees.

All three pigs turned to the sound. They made the exact same excited squeals. They all turned as if one pig and darted away.

"King Ruprick?"

All three pigs stopped, their ears perking up.

"Which one of you is Ambrose?"

All three pigs grunted and made little prancing motions with their front feet, bobbing their heads.

'Na's stomach clenched when their eyes got an even brighter red. All three in perfect unison leaped toward her. They skidded to a stop and grunted at each other and lowered their heads, wagging them threateningly. Those tusks could slice each other to ribbons in seconds.

"Zerocs?" Zella called as she stepped into the clearing.

All three pigs squealed in answer and again bobbed their heads. All three started drooling.

"Which is which?" She stepped up next to 'Na. "Which one of you is Zerocs?"

All three mouths dropped open and they made jabbering noises and bobbed their heads, and then turned on each other.

"Did you really think it would be that easy?" Circe-Beth sneered. She staggered into the clearing, covered with mud, her multiple gauzy veils torn and clinging to her.

"Zerocs?" Zella said, and went to her knees, holding out her arms.

All three pigs squealed delight, took two steps, ran into each other, and this time rammed against each other, trying to knock their competitors off their feet.

Circe-Beth cursed.

'Na choked on nasty laughter. That was something she had forgotten about her former classmate: she was always outsmarting herself. Every time she tried to cheat or claim credit for the work someone else did, she always tangled herself up and then blamed someone else. 'Na fought the urge to say, "Did you think it would be that easy to steal our sweethearts?" She knew better than to gloat. That was usually when things either fell apart or got a lot worse.

Then she had an idea. There was always a flaw in Circe-Beth's spells. The trick was finding the place where she created her short-cut and messed up.

"Which of you isn't Ambrose?" she cried.

All three pigs went silent. So, there was a crack in the nasty spell.

One pig squealed and lifted up off his front legs several times.

"Who isn't Zerocs?" Zella said, and caught hold of 'Na's hand.

A different pig this time responded, jumping up and waggling his ears.

The third pig stayed silent both times.

'Na hoped she was right, and King Ruprick was such a schemer and liar, he wouldn't be able to tell the truth.

"Who isn't King Ruprick?" she asked.

All three pigs responded with head bobs and squeals that certainly sounded a little frantic by this time.

"Oh, you think you're so clever!" Circe-Beth shrieked, and leaped over 'Na and Zella, to land across all three pigs with a huge cloud of sparks. "Hold still!" she snarled, and oophed a few times. A shrill sound filled the air and sliced into 'Na's ears. Hopefully, that was the sound of lots of expensive, fragile cloth tearing.

'Na choked on laughter as the sparks cleared away, to reveal Circe-Beth astride one of the pigs, several scarves around his neck to form a harness, while the pig squealed and grunted and wriggled and leaped and fought with sweaty, red-eyed terror. In seconds, the scarf tightened and choked him, cutting off his air. His legs wobbled.

"We don't have much time," Zella said. "Grab a pig, quick."

"What if we get the wrong one?"

"Are you Zerocs?" she asked the pig that was certainly looking at her with pleading eyes. In another second, he might burst into tears.

"What if they're spelled so they can't tell the truth?" 'Na said. She focused on the other pig, who was now down on the ground, wriggling, crawling and grunting toward her. He certainly looked like he was begging.

Would King Ruprick beg, even in pig shape? Would Zerocs? No, Zerocs was more likely to faint at the thought of anyone but Zella kissing him, and maybe even run away, squealing in utter terror.

A horrifying shrieking squeal shredded the air. 'Na looked over to find Circe-Beth had wrestled her chosen pig to the ground and had her mouth pressed hard against his bristly jowl. The pig sounded like he was on his death bed.

The pig in front of 'Na whimpered and tears filled his eyes.

"Who do you love?" Zella said, waving her hands to get the attention of both pigs.

One blushed a deep red, spreading from his snout backwards.

"That's got to be Zerocs," 'Na said, almost choking on the need to laugh.

To spare her friend, she flung herself at the other pig and kissed his snout. Then remembering the sacrifice Ambrose had made for her, the night of her seventeenth birthday when she had turned into a four-headed beast, she kissed one corner of his mouth, then the other. On the third kiss, the bristles softened under her lips. 'Na sat back, her hands framing the pig's face, and held her breath as he melted into Ambrose.

Zerocs melted back into his true form under Zella's kisses and sank into the grass as she kept kissing him.

"My darling!" King Ruprick trumpeted from the other side of the clearing, where Circe-Beth struggled to break free of the scarves that had bound her and the king together.

Nauseated horror competed with fury on her bright red face. King Ruprick caught a handful of her hair and brought her face down to his and planted a big, sloppy kiss on her lips. He roared laughter as she struggled free. Circe-Beth gagged and spat and brought up a knee between them. His laughter shattered and he let go of the scarves to roll away, folding himself into a defensive ball. Circe-Beth struggled to her feet, shuddering with nausea.

"No! This isn't how it's supposed to go! I'm supposed to get him!" She pulled out a wand to point at Ambrose. "If I can't have you—"

Zerocs snagged several rings from Zella's hands and tossed them all at Circe-Beth. They merged in mid-air and shot out a waterfall of bright green magic that turned pink as it fell down, enclosing Circe-Beth, and folding her to the ground. When the light faded, a little pink pig surrounded by muddy, gauzy scarves squealed and rolled onto its back and had a temper tantrum.

"Oh, my dove, my darling, my treasure," King Ruprick moaned, "what have you done?" He scooped up the pig and cradled it like a baby, then tipped his head back and wailed like a snotty four-year-old who had just had his lollipop yanked out of his mouth. The pig shrieked and wriggled, but couldn't escape, tangled up in the same scarves she had used to trap him.

~~~~~

There were times when Lady Ashlyn and Lord Zared's sense of nobility and fair play went just a little too far. This was one of them.

King Ruprick crooned over the little pink pig to the point of generating nausea in everyone, not just Phibbia. 'Na felt her parents should have just packed Circe-Beth and the king off to Rathelshiffen to deal with the twisted, nasty little curse, for however long she was a pig and he thought he was in love with her. Instead, they put both the king and the pig to sleep and packed them off to the Enchanter's Court to be dealt with. Considering that the members of the court lived inside time pockets with varying relationships to the normal stream of time, King
~~~~~

Ruprick and Circe-Beth might not return for years. If they returned at all. Sometimes the court's sense of justice could be rather vicious, or rather humorous. Even infantile.

Once that task was dealt with, a new crisis cropped up.

The efforts to nullify all the trouble Circe-Beth had been causing, setting herself up as maid of honor and event planner, had essentially notified the entire world of 'Na and Ambrose's betrothal. Protests and congratulations and betrothal presents and demands to meet Ambrose in ritual combat and offers to host the wedding were pouring in from every kingdom, both friends and enemies of Lady Ashlyn and Lord Zared.

'Na was well aware of the chaos that resulted when her parents gave in for the sake of peace. A prime example being the fuss of her christening. She could well imagine the wars that would break out between rival kingdoms trying to solidify their friendship with the enchanted castle through their involvement with the wedding.

"There's only one solution," Zerocs said, when their wedding party met in the tallest tower of the castle, to escape the noise of ambassadors spilling into the castle and messages coming into the mirror room from all over the world. He flushed a deep red and dropped to one knee and snapped his fingers, bringing a crystal betrothal band out of thin air. "Let's elope." He choked and gestured from him and Zella to 'Na and Ambrose.

"Oh, do," Princess Phibbia said. "Our wedding was so exhausting, I slept through the first week of our wedding trip. Getting married should be fun, not warfare."

"I'm all for that," Ambrose said, and wrapped his arm tight around 'Na's waist as they watched Zerocs, with trembling hands, slide the band onto Zella's wrist.

"You're sure you're not too tired? Being transformed into a pig—" 'Na squeaked when he caught her face between his hands and kissed her.

THE END

MEET THE AUTHORS

Kathleen Bird is the author of a completed Christian fantasy series (the *Adven Trilogy*), an ongoing series of steampunk fairytale retellings (the *Isles of Miadhra*), and a brand-new devotional series (*The Things God Does*). You can also find her writings included in a variety of anthologies, and as a fantasy reviewer for *Clean Fiction Magazine*. She loves traveling and seeing new places, which give her inspiration for her writing, but when she and her husband are not traveling the world, they live in Des Moines, IA. Be sure to check out her website (www.adventrilogy.wordpress.com) and her Instagram (@birdsthewords) for more information about her books and where to find them.

Jordan Campbell was born in California and moved to Maine when he was eleven. All through his childhood, Jordan had a book in his hand nearly continuously. Educated at the University of Maine, majoring in English, Jordan has had almost a dozen short stories published in the last two years. He is excited to bring his stories to the world. Jordan's first story for Ye Olde Dragon Books was *Neher, Demon of the River*, which was published in the 3rd Classic Monsters Anthology, ***Don't Go in the Water…***

Rosemarie DiCristo never wrote fantasy or speculative fiction, let alone dystopian stories, before she was influenced by her good friend Pam Halter, but now she can't stop coming up with ideas… and gleefully subjecting her characters to mayhem. She's delighted to be published in another Ye Olde Dragon Books anthology. Other stories she's written have been regularly published in *Havok* and *StarLight* magazines.

Jim Doran is a genre writer who enjoys transporting his readers into worlds of wonder, mystery, and danger. Whether it's the fairytale hijinks in his Kingdom Fantasy series or a centaur agent's daring adventures, Jim aims to entertain his audience with every word. His forthcoming YA horror novel, ***Forlorn Harbor***, will be published by Rowan Prose Publishing in 2026. Among his published shorter works, Jim has had five stories included in Ye Olde Dragon monster and fairy tale anthologies (always a thrill). If you enjoyed *Higpins*, Rebecca Eidelweiss will be featured in the novel *DEED*, publishing in summer 2025.

Arlan Gerig has stories published in Havok Publishing's *Animal Kingdom* and *Remember When* anthologies, as well as stories on *Havok's* website and *Every Day Fiction*. He participated in several mission trips to the Bahamas to meet the needs of impoverished Bahamians and Haitian refugees, leading to a series of stories about aliens landing in the Bahamas. After much prayer and consideration, Arlan left his job of nineteen years to return to teaching middle school students. He teaches students to read great literature, write great essays, and read his stories (at least a couple of them). When he's not spending time with his wife and family, reading, grading papers, or writing his next fantasy story, Arlan enjoys walking his two pit mixes around his Ohio neighborhood.

Pam Halter is not only an award-winning author, but also an award winning cook. Her recipe for Tomato Fritters won runner-up in a *Taste of Home* magazine contest! One of her favorite things to fix for dinner is sesame ginger ribs on the grill. Yeah, pork ribs. Shhhhhhhh … don't tell the pigs. If you want to learn more about Pam, you can subscribe to her email newsletter where she shares what she's up to, what she's writing, a recipe of the month, and more! www.pamhalter.com

Michelle Houston enjoys creating new worlds and civilizations and occasionally getting them on paper. She is a Christian, wife, mother, teacher, and scientist, who strives to connect young adults with the wonders found around us. She spends her free time reading everything in sight, going outside as much as possible (to the relief of the dust bunnies inside), and of course, writing. She would love to connect with you at *whichwaywriting.com*, where you can also find her other stories. (Editor's Note: Michelle is also one of our most prolific authors! She has been in almost every anthology since Ye Olde Dragon Books began.)

Michelle Levigne started writing for fanzines in college, while earning a bunch of useless degrees in theater, English, film/communication, and writing. Her first professional publication came from winning first place in the Writers of the Future contest in 1990. She has over 100 published books and novellas in SF, fantasy, cozies, and romance. Her Enchanted Castle Archives series started here with the fairytale and classic monster anthologies. Her most recent release is *Enchanting the Prince*, the Enchanted Castle Archives series, book 3. Look for a middle-grade tie-in about 'Na and her pet dragon Smedley this fall! A tea snob, she freelance edits for a living and terrorizes writers and readers through two small presses she co-owns: Mt. Zion Ridge Press and Ye Olde Dragon Books, as well as the storytelling podcast, Ye Olde Dragon's Library. Be afraid … be very afraid.

Stoney M. Setzer is a middle school special education teacher who lives south of Atlanta, GA. He has a beautiful wife, three wonderful children, and one crazy dog who has convinced himself that he is human. In addition to his work in the Ye Olde Dragons anthology series, he has had short stories featured in publications such as *Havok* and *Residential Aliens*. Many of his stories involve the citizens of Sardis County, Tennessee, and he has also the author of the Wesley Winter trilogy and the **Zero Hour** short story anthology. When he is not writing, he likes reading, drawing, and keeping up with the highs and lows of his beloved Atlanta Braves. Learn more at www.tinniepress.blogspot.com or on Facebook@ stoneymsetzerofficial.

Deborah Cullins Smith has been writing stories ever since she could hold a pencil, but she came to her actual career in writing rather late in life. In 2019, she published the trilogy, *The Last of the Long-Haired Hippies*, in a rapid-release timed for the 50th anniversary of Woodstock, which she covered in great detail in the second volume. *CWG Press* released **Shroud of Darkness**, **The Birth of the Storm**, and **Victoria's War** over a four-month period, a culmination of almost twenty years in development. Ms. Cullins Smith's first Mina Harker adventure, **Mina: Warrior in the Shadows** won the 2022 Realm Award for Horror Novel. Her next novel will continue the saga of Billy the Kid, which she began in the anthology **Moonlight and Claws** with the story *Habitations of Violence*, and continued in **Who's the Monster?** with the story *Phillippe*. Her love of historical research makes these books challenging, as she is devoted to maintaining as much historical accuracy as possible while sliding things sideways to suggest that a few characters might be more than we gave them credit for! (No disrespect intended.)

A childhood spent obsessing over fantasy and role-play while haunting the landscape of Central Europe resulted in **Etta-Tamara Wilson** having a deep fascination with rarely-told fairy tales. She's now preoccupied with reminding a whole host of fairy tale characters to mind their manners and be patient, while she thinks up future adventures for them. When not writing, she's usually off learning new skills or dreaming of travel in lands near, far, or fictional. She has additional stories in the **Tales from the Tower, Who's the Monster?** and **Don't go in the Water...** anthologies.